I0679330

CONTENTS

CRIME SPREE

A BUCK TAYLOR NOVEL

BOOK 9

BY

CHUCK MORGAN

Printed in the United States of America

First printing 2022

ISBN 978-1-7371584-7-9 (eBook)

ISBN 978-1-7371584-8-6 (Paperback)

ISBN 978-1-7371584-9-3 (Large Print)

ISBN 979-8-9862066-0-8 (Hardcover)

LIBRARY OF CONGRESS CONTROL NUMBER 2022908134

DEDICATION

This book is dedicated to the men and women, both professionals and volunteers, who conceived, built, maintain and hike the Continental Divide Trail.

CHAPTER ONE

Pine County Sheriff Jimmy Wechsler stepped into the media room and tried to focus on what he saw in front of him. He wasn't sure what was going on, but he felt dizzy as the flashing lights and the screaming coming from the video game on the eighty-four-inch TV at the front of the room penetrated his brain. At first, he didn't see anyone, and he yelled above the noise.

"Jenny, Rachel, what the hell is going on?"

As his eyes and brain focused through the sensory blitz, he spotted two bloody lumps in the middle of the floor, and standing over them were two blood-covered people dressed in black, and they were hitting the lumps with what looked like axes.

Jimmy couldn't comprehend what he was seeing, but he knew it wasn't good.

An hour earlier, Jimmy Wechsler had finished his daily report, shut down his computer, and grabbed the keys to his SUV. As he locked the door to the sheriff's office, he knew he was late for dinner, but he had one stop to make before heading home.

Jimmy Wechsler had only been the sheriff of Pine County, Colorado, for a couple of months. The twenty-six-year-old had been swept into office as part of a wave of ultra-right-wing election victories that changed the political makeup of rural Colorado.

The son of a local rancher, Jimmy Wechsler had been a probationary police officer with the Grand Junction Police Department when he was approached by one of the county commissioners and asked to run against the long-term sheriff, Bob Trowbridge.

The second-longest-serving sheriff in Colorado, Trowbridge had fallen out of favor with the commissioners. It didn't matter what he had done wrong. In their eyes, they felt he just wasn't conservative enough. So, Bob Trowbridge had to go.

Pine County is the second smallest county in Colorado and the fourth smallest by population. Located between Mineral and Saguache Counties, with a population of just a shade over 1,200, it had 824 registered voters.

The election was tight, and Bob Trowbridge was pissed when he lost the election by twelve votes. After all those years of serving the people of Pine County, he did not feel he could complete his term in office and effectively protect the people who voted against him. So, before the local newspaper had published the election results, Bob Trowbridge had slipped his letter of resignation under the county clerk's office door, packed his wife and two dogs into his RV, and headed for Arizona. He didn't even bother to lock the front door of the county-provided sheriff's residence. He was finished with Pine County.

Jimmy Wechsler was sworn in as the new sheriff the morning after the election and set about making the changes the county commissioners wanted.

The first thing he did was fire both long-term deputies for fear they would still be loyal to the old sheriff. He hired two friends he had made while attending the police academy. The second thing he did was move his wife and two daughters out of their apartment in Grand Junction and into the sheriff's residence. Jimmy Wechsler was now the man in charge, and he was scared to death. The one good thing was that there was very little crime in Pine County.

Jimmy had given his two deputies the weekend off as a reward for all the hours they had put in since they had been hired. He wasn't concerned about being the only person on duty, and he was looking forward to a little quiet.

On most days, they locked up the office at seven p.m. All calls to the office were rerouted to the on-call deputy's phone. This weekend, the sheriff would cover all those calls. So far, the weekend had been quiet, and Jimmy had spent most of his day sitting in his office reviewing resumes for an undersheriff.

The commissioners had authorized him to hire an experienced law enforcement officer to help run the department. By hiring his two friends as deputies at less money than the county had been paying the previous deputies, he had saved a significant amount of money from his budget, money he could now use to get some help.

Jimmy Wechsler slid his thin six-foot-five-inch frame into his SUV, pulled out of the parking lot, and did a tour of Silver City. Most people who met him thought he reminded them of Ichabod Crane from the various *Sleepy Hollow* movies. He had a long, narrow face with angular features, and he had grown a mustache after he was approached to run for sheriff to make himself look older.

With a population of 800, Silver City was the county seat and the only incorporated municipality in Pine County. Located on Highway 114 and with a history of mining and forestry, the city had seen a resurgence over the last decade as a stopover on the Continental

Divide Trail. Tourism had been good for Silver City.

There were still several mines operating in the area, although most of those were hobby mines. Many had played out a long time ago, but there were still reports of weekend hobbyists finding small veins of gold and making some decent money for a few hours' work. Even with gold prices up around $1,800 an ounce, most of the mines were not commercially viable, so the big investors and operators had kept their distance. Some of the mine owners had started offering tours to hikers and visitors on the Continental Divide Trail.

With the trail passing just three miles west of the city and as an easy entry and exit point, it had become a mecca for both section and thru-hikers. It offered guide services, supplies and a place to grab a hot shower and rest their weary feet.

With easy access from the trailhead and much of the trail in the area below the tree line, many novice CDT hikers started their journey from Silver City to get acclimated before climbing to the higher elevations in the next section. There was also access to several off-trail hikes that led to some small mountain lakes and one hike that led to a small waterfall with an incredible view of the valley below and the snowcapped mountain peaks in the distance.

Driving down Main Street, Jimmy waved at several shopkeepers as they were locking up for the night. He pulled into the gas station/convenience store at the edge of town, gassed up the SUV, and spent a few minutes chatting with Missy Halloran, the store owner.

Bidding Missy a good night, he pulled out of the lot and headed north on Highway 114. A mile out of town, he turned onto County Route 7 and headed deeper into the forest. His destination was the home of County Commissioner Lenny Carrollton.

Carrollton and his wife, Marla, had traveled back to Michigan for a wedding, and he had asked Jimmy Wechsler to check on his two daughters, who were home from college and didn't want to make the trip back east to attend the wedding. Both his daughters were capable of staying home, but he told Jimmy he would feel safer if Jimmy could do a drive-by once in a while just to make sure everything was fine.

The house sat at the end of a long dirt road, the nearest neighbor about a half mile away. There were no lights along the road, and without a moon, it was as dark as a cave. Many people came to the area to stargaze because of the almost total darkness that could be found in and around Silver City. Tonight, with no moon, the sky was brilliant, and it looked like you could reach up and touch the Milky Way.

The county was full of long, dark roads like this, and it made Jimmy uncomfortable driving them at night. He was glad he was armed, despite never having any trouble. It was a comfort just knowing his pistol was there.

Jimmy came around a slight bend and spotted the house sitting back fifty yards off the road. He knew as soon as he spotted it that something was wrong. He could see flashing blue, red, and green lights through the front window, and even though he wasn't close, he could hear the sounds. It was like someone was playing a movie or a video game and had the volume turned up all the way.

Jimmy pulled his SUV into the driveway, grabbed his flashlight off the front seat and headed for the front door. The front curtains were partially closed, but the lights flashing through the opening between the drapes hurt his eyes, and the vibration from the deep bass went right up his spine.

He reached for the front knob, found it unlocked and opened the door. The noise and flashing lights inside were several times worse than they were outside, and he called the girls' names. This was totally unlike the sisters.

When he knew them growing up, they had been studious and never got into trouble. Rachel could get a little crazy sometimes, but Jenny, the oldest, always managed to reel her back in. The noise and the flashing lights were so out of character that he wondered what the hell was happening. He made his way through the living room towards the noise coming from the back of the house.

Passing through the kitchen, he saw the half-open door that he knew led to the media room. He walked over and pushed the door open.

"Jenny, Rachel, what the hell is going on?" he yelled above the noise.

He recognized the video game *Viking Warrior* playing on the big screen. The noise was the Vikings sacking the city and killing the people as they ran from the streets. The people on the screen were screaming and dying. It was a bloody, violent game, but not as bloody or violent as the scene that played out before him.

Lying on the floor in the middle of the room were two blood-covered lumps of he didn't know what, and leaning over them were two people dressed in black, hitting the lumps with what looked like hand axes. The two figures with the axes ignored him and slammed away at the lumps. Blood and things Jimmy didn't want to think about were flying all over the room, and the floor was covered in blood.

Jimmy was stunned and unable to comprehend what he was seeing. He had never seen that much blood in his life, and with the flashing lights and loud noises, his brain wanted to shut down. He started to feel faint and nauseous, and he leaned back and pushed against the wall. He knew he needed to do something, but he wasn't sure what.

"Sheriff," he yelled.

Knowing before he yelled it that they wouldn't be able to hear him, he was surprised when the two figures stopped, stood up with bloody axes in their hands and looked at him. Blood was dripping off their clothes and hair, and it was hard to see what color their skin was or anything distinctive about them. They looked like foul creatures from someone's worst nightmare.

Shaking off the dizziness, Jimmy placed his hand on his holster and drew his pistol. With shaking hands, he raised it toward the two attackers.

Something hard slammed into his chest and penetrated his ballistic vest, and he fell back against the wall. He looked down and spotted a shaft sticking out of his chest, and he slid down the wall. The pain was intense. His pistol fell from his hands, and he stared in disbelief as blood dripped off the shaft.

He couldn't figure out who had shot him since the two attackers were still standing over the bodies, looking at him. Then he spotted a shadow to the right of the two attackers that walked towards him. The person was dressed in black and wore a black balaclava. Jimmy spotted the crossbow. That was the last thing he would ever see as the two attackers left the lumps and approached him, shrieking as they came.

The first ax blow hit Jimmy in the shoulder, and he screamed. The next blow hit him in the chest, and his final thought was that he would never see his daughters grow up. Then everything went black.

CHAPTER TWO

I n her run for freedom, she crashed through the scrub oak, the closely spaced branches tearing at her bare limbs. Even though she couldn't see in the inky blackness, she could feel the blood running down her arms and legs, but she knew she couldn't stop. If she stopped, she would die. She prayed she wouldn't bleed to death before she reached safety.

She hit her bare foot on a low branch and tumbled headfirst into more tangled branches. Blood dripped into her eyes. One of the boots she carried flew into the mass of trees, and fear set in as she tried to locate it. There was no moon tonight, and the darkness on the mountain made finding it difficult, but she was desperate.

Her hand touched the laces, and she pulled the boot through the branches. And then she heard them. Her pursuers were not even trying to be silent as they crashed through the trees. She couldn't tell how close they were, but she knew she needed to keep moving.

Mustering her last bit of strength, she pushed

through the edge of the scrub oak and saw nothing but black emptiness in front of her. Not knowing what direction, she was heading, she could only hope that her journey would take her to civilization. She started running, ignoring the pain as sharp stones slashed her feet.

She had no idea how far she'd run when she saw a small rock outcropping a short distance away. If she could make it to the rocks, it might give her enough protection that she could, at least, put on her boots and wipe the blood from her face.

She tripped over a large rock, slammed hard onto the rocks of the scree field and smacked her head on the ground. She knew she was hurt badly as she tried to lift herself off the ground. Fighting back nausea and dizziness, she convinced her legs that they needed to get moving. She shrugged off the dizziness and limped to the rock outcropping.

It seemed like she had been running for hours. She sat down on the ground, laid her head back to catch her breath and sleep grabbed her from behind, and she dozed off.

The day had started beautifully as McKenzie crawled out of her sleeping bag to the smell of bacon cooking. Mark knew it was her one indulgence in an otherwise healthy lifestyle, and he loved the joy he could see in her face every time he cooked it up.

The second morning of their honeymoon dawned clear and bright, with just a hint of a chill in the air. The wedding, three days before, had been picture-perfect, and the thought of them spending the rest of their lives together made her blush.

Their friends and families could not believe it when they told everyone that they would spend a wonderful week together hiking a section of the Continental Divide Trail. Her father was willing to send them anywhere in the world, as money was no object, but they insisted that this was the first item on the dream list together.

They had parked their rental car at the trailhead the morning before and had double-checked all their equipment and supplies. They were traveling light and would be eating an assortment of freeze-dried food, their only indulgences being the fresh bacon and a small bottle of champagne.

They had hiked farther than they planned on the first day, and when they set up camp, it was along a small stream below the tree line. They had sent the family a message on the GPS tracker, the one thing her father insisted they bring along, and spent the night watching the stars.

That night's lovemaking had been incredible, and they both fell into a blissful sleep.

They spent time on a leisurely breakfast of freeze-dried scrambled eggs, coffee and the bacon, which Mark had cooked to perfection.

Mark, a junior vice president in her father's development company, wasn't much of an outdoorsman, but he made every effort, knowing how much McKenzie loved the mountains. As a fitness trainer, she was in fantastic shape, and she could often be found trail running near their town house in Grosse Pointe, Michigan, after a hard day of working the fat off people who wanted to look like her.

Mark was content to sit in his office and review financial documents and blueprints all day. When they first started talking about their honeymoon, he hoped they would be going to some exotic location in Europe where they could spend time walking through art museums and eating in five-star restaurants. But McKenzie had other ideas, and she convinced him that a hike in the mountains would be perfect. Just the two of them communing with nature. An entire week with no family or friends wishing them the best, or having to attend the multitude of congratulatory parties her mother had planned with all her socialite friends.

Mark gave in, and here they were, standing on

a slight rise above the tree line, looking at their next destination: a small lake hidden away in a forested valley below them.

After finishing breakfast and breaking camp, they had checked their next destination on the trail app Mark had installed on his phone and headed out. The first part of the trail was relatively easy compared to what was to come in the following days, so they trudged along, hoping to make camp earlier than they had the first night.

They were surprised at how many people they met on the trail. It was still early in the season, but the weather had been incredible for the past couple of weeks, and they expected the trail would be busy. They had encountered another couple, a scraggly-looking team, who had started out the month before in New Mexico and hoped to reach Montana in the next week or two. They had lunched together on water and trail mix, exchanged their stories and then said their goodbyes.

McKenzie loved the trail names of many of the hikers they had met, and she was thinking about what their trail names could be. The couple they'd had lunch with were Snowflake and Dirt Crusher, and McKenzie wanted cool names too. She decided to work on that while they hiked to the next camp.

The small lake at the bottom of the steep trail was stunning, and Mark took some time to wade into the frigid water and take a quick bath. They made camp, cooked up some freeze-dried spaghetti and meatballs and had ice cream pellets for dessert. The day had been perfect, and they were both exhausted by the time they crawled into their sleeping bags, sent off a message through their GPS tracker and shut down for the night.

CHAPTER THREE

McKenzie knew something was wrong when they were dragged from the tent, still wrapped in their sleeping bags. She tried to focus and called out for Mark, trying to wipe the sleep from her eyes. She sat up, and that's when she saw the two dark shapes dragging Mark and his sleeping bag towards the fire. Her first thought was bears until they started yelling like crazy people.

Mark was trying to get out of the sleeping bag and was screaming for them to stop, but the two shapes kicked at him from both sides. Then one of the shapes held something up in front of his face and screeched. The light from the dying fire glinted off an object in his hand as he jumped on Mark and started raising his hand up and down.

McKenzie couldn't see what was happening, but she knew whatever was going on was not good. She also realized that she no longer heard Mark screaming. Her flight response kicked in, and she started crawling from the sleeping bag when the hand of another unseen being grabbed her hair and shoved her to the ground.

The two shadows that had taken turns sitting on Mark added some wood to the fire, and when the embers caught and exploded into a huge blaze, she saw that they were two young men. She also saw that Mark wasn't moving. The young men approached, and she shivered as she saw the liquid dripping from the axes they carried. She tried to scream, but the unseen hand punched her in the side of the head, and she blacked out. When she regained consciousness, she found one young man on top of her, penetrating her, and it took her a moment to realize she was being raped. She tried to fight but was punched again as the second young man took over.

She was raped for what seemed like several hours. How long, she had no idea, but when they were finished, they slid off her and threw the sleeping bag over her naked body. She was sore, and she could tell she was bleeding. She found her T-shirt and panties lying next to the sleeping bag, put them on, and curled up into a little ball. She had no idea when this would end, but she prayed for morning to arrive.

She must have dozed off because when she opened her eyes, she could see the two young men sleeping next to the fire. She had no idea where the third person was, but she knew she needed to get away. She slid out of the sleeping bag, making as little noise as she could, found her boots near the entrance to the tent and moved towards Mark, who still hadn't moved.

She reached for the sleeping bag to shake Mark to see if he was awake, but her hand came back covered in a sticky liquid. She recoiled and fell backward. She used her clean hand to stifle a scream. One man started to stretch, so she picked up her boots and ran into the woods.

McKenzie knew if she headed back the way they came, she should be able to run to the car, but she heard movement coming from the camp and decided the best thing she could do was to seek help. She knew they were about twelve miles from a resupply resort, but when she reached the main trail, she was unsure what direction she needed to go. Without a moon to give her some light, the forest was one large black void. She sat on a downed tree to put on her boots when she saw an even darker shadow cross the path. She grabbed the boots by the laces and took off down the trail.

She knew her pursuers were following her. She could hear them moving in the trees behind her, so she decided the best thing she could do was to get off the main trail and bushwhack through the trees. She needed to put some distance between her and her attackers.

After what seemed like miles of running, she

ran out of the forest into the scrub oak. The low-growing twisted shrubs were as thick as fleas, and they fought her every step of the way, but she knew that her attackers would also be slowed by the trees. That gave her hope until she realized they were not far behind her.

Falling several times, she gave it everything she had. She stopped several times to wipe the tears from her eyes. There would be time to grieve Mark later. Right now, she had to focus on surviving until she could get to the authorities.

She woke with a start and tried to remember where she was. She knew she had been running and was being chased, and she realized that she must have made it to the safety of a rock outcropping. Her entire body hurt, and she was covered in blood. She was exhausted.

For a minute, she broke down as tears filled her eyes. Her body shook, but she wasn't sure if it was from the events or the chill of the night. She wore a T-shirt and panties, which did not offer much protection in the cool night air. She held back screams as she put her boots on over her swollen and bloody feet. Once she had them tied, she fell back against the rocks, exhausted. It had taken everything she had not to let out a scream. She wondered if her feet would ever recover and then thought about how stupid a thought that was since she was still in mortal danger.

She pulled herself together as best she could and then listened for any sound that might tell her where her attackers were. She had no way of knowing if they had passed her by in the night or if they had stopped to wait for first light.

The sky in the east was starting to lighten, so she knew the morning was coming, and she also knew that she was headed in the right direction to get to the rest and resupply resort. That helped improve her mood, but she knew she needed to move. She would soon be better able to see her path, but that also meant that her attackers could see her as well.

Not hearing anything, she stood up and looked for any shadow that seemed out of place. Seeing nothing, she stepped from behind the rocks and stretched to relieve some of the stiffness. She took her first tentative steps to stretch her stiff muscles and was about to start running when something hard slammed into her left thigh, and she screamed.

She tumbled down the slope for five or six yards and lay flat on the ground. The pain was incredible as she pulled herself up and looked at her thigh. She couldn't believe what she saw. Sticking out of her leg by two or three inches was a shaft with a metal point. She reached down to touch it, screamed and fell back to the ground.

McKenzie could hear footsteps on the loose rocks, and she closed her eyes. When she reopened them, three people were looking down at her. Her mind hoped that they were rescuers until she saw the black crossbow in one person's hand. She knew what it was as soon as she saw it. Her younger brother had been into crossbows and had even shown her how to shoot one. She realized that the memory of her brother was the last memory she would have, and she started to cry.

The two younger men reached into their blood-spattered coats, and one of them pulled out a long knife. The other pulled out a bloody ax. They pulled back their hoods and smiled at her. She thought they looked very young. The two young men kneeled next to her and looked up and down her body. One of them took the knife, slipped it under her T-shirt, and slit the shirt from top to bottom, exposing her breast.

She forgot, for a moment, the pain in her leg and wondered if they were going to rape her again. The answer revealed itself as the man on the left slammed a gilded ax into her chest just below her breast. Then the frenzy began, and at some point, her world went black.

CHAPTER FOUR

B uck Taylor stood in the dark, pushed back as far as he could against the wall. He could hear his pursuer looking for him, and he hoped the spot he had chosen to hide would be enough to buy him some time to come up with a better plan.

He wasn't sure how he'd gotten into this situation. Unarmed and without his cell phone, he found himself in a position he had never been in before, and he was conflicted about what to do next. Evasion and escape were foremost on his mind, but first, he had to get past his pursuer.

This situation was completely foreign to him. Most of the time, he was the one pursuing someone into a dark building or, in several cases, into a cave or an old mine. He was never comfortable working in dark, tight spaces, but he did whatever the job required.

Now, the shoe was on the other foot, and he was the one being tracked. His nemesis was close. He could feel it more than he knew it. His senses were on high alert as he tried to stay as still as possible. He wondered if his pursuer could hear his heart beating.

He heard his pursuer stop at the door to the space where he was hiding. He heard the doorknob rattle, and then, by some stroke of luck, his pursuer moved on. Buck breathed a sigh of relief and thanked the gods for protecting him. For the moment, he was safe.

Buck heard a ringtone in the distance and moved closer to the door to see if he could hear what was being said. He cracked the door and listened.

"Grandpa Buck's phone, Rose speaking," said a soft voice. There was a pause while someone on the other end of the call spoke.

"We were playing hide and count, but I'll go find him. Hold on, please," said Rose.

She turned and saw Buck standing in the doorway, laughing. She was so adorable, and Buck loved her.

"Grandpa, Mr. Jackson wants to talk to you," she said, holding out the phone.

"Thanks, Rosie," said Buck as he took his phone from her, leaned over and kissed her on the top of her head.

"She sounds so grown-up, Buck. How old is she now?" asked Kevin Jackson as Buck put the phone to his ear.

Kevin Jackson, the director of the Colorado Bureau of Investigation, had been the youngest person to ever run the bureau when he was appointed by Governor Richard J. Kennedy. He'd had a stellar career with the Colorado Springs Police Department before being tapped for the top post at CBI. He was more bureaucrat than cop, having spent most of his career on the administrative side at CSPD, but he was well respected in the law enforcement community, and so far, Buck was impressed with him.

"She turned five a couple of weeks ago," said Buck. "She'll be going to kindergarten in the fall. What's up, sir?"

"I hate to take you away from your granddaughter, but we have a situation I need your help with. The sheriff of Pine County hasn't been seen in two days. He hasn't spoken to his wife or his deputies, and they can't locate his phone or his SUV. Neither were GPS enabled. It's like he fell off the face of the earth. I need you to head to Silver City and see if you can lend a hand."

"That's the young fella who replaced Bob Trowbridge. No problem, sir," said Buck. "Let me make arrangements for Rosie, and I'll head straight over there."

"Thanks, Buck. Keep me posted and call if you need anything."

The director hung up, and Buck looked up a number on his phone and hit the call button.

"Hi, Buck," said Rosalie Torres. "What can I do for you?"

Rosalie Torres was one of the elders of the community. She was also Buck's mother-in-law. Pushing eighty and five foot two, she was a force to be reckoned with. What she lacked in stature this still-active Latina more than made up for with drive. She was still on the organizing committee for the Labor Day picnic, and she served on almost every volunteer committee that functioned within the county. Nothing went on in Gunnison County that Rosalie was not a part of.

Rosalie and her husband, Fernando, had run a small horse ranch just outside the Gunnison city limits. Fernando had also been an outfitter and hunting guide. His love of the outdoors was something he was proud to have passed on to their two daughters, Lucinda, Buck's late wife, and Rachel, and their son, Michael. Life was not always easy for Fernando and Rosalie, but they did the best they could and made sure that their children never wanted for anything.

It was a sad day six years ago when Fernando suffered a heart attack while guiding a couple of hunters near Monarch Pass. Although the hunters had made a valiant effort to revive him and had succeeded several times, by the time search and rescue reached them, Fernando was gone. The family still missed Fernando every day, but it was okay. His daughter Lucy was with him.

"Hey, Rose. I just got called away, and I'm watching Rosie until her brother gets home from school. Any chance you could fill in for me?"

"To get to spend the day with my bisnieta. I'm on my way."

Buck disconnected the call, sat next to Rosie and explained that he had to leave. He told her someone was missing, and they needed his help, and that her bisabuela was going to watch her until her brother got home from school.

Rosalie was excited that her great-grandmother would be taking over from Buck. That meant an afternoon of shopping and lunch. She couldn't wait.

Buck walked over to the gun safe that was mounted to the wall inside the hall coat closet, entered the combination, pulled out his badge and holster and clipped them to his belt.

The gun safe was his gift to his son David and daughter-in-law Judith when they first moved into the house around the corner from Buck and Lucy. An odd choice for a housewarming gift until you realized how many guns were in the house.

David was Buck's oldest son and was a sergeant and night shift supervisor with the Gunnison Police Department. He looked just like his dad when Buck was his age, slightly taller at six foot two and a little heavier, but the resemblance was almost scary. He also played guitar in a local bluegrass/country band.

Since neither of them wore their guns when they were in David's house, Buck thought the gun safe would be a good idea.

Buck heard a low rumble and watched as Rosalie Torres pulled her fifteen-year-old Ford F-150 into the driveway and parked next to his state-issued Jeep Grand Cherokee. A minute later, Rosalie came in through the kitchen door, gave Buck and Rosie a hug and dropped her sweater and purse on the kitchen table.

They spent a few minutes catching up, and then Buck gave Rosie a big hug and headed out the door. He called David and Judith and let them know what was going on and that he wasn't sure when he would be back, but he would call them later and fill them in.

He slid into his car, pulled up the directions to Silver City on his GPS and pulled out of the driveway. He drove through the neighborhood, pulled onto Highway 50 eastbound and headed for Highway 114. The GPS told him the drive would take about forty-five minutes.

He sat back and thought about the missing sheriff, and he hoped the next couple of days wouldn't end badly. He always dreaded situations that involved law enforcement officers. In his experience, most of them did not end well. He took a drink from the ever-present bottle of Coke in his center console and focused on the drive. He hoped today would be a good day, but he didn't realize how wrong he would be.

CHAPTER FIVE

Buck was almost to Silver City when his phone rang. He saw the caller's name on the entertainment screen in the dashboard and answered. "Yes, sir?"

"Buck," said Director Jackson. "I just got a call from the coroner in Silver City. They found the sheriff, and it doesn't sound good. I'm sending you the address of the scene."

"Can you call and roll the forensic team from Grand Junction?" asked Buck.

"Already done. They're about an hour and a half behind you. I also called Bax and told her to meet you there. Anything else?"

"Not right now, sir. I'll fill you in once I get there."

Buck hung up and wondered why the county coroner had been the one who called the director. Colorado was one of about a dozen states that still used the coroner system instead of the medical examiner system. The coroner for each jurisdiction was an elected official, and that person did not have to have any experience or even be a medical professional. Anyone could run for coroner.

The system was evolving so that the coroner was required to complete a formal training program in death investigations, but it was a slow legislative process. Unlike in the medical examiner system, and since the coroner did not have to be a doctor, coroners would contract with a licensed forensic pathologist to handle any investigations that required an autopsy.

These forensic pathologists were highly trained doctors who, in some cases, split their time among several jurisdictions to keep costs down. Almost all the forensic pathologists were current or former medical examiners, and several were retired, working part time to keep their hands in the game.

The GPS alerted Buck to an upcoming turn, and the arrow pointed to the left. Buck turned onto County Route 7, about three miles from his destination, and he steeled himself for what he might find when he got there.

The GPS indicated a right turn onto a dirt road, and as he drove around a slight bend in the road, he spotted a sheriff's patrol SUV blocking the road. The young deputy leaning against the vehicle stood up, hiked up his gun belt and held up his hand for Buck to stop. Buck came to a stop and rolled down the window.

"Sorry, sir. Can't go any further; you'll need to turn around and head back the way you came."

Buck had been prepared, and he pulled his credentials out of the extra cupholder in the center console and held them up for the deputy.

"Buck Taylor, Colorado Bureau of Investigation."

The deputy reached for the credentials, and Buck pulled them back, just out of his reach. "I'm looking for Marvin Willets." He put his credentials back in the cupholder.

"You'll find Mr. Willets in the house at the end of the road. Can't miss it."

He stepped back and waved him forward. Buck noticed the slight sneer and how he emphasized the word Mr. He wondered what that was all about. He spotted another SUV along with two civilian cars. He pulled down the driveway, parked and slid out of his Jeep.

Buck wasn't an imposing figure, but when he was on a crime scene or running an investigation, there was little doubt about who was in charge. At six feet tall and one hundred eighty-five pounds, Buck was in the best shape of his life. He looked like he could still play football for the Gunnison High School Cowboys.

He wore his salt-and-pepper hair, which had a

lot more salt than pepper in it, longer than the style of the day, and considerably longer than when his wife of thirty-four years, Lucy, had still been alive. Today he wore a T-shirt and jeans. His Carhartt vest was unzipped, and his gun and CBI badge were clipped to his belt.

Buck was an investigative agent for the Colorado Bureau of Investigation. He was currently assigned to the CBI field office in Grand Junction, Colorado, but he hadn't been in the office much during the past couple of years. Somehow, he had become the favorite "go-to" guy for the governor of Colorado, Richard J. Kennedy, who was, in fact, one of "those" Kennedys. The governor had been in office about three years, and Buck had been instrumental in closing several high-profile investigations during that period; that made the governor look good, and as a result, when a situation came up that might get a little hairy, the governor always asked to have Buck assigned.

As he walked towards the front porch, the door opened, and several people walked out of the house. If this was the crime scene, and he had no reason to doubt that it was, he was dismayed by all these people.

The first person out the door was another deputy in the same brown shirt and tan pants uniform that the other deputy was wearing. Also, like the other deputy, this one didn't look old enough to shave. The deputy was followed by a short man with short blond hair. He had a badge clipped to the lapel of his suit jacket. He was helping a woman down the stairs who looked like she was in a state of shock, the way she shuffled along. Her head was down, and she held a handkerchief to her face. Another man, older than all the others, with gray hair and wearing jeans and a button-down shirt, was holding up the woman on the other side.

The man with the badge spotted Buck, said something to the other man, who nodded, and he let go of the woman's arm and headed towards Buck.

"Agent Taylor, Marvin Willets. Director Jackson told me to expect you. Glad you're here."

He held out his hand, and Buck shook it. Buck pointed to the sheriff's department badge. "Mr. Willets, I was told you were the county coroner."

"Long story. Would you like to see the crime scene?" He pointed towards the house.

Buck took Marvin Willets by the arm and led him away from the others. When they were out of earshot, he said, "Marvin, may I call you Marvin? Who are all these people, and why were you all inside the house?"

Marvin Willets looked dismayed, like he wasn't sure what Buck was asking. "Sorry, Agent Taylor. That's County Commissioner Lenny

Carrollton and his wife, Marla. This is their house." He pointed to the man and woman standing against the sheriff's department SUV.

"Marvin. I assume the body is inside the house, correct?" asked Buck.

Now, Marvin Willets looked bewildered. "The bodies are inside the house. There are three of them. Quite the mess."

"What do you mean, three bodies? I was told that the sheriff was missing, and his body had been found. The house is a crime scene. Who do the other bodies belong to?"

"Perhaps I should explain."

"Perhaps you should," said Buck.

Buck was a patient man, but he was starting to get annoyed. He had made patience into an art form. There had been a story circulating the CBI offices for years about Buck getting a murderer to confess just by sitting at the table opposite him and not saying a word for four or five hours. Of course, the time got longer or shorter depending on who told the story, but it was always told as a sign of respect.

"I'm sorry, Agent Taylor. I thought you were told." He hesitated for a moment. "I was very rattled when I spoke with Director Jackson. I can't recall whether I told him about all the bodies or not."

He turned pale and looked like he wanted to throw up. Buck noticed the stain on his jacket and assumed that he already had.

"There are three victims. Sheriff Wechsler, Jenny Carrollton, and Rachel Carrollton. It's just horrible."

Tears filled Marvin Willets's eyes, and he excused himself and ran to the bushes on the side of the driveway with his hand covering his mouth. Buck waited until Marvin returned, wiping his mouth.

"Sorry, Agent Taylor, this is all new to me. Mr. and Mrs. Carrollton were out of town for the weekend. When they returned home this morning, they walked into a horrific scene. Mrs. Carrollton passed out, and Lenny carried her to their bedroom and laid her on the bed, and then he called us," said Marvin Willets.

Buck could see how much distress Marvin was under. "Marvin, why don't you go join the Carrolltons over by the SUV, and I will go take a look."

Buck walked onto the porch and put his backpack on the small table in the corner. He opened it and removed a pair of blue booties, nitrile gloves and a face mask. He put them on, grabbed his flashlight from the backpack and opened the front door. The first thing he noticed was the coppery smell of blood and the smell of decomposition. The weekend had been mild, and the higher temperatures sped up the decomp.

The house was dark for the time of day, and Buck noticed that the front drapes were partially closed. He turned on his flashlight and shined it around the room. Buck used the flashlight to focus his attention as he scanned the room. He spotted several bloody footprints on the hardwood floor and on the throw rug by the door. He stepped around them.

Moving through the house, he followed the footprints through the kitchen, ending at the entrance to a media room or home theater. The smell was terrible, and he wondered how the Carolltons managed to make it this far without being repelled by it. He stepped into the media room.

He was not happy with what he saw.

CHAPTER SIX

I t wasn't the blood that covered the wall, floor and furniture that upset Buck. It was the fact that all three bodies were covered with sheets or blankets.

He stepped over to the first body, took out his phone and took several pictures of the body and the surroundings. He pulled back the bloodstained sheet. The first victim was a young male with a thin, angular face and a mustache. His eyes were open, and Buck could feel the pain he must have felt during the attack.

It was hard to tell where the wounds were from the initial look. The body was covered in blood. Buck pulled the sheet back further and noticed that the sheriff—he assumed this was the sheriff—was naked. His clothes were torn and bloody and lying next to the body. Buck pulled out his phone and took several pictures of the body.

He kneeled next to the body and inspected the wounds. He couldn't be sure because of all the blood, but it looked like the young man had been hacked to death. By what, Buck had no idea. He left the sheet lying next to the body and made a mental note to find out where the sheriff's weapon was.

He ran his flashlight over the walls and ceiling. There were blood and body pieces on every surface. The savagery of the attack was brutal. Whoever did this must have been covered in blood. He would have the forensic team check the area around the house for bloody clothes.

He moved deeper into the room. The lights were on, but the big-screen TV that covered a good portion of the wall at the front of the room was off. The room was set up like an expensive movie theater with several rows of leather seats. Each row of seats was raised above the one in front of it. The seats were covered in blood and pieces of what used to be a person.

In the corner of the room was an old-style popcorn maker. The kind that could make a large amount of popcorn and display it behind a Plexiglas panel, with a heated butter machine above the popcorn. The multicolored popcorn bags were lying all around the machine.

The popcorn no longer smelled fresh, and the butter had congealed on the side of the heated container, on the walls of the machine and on the Plexiglas front. He wondered if the killer or killers had enjoyed themselves or if the victims had made popcorn before everything in their lives went wrong. He took a series of pictures around the room and then switched the camera to video mode and scanned the room.

He stepped over to the first lump on the floor. This one was covered by a red-and-black tartan print flannel blanket. He took a couple of pictures and then pulled back the blanket, taking several photos of the body. Just like the sheriff, the body of this young woman—he didn't know if this was Rachel or Jennifer—was covered in blood from head to toe and had many open wounds. He left the blanket next to the body.

The second lump was more of the same, another young woman, covered by a floral print sheet, who had been hacked to death. He repeated the picture-taking process and then finished scanning the room with the light from his flashlight. He spotted something tiny lying on the floor next to the leather chair and the second body. He kneeled, took a picture of it, and pulled a small evidence bag from his pocket. He placed what turned out to be a tiny lavender-colored pill in the bag, made a notation on the bag and placed it in his vest pocket.

He headed back towards the door to the media room, being careful where he stepped. At the door, he turned and looked back into the room. The fury of the attack was horrendous and personal. He did not believe the attack was random, and he believed the victims knew the attacker or attackers.

He walked through the kitchen and stepped out onto the front porch. He removed the booties, the mask and the nitrile gloves, pulled an evidence bag from his backpack and placed them inside. He sealed the bag, noting the day and time, and signed his name over the flap.

He looked up and noticed that the Carrolltons were no longer standing next to the SUV. He walked over to Marvin Willets and the deputy, whose name tag read tortelli.

"Where did the Carrolltons go?" he asked.

"I called my wife and asked her to come pick them up and take them back to town. She was going to arrange a motel room for them since they can't come back here," said Marvin Willets.

Buck looked at the young deputy. "Were you first on the scene?"

The young deputy stood up straight and puffed out his chest. "Yes, sir. Michael Tortelli." The deputy reached out his hand, but Buck was in no mood to be friendly.

"You covered the bodies?" The deputy could tell by Buck's voice that he wasn't pleased. He took a step back and looked deflated.

"Yes, sir. The girls and Jimmy, Sheriff

Wechsler, were naked. Mr. and Mrs. Carrollton were a mess, and I didn't want them to have to look at the bodies. I . . ."

Trying not to raise his voice, Buck said, "Did you forget everything they taught you at the police academy about crime scene preservation? You walked through the entire crime scene, you covered the bodies, and you allowed the victim's parents to remain in the house. You may not have contaminated the entire crime scene, but you sure made a good effort."

The smile disappeared from the young deputy's face. "I, uh, I . . . uh, was embarrassed."

"Embarrassed for who?" asked Buck. "The victims were already dead. They weren't going to be embarrassed. For the parents, who you should have escorted from the house as soon as you got here and saw it was a crime scene. They had already seen the damage. What the fuck were you thinking, or weren't you?"

The deputy started to stutter, and Marvin Willets stepped up, but Buck held up his hand. He looked back at the deputy.

"What else did you touch?" he asked.

The deputy thought for a minute. "Nothing," he said. Buck could see the fire in his eyes. He didn't like being dressed down. Then something crossed his face.

"Mr. Carrollton told me he turned off the TV because the noise was deafening." He lowered his eyes to the ground and scuffed his feet on the dirt driveway.

Buck ran out of patience. "So, the victim's father also walked through the fucking crime scene?"

The deputy slunk back against the SUV.

Buck then turned his attention to Marvin Willets. "You should have known better. You're the coroner and the acting sheriff. How the hell that happened, I'll never know. Did you forget what you learned in your death investigation classes?"

Marvin Willets diverted his eyes. "I never finished the classes," he said in a whisper.

Buck stared at him without saying a word. He was looking for more information. After a long, uncomfortable minute, Marvin spoke.

"I've been the coroner for four months, and I only took the job because no one else wanted it. I figured I'd sign a few death certificates and go about my business. I'm an accountant, not a doctor. And as far as being sheriff. I didn't ask for this job. The other commissioners and the city attorney said it was some old law. The closest I ever came to law enforcement was reading mysteries and watching cops on TV."

Buck stopped for a minute and thought back. He remembered a couple of cases over the past couple of years where a county sheriff was unable to fulfill his duties. He pulled out his phone, opened Google and found what he was looking for.

In 1877, two years after Colorado became a state, the state legislature had passed Colorado Revised Statute 30-10-604. This law said that anytime a sheriff was unable to perform his duties, the county coroner would be appointed to the position of sheriff. There was also a conflicting law C.R.S 30-10-505 that said that in the event the sheriff could not perform his duties, the undersheriff would be appointed sheriff.

Buck put away his phone. "Does the county not have an undersheriff?" he asked.

"No," said Marvin Willets. "Jimmy was in the process of looking for one, but he hadn't gotten around to hiring one. Now, I'm stuck being sheriff because of some ancient law. It's ridiculous. I have no experience." He pointed back towards the house. "And now, this."

Buck was about to say something when a white Ford cargo van pulled into the parking lot, followed by a black Jeep Grand Cherokee. The cavalry had arrived.

CHAPTER SEVEN

Franklin Williams, the lead forensic tech based out of the CBI office in Grand Junction, slid out of the Jeep and walked towards Buck. Franklin was a distinguished-looking black man who stood about four inches taller than Buck but weighed about the same. He had short gray hair and a gray goatee. He stepped up to Buck, and they shook hands.

"What do we have, Buck?" he asked.

"What we have is a mess. Besides the three bodies inside, those two." He pointed towards Tortelli and Willets. "Walked through the entire crime scene and covered the bodies. The parents who discovered the victims also walked through the scene. You'll need to process them as part of the scene." Buck smiled.

Franklin smiled back. "No problem, Buck. I'll help them understand that they shouldn't have done that."

Franklin walked over and introduced himself and, with his best authoritative voice, said, "So, you two contaminated my crime scene. I'm going to need your clothes, shoes and we're gonna need your fingerprints and DNA."

Without waiting for a response, he turned and called to a blond woman in a white Tyvek suit, who was just stepping out of the van.

"Marcie, I need these two processed. Clothes, shoes, DNA and fingerprints. The works. Give them each a pair of those disposable scrubs and a pair of booties to wear."

"You can't be serious?" said Tortelli.

They both looked stunned and were about to say something in protest when Franklin held up his hand.

Franklin looked into Tortelli's eyes. "You were in the house and covered the bodies. You are now part of the crime scene. If you play nice, I might let you keep on your underwear." He pointed towards the van and the waiting Marcie. "Go, now."

Franklin walked back to Buck, a big grin across his face. "Now, let's go see what we've got."

They walked up onto the porch, and Franklin stopped to zip up his Tyvek suit and put on his gloves and booties. He handed Buck clean booties and a pair of nitrile gloves. They stepped into the nightmare that was the crime scene.

Buck turned back towards the door. Tortelli

was just walking towards the van. "Deputy. Do you have the sheriff's weapon and phone, and where is his SUV?"

Tortelli looked back as Marcie handed him the folded blue disposable scrubs.

"I have his weapon locked in the safe in my SUV. We haven't been able to locate his SUV or his phone. I sent out a BOLO, so the information about his SUV is circulating statewide."

"Does the SUV or the phone have GPS?"

"The SUV does not, but the phone might." He turned and climbed into the van.

Buck stepped back into the house and headed towards the media room, where he found Franklin taking pictures of the scene with a Nikon DSLR camera. He lowered the camera.

"Holy shit, Buck. This is fury on steroids. This is gonna take a while."

"I know. There's so much blood on the victims that I can't even see the wound or wounds. What a mess."

"Did you call the pathologist?" asked Franklin.

"That's what I was heading to do when I started jumping on those two. So, if you're good here, I'll call now. I'll use Garrett from Gunnison. He's the closest."

Buck walked back through the house and

stepped onto the porch. He pulled off his gloves and pulled out his phone. Dr. Garrett Parkinson answered right away.

"Hey, Buck. What's going on?"

"Hey, Garrett. Didn't catch you on the golf course, did I?" asked Buck.

"Nah. Just sitting in the sun, reading the paper. What can I do for you?"

Dr. Garrett Parkinson was a semiretired emergency room doctor who picked up a couple of shifts each week at the Gunnison Valley Health hospital. He was also a board-certified forensic pathologist who did autopsies for Gunnison County and several of the smaller counties in the area. He was a longtime friend of Buck's.

Buck explained the situation and what he needed, and Garrett listened without saying a word until he finished.

"Sounds like quite the mess. Let me call the transportation department at the hospital and see if they have an ambulance crew to bring the bodies back here. I'll head down right away so you can release the scene to Franklin. See you soon."

Buck thanked him and hung up.

Franklin stepped through the door, removed his gloves and took a deep breath. He had seen almost everything in his thirty years as a forensic technician, but he looked a little green.

"You, okay?" asked Buck.

"Yeah. Shouldn't have stopped for that breakfast burrito on the way here."

"Docs on the way," said Buck. "First blush, what'd yah think?"

"From what I can see, the bodies were cut to pieces with a bladed instrument. Not a knife, unless it was a meat cleaver. Something with more heft. Something like an ax. You know, Buck, I've seen a lot of destruction in my day. We both have. This is beyond any of that. This was a frenzy. I just hope they were dead while most of it happened. We'll get started in the living room and kitchen while we wait for the doc."

Franklin walked towards the van. He turned back towards Buck. "By the way. Someone vomited in the kitchen sink. Could be the perp, or it could be one of those guys."

Buck nodded and walked past him to where Deputy Tortelli and Marvin Willets were standing in their clean blue scrubs and booties. "Either of you throw up in the kitchen sink?"

Deputy Tortelli lowered his head. "That would be me. Tried to make it outside."

Buck nodded to Franklin, who had walked up behind him. "Check the DNA anyway, just to be sure."

Franklin headed to the van and huddled with his team. Buck looked at the two sad figures in front of him. He almost felt sorry for giving them a hard time, but it was a lesson they needed to learn.

"I know this is hard. These people were your friends and neighbors, but if you want to help find who did this, you need to screw your heads on straight. We have a lot of work to do, and we don't have a lot of time. I want you to go home, grab food or a shower, whatever you need, get dressed and head back to your office. Is the sheriff married?"

Marvin Willets looked horrified. "Oh my god, Felicity. Someone has to tell his wife." He looked pleadingly at Buck.

"I'll take care of that. Text me her address. Next, I want some background on all the victims. Friends, local relatives, jobs. Anything you can find. You may also want to put out a statement telling people what happened. Leave out the details. Short and sweet. Ongoing investigation. Blah, blah, blah. Don't talk to anyone about any of what happened here today."

They both nodded, and Buck turned towards his Jeep when the deputy who had been blocking the road came running down the driveway in a panic. "Marvin, Agent Taylor, we may have another body. Just got the call on my phone."

He stopped to catch his breath. Marvin Willets looked like he wanted to crawl under a rock and hide. Deputy Tortelli turned pale.

"Tell me what you know, Deputy," said Buck. Franklin and his team had gathered around them. Everyone listened while the deputy spoke.

"Got a call from Mrs. Groves. She said she went to check on her son Mitchell since she hadn't been able to get hold of him since Saturday night, and when she walked into his house, there was blood everywhere. She said she ran back outside, slammed the door behind her and called me."

The deputy stopped to catch his breath. Buck turned to Franklin. "You guys okay here without an escort?"

"Yeah, we're all armed. We'll be fine." Franklin and his team, besides being forensic technicians, were also certified law enforcement officers. They were trained just like everyone else who worked at CBI.

He turned to Marvin Willets and Deputy Tortelli. "Skip the food and showers. Go get dressed and meet me at the Groveses' house.

"Deputy . . . ?"

"Jefferson, sir. Tommy Jefferson."

"That's a name that should be easy to remember. You're with me," said Buck. "You lead the way. I'm right behind you."

The deputy raced to his car, and Buck stepped to the side with Franklin. "Get your guys working, and then follow us; I'll text you the address. This could be nothing, but I'm getting the feeling that this is going to be a bad day."

CHAPTER EIGHT

B uck followed Deputy Jefferson back down County Route 7, turned left onto Highway 114, and sped through town, the deputy with lights and sirens on, Buck with his flashing lights on. They turned right onto Second Avenue and then right again onto Third Street.

The town was laid out on a grid. East–west streets were numbered avenues, even on the north side of Highway 114 and odd on the south. The cross streets were numbered streets. They pulled in front of a small, faded gray house with a broken-down front porch and a car up on blocks under an open-sided metal building.

An elderly woman hobbled towards the patrol SUV as Deputy Jefferson opened his door. She was holding one hand against her heart. She looked frantic. Several of the neighbors were with her, trying to calm her down. Buck could hear her babbling incoherently, and he stepped up to intervene. He held her by her upper arms as gently as he could to keep her from moving.

"Ma'am. My name is Buck Taylor. I'm an investigator with the Colorado Bureau of Investigation. I need you to try to calm down so we can find out what's going on."

Buck led her over to the passenger side of the SUV, opened the door and helped her sit on the seat. He was about to try again when an elderly man stepped up.

"Agent. I might be able to help."

Buck stood up, and the man held out his hand. Buck shook it.

"My name's Trudeau, Raymond Trudeau. I live next door. I was working in the yard when I heard Edna scream. She slammed the door and ran across the yard, screaming that Mitchell was dead. I sat her down and told her to call the deputy while I went to see what she was screaming about. I opened the door, and the smell was terrible. From what I could see from the front door, there was blood spatter all over the house. I closed the door. When I got back to her, she was on the phone with the deputy."

"Mr. Trudeau, did you see anyone around the house, and did you go any farther inside than the front door?" asked Buck.

"No, sir, to both questions."

"One more thing, Mr. Trudeau, when was the last time you saw Mitchell Groves?"

Mr. Trudeau thought for a minute. "Must have been Saturday night. I had just let the dog out in the backyard when I heard him pull up on his motorcycle. That would have been right after the ten o'clock news."

"Did he leave after that, or did you hear anyone else stop by?"

Mrs. Trudeau walked up and joined them. "I'm a light sleeper, Officer. I heard a car pull up out front about an hour after we went to bed. When I looked outside, I saw the sheriff's SUV parked at the curb. I just assumed he was arresting Mitchell."

She leaned in closer so only Buck could hear. "We think Mitchell might be selling drugs. Lots of cars pull up to the house at all hours of the day and night, but they only stay a minute or two. I spoke to the sheriff about it a couple of times, and he said he would investigate it. Thought that's what he might have been doing that night."

Buck leaned back. "Ma'am, could you sit with Mrs. Groves while we check out the house?"

She nodded, and Buck signaled to the deputy to follow him. As they approached the door, the deputy told Buck that he had called her doctor, who was on his way over. Buck nodded.

Buck stepped up to the front door and pulled his pistol from his holster. The deputy watched

Buck and then pulled his gun. His hand was shaking, and Buck put his hand on top of the deputy's and pushed down so the gun was pointing towards the ground.

"I want you to stay here by the door and make sure no one comes up behind me. I'm going to clear the house. Do not come inside."

The deputy nodded, and Buck pushed open the front door. The house was dark, with all the curtains closed, so he pulled his flashlight from his belt, and with his gun leading the way, he stepped into what he assumed was the living room.

Mrs. Groves had been right. There was blood spatter all over the living room walls, floor and ceiling. And he spotted a dry puddle in front of the sixty-five-inch TV, which looked like the only decent piece of furniture in the house.

Buck, watching where he stepped, continued to move through the house. There was less blood in the kitchen, but it was hard to tell with all the dirty dishes in the sink and on the counter. He turned towards the hall and noticed a bloody drag mark down the center. He stepped to one side and followed the trail. He cleared a bedroom, which was filthy, and a bathroom that made Buck cringe.

At the end of the hall, he came to a closed door. He turned the knob and pushed the door open.

The first things he saw were shelves of chemicals and boxes of cough syrup. A small table in one corner held a cooking pot, test tubes and a Bunsen burner. It looked like a small chemistry lab, but Buck had seen meth labs before, and he had no doubt that this was what he was looking at.

He felt a presence behind him, and he turned, raising his pistol as he did. He stopped moving and stared. He was having trouble comprehending what he saw on the opposite side of the room.

Buck moved closer. The body was lying facedown on a wooden table. Its hands and feet were tied to the four table legs. The amount of blood was incredible, but the most striking detail was what had been done to the body. All the person's ribs had been cut from the spinal cord, pulled away to form a large cavity, and the lungs were spread out on top of the ribs. Buck had never seen anything like it.

He holstered his gun and pulled out his camera. He put the camera on video and scanned the room, paying close attention to the body. He then ran the camera along the shelves and scanned the table with the test tubes. He turned off the video, walked back to the body and took several detailed pictures of the body.

He shut off his camera and put his phone back

in his pocket. He stepped over to the small lab setup and looked around. Under the table, he found several more of the same lavender-colored pills that he had found at the Carrollton house. He pulled a pair of nitrile gloves out of his pocket, put them on and picked up the pills, placing them in the bag.

He stood up and stepped to the door. He heard Franklin calling his name, so he yelled for Franklin to stay where he was. He followed his original path back to the front door and stepped outside. He told the deputy it was okay to holster his weapon.

"You okay?" asked Franklin.

Without answering, Buck pulled out his phone, opened his gallery and showed Franklin the pictures he had taken in the lab.

"Fuck, Buck. What the hell did we walk into? This looks like we're dealing with a homicidal maniac. Who could do such a thing? Who could even think up doing such a thing to another human being?"

He handed Buck back the phone, and Buck clipped it on his belt. He headed back to the SUV, where a young man with longish hair and glasses was checking Mrs. Groves's blood pressure. He stood up and walked over to Buck. "Is it her son, Officer?" He held out his hand. "Sorry, Officer. Dr. Ken Maxwell. I'm Mrs. Groves's doctor." Buck introduced himself, and they shook hands.

"It looks like it might be, Doctor. I need to tell Mrs. Groves."

The doctor pulled his arm. "Let me do that, Agent Taylor."

He walked back to the SUV, kneeled and spoke to Mrs. Groves. Her eyes filled with tears, and she let out a bloodcurdling scream that made all the neighbors who had gathered jump. The doctor reached into his black bag lying on the ground, pulled out a bottle, dumped two pills in his hand, took a water bottle from one of the neighbors and gave the pills to Mrs. Groves.

He walked back to Buck. "I gave her a sedative to calm her down. I'm worried about her heart, so I'm going to drive her to the hospital in Saguache. I know you will need to talk with her."

He pulled a business card from his pants pocket and handed it to Buck. "Call me, and I will let you know when she is ready."

He walked back to the SUV, gently lifted Mrs. Groves and led her to his car parked behind the SUV. He put her in the front seat, slid into the driver's side and pulled away from the curb.

Buck turned to Deputy Jefferson. "I need you to stay here and wait for the forensic pathologist. Franklin will stay with you. No one goes into the house. I need to meet the pathologist at the other crime scene; then, we'll head over here."

Buck nodded to Franklin, headed for his SUV and slid into the driver's seat. He checked the text from Marvin Willets and entered the sheriff's address into his GPS. The house was about four blocks away. It was time to let the sheriff's wife know that her husband would not be coming home. This was the part of the job he hated most. There was never a good way to tell people that their loved ones had passed away, especially when it was so unexpected.

He thought about the night he'd had to tell his own children that their mother had passed away. They were all adults, and they had been expecting it for five years, but it was still difficult when the end came. Buck was amazed that after all this time, he still missed Lucy.

CHAPTER NINE

I f you asked Buck, he would tell you that he fell in love with Lucinda Torres on the first day of their senior year in high school. Lucy always told people that Buck stalked her the entire senior year before she gave in to shut up her friends and agreed to go to the movies with him. She had always considered him just another jock, another football player who was too full of himself. What she found on that first date was a shy, unassuming gentleman, for lack of a better word, who, it seemed, cared more about pleasing her than bragging about his prowess on the football field. She would tell people it was love at first sight that had taken a year to accomplish. From that day forward, they were inseparable.

During senior year Buck had been approached by several college football scouts who wanted to sign him to play for their schools. Gunnison High School was a small school back in 1978, and Buck and his family were amazed at how many schools had recruited him, but for Buck, college just wasn't in the cards.

Buck hated school and spent a lot of time getting himself out of trouble instead of getting an education. When he found something that interested him, he had no problem learning all he could about the subject, but regular schoolwork just bored him. After several long heartfelt discussions, first with Lucy and then with his parents, he had decided to join the army after graduation. Surprisingly, no one was surprised.

Buck spent four years after high school in the army, and by the time his enlistment was up, he had been promoted to First Sergeant. He spent three years of his enlistment in the military police and really took to police work. That was when he decided to apply for a position with the Gunnison County Sheriff's Office.

Since he was already well known in the county, he had no trouble getting a job as a deputy. He proposed to Lucy on the night he received the call that he had gotten the position. His life and career were set. He made the most of his time with the Gunnison County Sheriff's Office, eventually becoming the undersheriff in charge of the Investigation Division and coming to the attention of the Colorado Bureau of Investigation.

Buck had worked with the Colorado Bureau of Investigation on several cases inside the county and had earned the respect of the investigators he had worked with.

As twilight started to fall on Buck's career, he knew that unless he wanted to go into politics and run for sheriff, he had reached the highest position in the sheriff's office that he could obtain. He loved his job, but when the first offer came in from the CBI, he sat down with Lucy and had a long heart-to-heart talk.

He'd spent seventeen years in the sheriff's office and had always figured he would retire from that job. They had three children, two in high school and one not far behind, and he was a well-respected member of the community. Did he have the right to disrupt their lives, pick up and move someplace else and start all over? The kids had friends, Lucy owned a small deli/ice cream parlor, and they had a nice life.

He could stick it out for another ten years and retire, and they could travel and see the world like they had always planned. Twice he turned down the offer from the CBI, although more and more, he felt like he was trapped behind a desk instead of doing what he loved, which was investigating crime.

The final offer came from Tom Cole, then-director of the Colorado Bureau of Investigation. Buck always remembered that day. The Denver Broncos had just lost another game, the third one in a row, and his friends had all packed up and headed home when there was a knock at the front door.

Anyone living in a small community knows that no one ever uses the front door, and no one knocks. So, who could be knocking this late on a Sunday evening?

Buck answered the door and was surprised to see the director of the Colorado Bureau of Investigation standing on his front porch. The director smiled and said, "Before you close the door in my face, please listen to my offer."

Buck invited him in, and he and Lucy sat on the couch and listened as the director laid out his plan. He was opening a new branch office in Grand Junction, Colorado, that would house five agents and a small forensic unit. Buck could continue to live in Gunnison but would have to report to the office in Grand Junction twice a month. Otherwise, he would be free to work out of his house. There would be no disruption in his life other than having to spend some time on the road as his investigations warranted. He would work alone, but he would have all the branch office's resources at his disposal.

Before Buck could say a word, Lucy said, "Buck, this is what you have been waiting for, a chance to be a real investigator again. You have to take this." That was one of the things that made him love Lucy every day. She always knew what he was thinking, and she always understood what drove him. She had nailed it this time. Buck looked at the director and replied, "Well, I guess it's settled; looks like you have a new investigator on your team."

That was twenty-four years ago, and Buck had never looked back. He had made the most of those years and was one of the most respected and feared investigators in the state, but all that work couldn't make up for the loss he suffered.

Lucy was diagnosed with metastatic breast cancer following a routine mammogram, and they set off together on their next adventure: the quest to beat the dreaded disease. After a double mastectomy and five years of chemo, they knew their time was drawing to a close when the cancer returned several times to her brain and was no longer controlled by the radiation.

They decided together to stop all treatments, even though they had always told the family that the decision was Lucy's alone to make. Lucy spent the last couple of months of her life taking care of her small business and spending as much time as she could with her children and grandchildren.

The end came one spring night. Lucy had been sleeping on and off for twenty hours a day in the end. The night she died, Buck had been lying in bed next to her, reading a report, when she snuggled into his arms and rested her head on his shoulder. Sometime during the night, Buck had fallen asleep. When he woke up, Lucy was gone, and his world was shattered.

They say that time heals all wounds, but Buck wasn't sure that was the case when you lost your closest friend. And even now, all these years later, he missed her more and more each day.

Buck always thought back to that Sunday morning when the family had gathered for a private ceremony at the little dock along the Gunnison River to scatter Lucy's ashes. Each family member got to say a few words about Lucy, and when they finished and turned to go, they were stunned to see several hundred of their neighbors and friends standing silently behind them in the park. Word had gotten out about their private service, and everyone turned out to pay tribute to Lucy. The affair turned into a huge party, with plenty of food and drinks. Lucy never wanted any kind of service, but Buck figured she would have loved this spontaneous outpouring of love.

CHAPTER TEN

B uck pulled into the driveway of a small light blue house on Fifth Street. He sat for a minute and mentally prepared himself. Looking at dead bodies was one thing. Telling a family that one of their loved ones was never coming home was something else entirely. He slid out of his Jeep and watched as a short blond woman and an older man and woman stepped out onto the front steps. Buck steeled himself and walked to the group. He reached the steps, and he saw Felicity Wechsler begin to shake. The older man wrapped his arms around her.

"Mrs. Wechsler, my name is Buck Taylor. I'm with the Colorado Bureau of Investigation."

Felicity Wechsler screamed, collapsing into the older man's arms, while the older woman fell to her knees and sobbed. Buck reached the older woman and helped her settle onto the stairs. He looked at the older man, who said with tears in his eyes, "I'm George Wechsler, Jimmy's dad. It's bad, isn't it?"

Buck, still kneeling and holding the older Mrs.

Wechsler's hand, said, "Yes, sir. We found Jimmy at a crime scene. There's no easy way to say this. Your son was murdered."

Tears flowed down George Wechsler's face as he tried to comfort Felicity. The older woman stood on shaking legs and came over and sat on the other side of Felicity, and they held each other.

Buck looked up and saw two young girls standing in the open doorway. They couldn't have been more than four or five. They had tears in their eyes, and they looked lost. The older-looking girl ran from the door, and Buck heard a door slam somewhere deeper in the house.

He stood up and started to step onto the front landing when a middle-aged woman came up, grabbed his arm and said, "I'll look after the girls. I'm Judith Ingraham, from next door. Such a tragedy. Jimmy was a wonderful husband and father. We're going to miss him."

She ran up the steps, took the younger daughter by the hand and moved deeper into the house. Buck stepped back down the stairs and kneeled in front of Felicity.

"Ma'am, I know this is a horrible time, but would it be all right if I asked you a couple of questions?"

Felicity Wechsler nodded, wiped her eyes, stood and led Buck into the house, followed by Jimmy's parents. Buck looked back at the small crowd that had gathered on the street. He nodded towards them and stepped into the house.

The small living room was bright and airy, and Buck walked over and closed the front window drapes to give the family some privacy. Then, he sat in a recliner opposite the couch.

"Mrs. Wechsler, when was the last time you heard from your husband?" he asked.

She wiped her eyes and looked at Buck. "He called me just as he was locking up for the night. That was Saturday night, about seven. He said he had one stop to make, and then he would be home." Tears rolled down her face.

"What did you do when he didn't come home?"

"I called Tommy and Mike to see if they had heard from him. They had the weekend off. They said they would look for him. When they hadn't called me by ten p.m., I feared the worst and I called George and Carol. They drove up from Farmington."

"One last question, ma'am. Did Jimmy tell you where the one stop was that he had to make?"

She shook her head and rested it on George Wechsler's shoulder. Buck turned to go and saw Marvin Willets standing in the doorway. Buck excused himself and stepped outside, followed by Marvin.

"Agent Taylor. Is there a madman loose in our town? I've lived here a long time, and nothing like this has ever happened before. People are scared. What do I do? I feel overwhelmed."

Buck put his hand on Marvin's shoulder. "Right now, Marvin, I'm not sure what to think. If anyone asks, tell them we are still investigating and will make an announcement once we have a clearer picture. I'm going to head back to the first crime scene. Why don't you stay here and see if you can help these poor folks? I will also call and see if I can get some state troopers to come up here and help you out. That should help put some folks at ease."

Buck turned to leave, then stopped and walked back to Marvin Willets. "The sheriff's SUV was seen late Saturday night in front of Mitchell Groves's house. Most likely after he was already dead. We need to know where that SUV went. When you leave here, get your deputies and check every store and residence in the area and see if anyone has a picture from a doorbell cam or CCTV, and let's see if we can figure out where the SUV went after it left the Groves house."

"You think the killers may have been driving the SUV?" asked Marvin.

Buck nodded. "I think it's a very real

possibility."

Buck walked down the steps, slid into his Jeep, and pulled out his phone. He speed-dialed the first number in his phone directory.

"Hey, Buck. Did you find him?" asked Director Jackson.

"Yes, sir, but it's bad."

Buck gave the director a quick debrief on what they found at both crime scenes. There was silence on the other end of the phone.

"Shit. Four bodies all hacked to death. What the hell is going on up there?" asked Director Jackson.

"Not sure, sir. I've seen a lot of death and destruction, but this ranks right up there with the worst I've ever seen."

"Where are you taking the bodies?" asked Director Jackson.

"We're gonna take them to Gunnison. Dr. Parkinson should already be on-site. I'd like to get them out of here as soon as possible. It's unusually hot up here for this time of the year, and decomp was moving fast."

"Let me know when you plan to transport, and I'll arrange an escort. Okay, Buck. What else do you need?"

"Can you call Paul and have him head this

way? Also, I'd like to get a couple of state troopers to help the sheriff. Last night he was the coroner, and today, he's the sheriff in a town with four gruesome murders. He's in way over his head, and I think it might help the townspeople sleep a little better. That should be it for now. I'll know more once we can get deeper into this thing."

"Okay, Buck. I'm on it. Stay safe."

The director hung up, and Buck backed out of the driveway and headed back to the first crime scene. He wasn't sure where this investigation would lead, but the little bug that danced around in his brain during an investigation was jumping around like crazy.

He did know one thing for certain, and that one thing made him cringe. These four murders were not going to be the last in this sleepy little county. Whoever committed these murders liked what he or she was doing, and that thought scared Buck.

CHAPTER ELEVEN

B uck pulled into the driveway of the Carrolltons' house and was glad to see the silver Jeep Grand Cherokee parked next to the dark green Ford F-250. He pulled in behind them, parked and slid out of the front seat. He grabbed his backpack off the passenger seat, slung it over his left shoulder and headed for the door.

He had just reached the steps when Ashley Baxter stepped out onto the porch, followed by Dr. Parkinson. They pulled off their masks and shook hands with Buck.

CBI Agent Ashley Baxter had worked with Buck on many interesting cases over the years, besides working on her own cases. At thirty-two years old, she was the youngest agent in the Grand Junction Field Office. She'd joined CBI straight out of college and, having had no experience in the field, she valued the time she got to spend with Buck because she learned so much about running an investigation.

Bax stood about five foot six with blue eyes

and blond hair that she often kept tied in a ponytail that hung through the hole in the back of her CBI cap. She was what some people would describe as husky, or what used to be called having a "mountain girl" figure. She wasn't gorgeous, but she was pretty enough to turn men's heads when she walked into a room until they spotted the badge and gun clipped to her belt. She had been with the Colorado Bureau of Investigation for nine years, and she had earned Buck's respect.

She was also a whiz at doing deep background searches—a talent Buck did not share—so he relied on Bax to help him out. They worked well as a team and collaborated more and more as the years rolled by.

"Fuck, Buck," said Bax. "What have we gotten ourselves involved in this time? What a mess."

The doctor agreed. "Buck, I've seen some horrible shit in my time, but this is gonna stick with me for a long time. It always amazes me what one human being can do to another."

"Yeah," said Buck. "What do you think, Garrett? What the hell are we dealing with?"

Dr. Parkinson shook his head. "I wish I knew. It looks like someone used a heavy-bladed weapon; my guess would be some kind of ax. I'll know more once I get them on the table. The fury that this took, though, that's the scariest thing of all.

This was way more than personal."

An ambulance pulled down the driveway, and Dr. Parkinson stepped away to talk to the two EMTs. They listened and then moved to the back of the ambulance to gather their gear. Dr. Parkinson walked back over to Buck and Bax.

"Your forensics folks said there's another body?"

Buck pulled out his phone and opened it to his gallery. He handed the phone to the doctor, who flipped through the pictures. When he finished looking at the pictures, he handed the phone to Bax.

"Shit, Buck. They don't teach you about that in the pathology classes. What the hell? That looks almost ritualistic."

"That's what I thought too," said Buck. "Franklin is there waiting for you." He texted the address to the doctor.

Dr. Parkinson looked at his watch. "I'd better get over there. I've got a long night ahead of me. I'll say one thing, Buck. You always make things interesting. I'll see you back at the hospital for the post."

He led the EMTs inside and walked them through the crime scene, making sure they stepped only where and touched only what the forensic techs told them to. After he finished, he headed to his truck, slid in, entered the address in the GPS on his dash and pulled out of the driveway.

Bax handed Buck back his phone. "What's your first impression? Do we have a madman on the loose, or is this something else?"

"I don't think this is the last. Whoever did this likes it. I'm going to follow the ambulance to Gunnison. I asked the sheriff and Deputy Tortelli to put together some background on the victims. Why don't you head over to the sheriff's office and see what they've got? Reach out to the FBI and see if they have anything in their files that looks like this. Go ahead and put together the investigation file. I'll upload pictures to it later."

He reached into his pocket, pulled out the bag with the pills and handed it to Bax. "Any idea what these are? Found one here and a bunch at the second scene."

Bax looked at the pills. "Nothing I've seen before." She handed the bag back to Buck.

"I'll send a picture over to Jess and see if she can identify them."

He opened his text app, picked a name from his contact list and sent the pictures to Jess Gonzales. As the deputy director of the DEA's western regional office, based out of Grand Junction, she might have come across these pills before. Buck wasn't sure if they were related to the case, but at this point, evidence was evidence, and he needed to follow it.

Buck and Bax stood back as the EMTs carried out one body bag after the other. It was getting late, and Buck realized he hadn't eaten since breakfast. He also needed a place to sleep, not that he would get much sleep tonight. If he needed to crash for a couple of hours, he would head home and sleep in his bed. Something that didn't often happen when he was working on a case.

He tapped Bax on the arm. "See if you can get us a couple of rooms in town. Gunnison is an hour away if you can't get something close to here. Call me, and I'll get you set up with a hotel there. Get a room for Paul as well."

He turned to head for his Jeep, then turned back around. "One last thing. We need to track down the sheriff's SUV. One neighbor said she spotted the SUV parked in front of the Groves house late Saturday night. She thought the sheriff might have been investigating a complaint that Groves was selling drugs. If the time is correct and the witness was certain, then I think the killers drove the SUV. The sheriff was probably already dead by then. I asked Marvin Willets to get with his two deputies and check the area around the scene for any video footage they can find. We need to figure out where the SUV went when it left the crime scene."

The EMTs carried out the last body bag and told Buck they were heading over to the second crime scene. Bax told him she was going to stay at this crime scene for a little while and work with the forensic team before heading to the sheriff's office. She'd send Paul to the second scene as soon as he arrived.

Buck wished her a good night and walked to his Jeep. It was going to be a long night.

Buck sat for a moment and listened to the sounds around him: the various birdcalls, and a bullfrog somewhere in the distance. He pulled out his phone and dialed the director.

"Hey, Buck. What can you tell me?"

"Well, sir. The crimes are related. Of that, there is no doubt. Dr. Parkinson said we are looking at an ax as the murder weapon. I'll upload the pictures of both scenes into the investigation file tonight when I get to the hospital in Gunnison. We should be ready to transport in half an hour or so."

"Okay, Buck. The troopers should already be there. I told one of them to escort you to the hospital. Give me a report as soon as you can."

Buck took a sip of the warm Coke sitting in the center console. "Yes, sir. And thanks for the troopers. This town is going to be on edge once all the details come out."

Buck disconnected the call, started the Jeep and pulled out of the driveway. He drove through town and noticed all the people gathering outside the Groves house. He also noticed that several of the people in the crowd carried rifles or had sidearms. This could get ugly.

He pulled in behind a state police car, walked up and introduced himself to the trooper. "Glad you're here, Trooper. From the looks of some of the people gathered, they are ready to protect themselves."

"Yes, sir, Agent Taylor. That's okay. I can understand why they're scared, but my boys will watch them and make sure things stay quiet in town tonight."

Buck thanked him and headed to the house. Dr. Parkinson was just stepping through the door. "It's even more horrendous up close. One thing you should be aware of. The victim's hands and feet were tied to the table legs. There was a gag in his mouth. He was alive when someone started hacking on him. There was no medical precision here, just brute force to cut through the ribs, so you are not looking for a person with medical training."

Buck thanked the doctor and stepped back as the body bag was carried from the house. Once the bodies were secured in the ambulance, Buck signaled to the trooper he had been talking with, and the trooper nodded and headed for his car.

The ambulance pulled out behind the state trooper's car, and Buck fell in behind. They all had their flashers on. The procession pulled onto Highway 114 and headed towards Gunnison. Several people stood along the sidewalks in town and waved American flags. The people of Pine County were giving their sheriff a dignified send-off.

A solemn voice came over Buck's police radio. "Dispatch to Sheriff James Wechsler . . . No response. Dispatch to Sheriff James Wechsler . . . Show Sheriff James Wechsler out of service four-twenty-seven p.m. . . . We have the watch. Godspeed."

As they reached the outskirts of town, several law enforcement vehicles from the neighboring counties joined the procession. They picked up more vehicles as they entered Gunnison County, and several patrol cars from the Gunnison Police Department escorted them to their destination.

At the hospital, the procession stopped, and the officers all lined the sidewalk outside the emergency room entrance and stood at attention as the three body bags were loaded onto gurneys and rolled into the hospital. The officers saluted as the flag-draped body bag containing Sheriff Wechsler was loaded onto a fourth gurney for the final leg of this part of his journey.

Buck and Dr. Parkinson followed the now-smaller procession through the hospital and into the elevator that would take them to the basement morgue.

Buck stepped to the side and watched as the first body, that of Sheriff Wechsler, was laid onto the cold stainless steel table by the two morgue orderlies. They removed the body from the black bag.

Dr. Parkinson excused himself to get changed, which gave Buck a chance to stand with the body as the orderlies removed the bloody remnants of clothes. They placed the clothes into several evidence bags, sealed and signed them and set them on the counter next to Buck.

One of the orderlies, a middle-aged dark-haired woman, broke the seal on several sterilized five-gallon buckets, removed the lid from the first one and set it under the drain at the end of the table. She picked up a hose from under the table, turned on the water and washed the body, giving Buck the first good look at the wounds. He watched as the red-tinted water ran down the drain and then stepped closer to the body.

The amount of damage to the body was incredible, and he hoped the sheriff had died with the first blow. The pain, he thought to himself, must have been incredible. He stepped back as Dr. Parkinson stepped up to the table in a pair of blue scrubs. He directed the second orderly to take pictures and pointed out where he wanted close-ups.

While the pictures were being taken, he asked the first orderly to melt down some paraffin, and when she was finished, he poured the melted mixture into one of the wounds and let it sit for a few minutes to harden.

Buck pulled out his phone and stepped closer to the table. He took pictures of several of the wounds, now that they were no longer covered in blood. The blows were deep and narrow with clean edges on the sides, but many of them appeared to have been torn at the bottom of the cut. It looked to Buck like the weapon might have had a hook at the bottom that ripped the flesh as it was pulled free.

Dr. Parkinson used a pair of tongs to pull out the paraffin mold and set it on the counter, so Buck and the orderly could take pictures. He then placed it in an evidence bag, and Buck sealed and signed it, adding it to his pile. It was a strange shape. It looked like an ax, but it had a tail or a hook on the lower end.

Buck stopped and glanced at the wound in the center of the chest. He took a couple of close-up pictures and then looked at Dr. Parkinson.

"What do you make of this wound, Doc? It's

different from the others?"

Dr. Parkinson leaned close to the wound and then pulled a magnifying glass from the array of tools above the exam table. He moved it around to get the best look. He pulled back so Buck could get a better look. He studied the wound for several minutes.

"It looks square," said Buck. "What kind of weapon makes a square hole?"

"I don't know, Buck. I've never seen anything like it. Could be something custom-made, I guess. That's strange." He had the orderlies help him roll the body on its side, and he examined the back. "Whatever made the front hole didn't exit out the back, so it was removed by the killer, or it is still in the body. If it's the latter, we'll find it."

The orderly melted down another stick of paraffin and poured it into the square hole. They waited a few minutes for the paraffin to harden, and then, using the tongs, Dr. Parkinson pulled the mold from the sheriff's chest. They both stared at it for a minute.

"Well," said Buck. "It's not a bullet. Looks like some kind of arrow. Nothing like I've seen before."

He took some pictures, and then Dr. Parkinson placed it in an evidence bag, sealed and signed the bag.

Buck stepped back from the table. He had taken a close-up of the paraffin replicas with a small ruler sitting next to them and saved them and the picture of the square hole to his phone. He opened his email app, chose a recipient from his contact list, loaded a couple of pictures and a brief message and hit send.

Dr. Parkinson instructed the female orderly to turn on the recorder, and he pulled the microphone down from where it was hanging above the table. Their long night was about to begin.

CHAPTER TWELVE

Bax pulled her Jeep into the parking space in front of the sheriff's office, grabbed her backpack and slid out of the car. A memorial covered the sidewalk in front of the office's picture window, and she stopped for a minute to look at the flowers and the notes of appreciation and love that filled the area. The sheriff had only been on the job for a short time, but it looked like he had made an impression.

She pushed open the door and heard the bell above the door clang. She loved walking into small-town law enforcement offices. So many of them had the feel of the Old West, right down to the musty smell and the dust. This one had authentic charm. It had dark pine paneling on the walls, and the floor was made of wide plank flooring of various sizes that were well worn and had a great patina.

Just inside the door was a small waist-high counter, and behind it were two desks in a large area and a small office behind those. She stepped up to the counter and tapped the bell.

A young deputy came walking from behind a wall carrying a water bottle. "Can I help you, ma'am?"

"Yeah," said Bax. "You can start by not calling me ma'am. Makes me feel old."

She held up her credentials. "Ashley Baxter, Colorado Bureau of Investigation. You can call me Bax; everyone does." She held out her hand. "My condolences for the loss of your sheriff."

The deputy lowered his eyes and nodded. Then, he walked up to the counter and shook her hand. "Deputy Tortelli, most folks call me Tort. What can I do for you?"

"First, I need a place to set up, some desk space and room for my laptop. Second, Buck said he asked you to put together some background on the sheriff and on the three other victims. Have you been able to work on that?"

He looked embarrassed. "As you can imagine, things have been crazy around here. I was just going to get started." He pointed towards a small wooden desk next to the front window. "Will this work for you?"

Bax told him it would. She set her backpack on the desk and pulled out her laptop. She connected to the Wi-Fi, logged into the CBI website, and opened the next investigation file.

CBI had gone digital a couple of years back,

so instead of having a blue binder for each case, Buck and the team just had to open a program on their laptops. The new case was automatically assigned a case number, and Bax would list everyone who needed access to the file and send them email invites. All evidence, lab reports, photos, etc. that were part of the case would be uploaded into the file, and anyone who needed access just had to open the file. That was much better than the old system, where everything had been placed in the binder by hand. Buck used to complain that he would spend half his time trying to track down who had the binder.

For a technological dinosaur like Buck, this made his life so much easier, and he had ready access to anything he needed. Bax clicked on the file and opened the chronology page, which was the first page in the file. Nothing was ever entered into the file without a note being entered into the chronology page first. The chronology kept track of everything that happened in the investigation.

Buck was meticulous about his case files, and he demanded the same thing from his team. He had never lost a case in court in all his years in law enforcement because something was missing from his files. Next, she clicked on the email addresses of everyone she wanted to have access to the file and hit send.

She opened a small notebook she carried in

her pocket and, working down the notes she had made, entered all the pertinent information into the file; the who, what, where, and when of the case. The why was still to be determined.

She stood up and walked over to Deputy Tortelli, who was sitting at another desk, clicking away on his laptop while talking on the phone. He thanked the person on the other end and looked up at Bax.

"Any word on the sheriff's SUV?" she asked. "One of Groves's neighbors said it was seen late Saturday night. She thought he was there to investigate Groves for selling drugs. Buck asked Sheriff Willets to search the town and see if there was any video of the SUV leaving the crime scene. Do you have a file on Groves?"

Deputy Tortelli dropped his eyes to his keyboard. "There were rumors and accusations, but they were unsubstantiated. The sheriff spoke with Groves a couple of days ago, and nothing came of it."

Bax had to keep from laughing. "Well, I guess you were wrong about *that* since the back bedroom was a well-equipped meth lab."

Deputy Tortelli looked up from his keyboard. "What are you talking about? What meth lab?" He sounded defensive.

"The one," said Bax, "that's been operating right under your noses for God knows how long."

He looked shocked, and Bax could tell from his facial expression that he didn't know anything about the lab. He looked like he was about to get defensive, so she walked away and turned. "Can you get me Mrs. Groves's home address? I'd like to talk to her and see if her son's drug dealing had anything to do with these murders. And please work on the background for the other victims."

Deputy Tortelli wrote the address on a sticky note and handed it to her. She placed her laptop into her backpack and headed out the door. She could feel Deputy Tortelli glaring at her.

Once in her Jeep, she plugged the address into her GPS, drove the six blocks to the opposite end of town and pulled into the driveway of a modest-looking mid-century modern ranch. She grabbed her backpack, slid out of the Jeep and walked to the front door.

A young, dark-haired woman, who looked a little older than Bax, opened the door as Bax approached. Bax held up her credentials. "Ashley Baxter, CBI. I'm looking for Mrs. Groves."

"I'm Carol Groves," said the woman. "Mom is in the living room. The doctor just brought her back from the hospital in Saguache. They gave her something to calm her down. Come in."

The entry was part of a large, well-appointed living room area, complete with white wood paneling and a wall that included a large-screen

TV, wood-burning fireplace and bookshelves from floor to ceiling, filled to overflowing with books of all shapes and sizes.

"Mom," said Carol Groves. "The police would like to talk with you." She led Bax into the room and pointed towards a high-back chair opposite the one Mrs. Groves sat in. Bax sat, and Carol Groves stood behind her mom.

Mrs. Groves had short silver hair, and she wore jeans and a floral print top. She looked right at home in the high-back chair, and Bax could picture her sitting there with the fire going, a glass of wine and reading one of the huge number of books lining the shelves. She had tears in her eyes, and she held a handkerchief balled up in her hand.

"Mrs. Groves, my name is Ashley Baxter. I'm with the Colorado Bureau of Investigation. First, I'd like to offer my condolences for the loss of your son." Mrs. Groves nodded and wiped her eyes. "I'd like to ask you a couple of questions about Mitchell if that would be okay?"

Receiving no verbal reply, Bax pulled her phone from her pocket and opened the recording app.

"Mrs. Groves, when was the last time you saw or spoke to Mitchell?"

Mrs. Groves thought for a minute. "It must have been Saturday morning. He called to ask me what kind of wine he should pick up."

"Sunday was Mom's birthday," said Carol. "When he didn't show up, she got worried. When he hadn't called by Monday, she thought something was wrong."

"Mrs. Groves, tell me about your son. What was he like? Things like that," said Bax.

She wiped the tears from her eyes. "Mitchell was a good man. He took good care of me and made sure I never needed anything. You couldn't ask for a better son." She spent the next few minutes telling Bax about her son's life, up till now.

"How did he make his money?" asked Bax.

Mrs. Groves grew agitated. "Don't you listen to that white-trash talk about Mitchell. He wasn't an angel, but he loved his mother."

Bax could see that Mrs. Groves had shut down, so she turned off the recording app on the phone, stood up and grabbed her backpack.

"Again, Mrs. Groves, my condolences on your loss."

Carol led her to the front door, followed her onto the porch and closed the door.

"Mitchell was a total shit," said Carol. Bax could see the anger on her face. "He's worthless and always has been. Mom thinks the sun rises and sets on her little boy, and she refuses to face reality. My brother is, was, a drug dealer, but he comes by now and then with something nice for Mom, and she fawns all over him. She refuses to believe what everyone else in town knows."

"How does he survive in a small town like this one, selling drugs? He can't have many customers?"

"I think he does more than just sell drugs," said Carol. "I suspect that he either manufactures drugs or deals for someone bigger. Someone not local. He lives in that shithole of a house, but his bank account is full."

Bax heard Mrs. Groves calling from inside for Carol, who looked perturbed. "The queen calls. I need to run. One word of advice, Detective, don't listen to a word my mother says when it comes to Mitchell."

Bax thanked her, and Carol pushed open the door and disappeared inside. Bax walked to her car and stood for a minute. Something Carol said was gnawing at her. She said her brother either manufactured or sold drugs for someone else, someone bigger. Bax knew he manufactured drugs, which was evident from the room where he died. So, the question was, who was he manufacturing for, and did that relationship contribute to his death?

It was time to dig deeper into Mitchell Groves.

CHAPTER THIRTEEN

They drove past Mitchell Groves's house, parked down the street and walked back to the crowd still standing outside the house. They asked a couple of the neighbors what was going on. At first, the neighbors looked at them like they had two heads. It was a small town; how could they not have heard what was going on?

Eventually, one of the neighbors, an older gray-haired man, told them about the murder of Mitchell Groves. They asked if it was a random crime or did he do something to piss someone off? The neighbor just shook his head.

They tried to get closer to the crime scene tape but were pushed back by a state trooper. They looked around and were amazed at the number of police vehicles on the scene. They had never seen that many cops in town. It looked like a cop convention.

They watched a blond-haired lady cop walk around the crime scene, looking in bushes and under the porch. They looked at each other. Had they forgotten something?

They saw the crime scene techs carrying out bags of evidence, but they didn't see anyone bringing out the body. They were hoping for a big crowd reaction, and they were disappointed. They headed back to their car and drove two blocks.

They pulled into the driveway of a nice two-story, Cape Cod-style house on the next block over, with a red front door and two dormers overlooking the street. They grabbed their backpacks and pushed open the front door.

"Hey, Mrs. Florence, we'll be upstairs."

A voice yelled from the kitchen. "You fellas want anything to drink or some snacks? And remember to close the front door, there's a psycho running around town, and I don't want him coming into our house."

She heard them charge up the stairs, and she walked from the kitchen, wiping her hands on a dishtowel and pushing the front door closed. She stopped to listen at the bottom of the stairs, heard nothing and went back into the kitchen.

Upstairs, they closed the door to the bedroom on the left, dropped their backpacks and pulled up a game for the gaming system that belonged to the third person in the room.

They grabbed the game controllers and

plopped down onto two big beanbag chairs in front of a forty-six-inch TV. The game started, the volume way up, and they remembered where they were, so they lowered it.

The Vikings on the screen had captured the British prince and had him lying on his stomach on a long wooden table. His hands and feet were tied to the table legs. They had stripped off his clothes, and player one began using an ax to cut his ribs from his backbone. It was like reliving the excitement all over again.

The funny thing was the game made it look so easy. It was a lot harder to do in real life, and even cutting all the way through, the ribs were still hard to pull away from the spine. They smiled and cheered on the Vikings as the game progressed, and their excitement grew as the Vikings moved from town to town, raping and pillaging.

They had switched players and had started the next level when they heard Mrs. Florence yell up the stairs that dinner was ready if they were staying to eat. It was hard to leave the game, but they needed to keep up appearances, so they paused the game and headed downstairs for dinner.

They didn't cook many meals for themselves, and it was nice when Mrs. Florence invited them to stay. Mr. Florence asked them if they had any plans for the evening. He wanted them to be careful going out at night, at least until the killer was found. Everyone in town and around the table was scared shitless. Well, not quite everyone.

They told him it was going to be an early night since they all had work in the morning, but they were going to head to a bar in Saguache. It was a hangout for gamers, and there was a tournament going on that they didn't want to miss. The first prize was a hundred dollars.

He asked about the game, and when they were finished explaining it to him, he asked them if they were the hunters or the hunted. They each chuckled.

Tonight, they were the hunters.

CHAPTER FOURTEEN

Snowflake and Dirt Crusher couldn't have been more different. Snowflake was in her early thirties and had been long-distance hiking since her first year in college. She'd completed school that year, but against her parents' wishes, she packed up her meager belongings and headed for Europe. She spent several years skiing professionally until a bad crash ended her career. Her rehabilitation included hiking, and she got hooked—the longer and the more demanding the trail, the better.

Two years earlier, she had completed the Pacific Crest Trail as a solo woman. She had hooked up for parts of the trail with other hikers, either segment or thru-hikers, but for the most part, she enjoyed the solitude of solo hiking.

When she started on the Continental Divide Trail, just north of the Mexican border, she intended to hit the Canadian border by the end of the summer and before the snow started to fall.

She met Dirt Crusher during her second week on the trail. He was over fifty years old, and she thought he might be over sixty, but he was one of the fittest people she had ever met on the trail. He was over six feet tall and weighing around one hundred ninety pounds, and she couldn't believe his strength and stamina. He had a short gray beard, and his gray ponytail hung almost to his waist. He could hike all day through some of the most challenging terrain around and never look winded.

Dirt Crusher was on the final leg of the triple crown of hiking. He had already completed the Pacific Crest Trail and the Appalachian Trail. The Continental Divide Trail would be the pinnacle of his time hiking in the United States, but it wouldn't be the end. He already had plans to head south of the border and hike from the United States to the southernmost point in Chile. He figured it might take him ten years, but no matter how long it took, it would be an incredible adventure.

They'd intended to keep hiking until they reached the Conway Hiker's Resort, just outside Silver City, Colorado. Then, the plan was to stop for a couple of days to rest and resupply before pushing on to Wyoming. However, that plan had changed last night when they took a short side hike to the Miner's Falls overlook.

The view from the overlook above the falls was incredible. The thin ribbon of water fell over two hundred feet before landing in a small lake with the clearest water you could ever imagine. The view of the lush valley and steep canyon below was incredible, but it was the stars that made the side hike worth it. From their perch on the overlook, they could see the Milky Way, and it seemed so close they could almost reach out and touch it.

They decided to spend an extra night on the trail, sleeping on the rock outcropping over the falls. They had heard from a couple of other hikers they met that they might be able to see the northern lights, which was rare in Colorado.

Their campsite on the outcropping was more bare bones than any of their other campsites. Instead of pitching their small one-person tents, they decided to sleep under the stars, so they built their campfire on top of the big rock and positioned their sleeping bags next to the fire. They removed the last packages of trail food from their backpacks and created a small feast that they enjoyed while lying back looking at the stars. The night couldn't have been more perfect.

A little after midnight, Dirt Crusher woke up with that urge that afflicts many men his age. Nature was calling. He stood up and stretched out the kinks. He thought he saw a faint greenish wave in the northern sky, and he tapped Snowflake with his foot.

She stirred and sat up. "What's up?"

He pointed to the north. "I think I see the northern lights. Real faint, but very cool."

Snowflake looked towards where he was pointing and sat mesmerized. The ribbon of green brightened as it moved across the sky, flowing like water. They stared until it faded out of sight.

Dirt Crusher turned to head towards the nearest trees when he stopped and grabbed his chest. He let out a grunt, and pain filled his eyes. He looked down to find his hands wrapped around a long metal point sticking out of his chest.

Snowflake heard a low thump and looked up to see him grab his chest. Her first thought, because of his age, was that he was having a heart attack until she saw the blood leaking from under his hands. She stared in disbelief until she heard someone crashing through the trees behind them.

She threw off her sleeping bag and watched in horror as Dirt Crusher fell backward and disappeared. She screamed, and then the lights went out as something crashed into her head.

She woke up, unsure of the time. It was still dark, and the sky was just as beautiful as it had been, but something was different. Then she remembered what she had seen, right before Dirt Crusher went over the edge, and she started to shake.

She tried to sit up, but she couldn't move. Something was holding her down. Her head hurt like hell. She reached with her hand, but it only moved as far as the rope that was tied around her wrists would allow. She didn't have a clue what was going on.

Behind her, she heard low voices talking. The conversation did not sound friendly.

"You stupid shit, I told you to get to him before he went over the edge," said one voice.

The other voice, more agitated, said, "If you hadn't been in the fucking way, I might have reached him. So now you need to climb down to the bottom and get the bolt."

"Yeah, well fuck off," said the first voice. "I don't take orders from you. You want the bolt so badly, you go down there and find it; otherwise, get out of my face."

A third voice, louder, entered the conversation. "Knock it off, both of you. She's awake, finish with her and let's go before someone hears you arguing. Forget about the bolt."

Snowflake shook even more as two shadows passed over her. She tried to yell, but a hand clamped down over her mouth. She tried to scream through the hand when she saw one of the shadows pull out a long knife.

She looked up into eyes that looked like they were on fire. The person kneeling next to her took the knife, lifted the bottom hem of her T-shirt and slit it to the neck. The shirt fell open, exposing her petite breast. The shadow took the knife and circled it around her nipples. He smiled through crooked yellow teeth as her body shook with fear.

He then took the knife and slit her sweatpants from the waist to her crotch. The other shadow grabbed the pants by the cuffs and pulled them down to the ropes holding her feet spread apart.

Snowflake started to fight against the ropes and curse at her attackers, but the hand that covered her mouth clamped down harder, and she was having trouble catching her breath.

The shadow with the knife then cut off her panties and threw them over the edge. Snowflake couldn't believe this was happening. She had hiked alone for years and had never been bothered by anyone she had met on the trail. Sure, she had heard stories from other female hikers about being harassed, but she had never heard of anything even remotely like this.

She watched as the second shadow pulled down his pants, exposing himself, and then he climbed on top of her and forced his way into her. She tried to scream, but the hand over her mouth shoved a gag into her mouth. Once the first shadow finished, the second shadow did the same thing. And this went on for some time. How much time she didn't know.

They finished raping her and sat next to the fire laughing about what they had done. They had tied her T-shirt across her mouth as a gag, and her mouth was as dry as sand. She prayed they would give her a drink. She also prayed that her ordeal was over, but that wasn't to be.

Shadow One stood up and pulled a wicked-looking hand ax out of a backpack that was sitting by the fire and stepped over to her. The other shadow followed. She stared at the blade, and tears filled her eyes. She tried to plead with them, but only grunts came from behind the gag, and they seemed oblivious to her plight.

Shadow One stood over her, the ax glinting in the firelight. He looked into her eyes, smiled and slammed the ax into her chest. The pain was excruciating. He raised the ax and hit her in the shoulder. Shadow Two, standing next to her, hit her in the other shoulder, and then the frenzy began.

Mercifully she never felt the rest of the blows as they hacked at her, blood and guts flying everywhere. When they stopped, the rock outcropping was covered with blood. They stood over her and admired their handiwork. She was unrecognizable, and they high-fived and put their axes back in their backpacks.

Shadow One took the knife and cut the ropes that held her down and threw them over the edge. Slipping on the wet blood and entrails and being careful not to slip off the rocks themselves, they took hold of her arms and legs, and they threw her over the edge. They heard her crash into the rocks below.

They looked at the blueish tint working its way into the dark eastern sky. It was later than they thought, the drug rush having lasted longer than it had the first time they tried it. It was a hell of a rush, and once it was over, they felt no remorse for what they had done. They didn't feel anything at all.

They needed to get to work, and they hoped that by the time they reached their destination, the drug would be out of their systems. They felt giddy, and even the sight of all that blood and gore lying on the rock didn't bother them. They grabbed their backpacks and dashed off into the woods, like a couple of kids heading out to recess, whooping and hollering as they disappeared into the trees.

CHAPTER FIFTEEN

D r. Parkinson finished up the autopsies at about sunrise the following morning. The initial findings were hard to believe. The two young women, Rachel and Jenny, had been sexually assaulted multiple times. Their bodies showed signs of both vaginal and anal tearing.

Rachel suffered twenty-six what the doctor described as ax wounds, as well as five stab wounds. Jenny suffered thirty-four ax wounds. Both women died from massive blood loss, and Dr. Parkinson believed they were alive during the initial attack. It was impossible to determine the fatal wound.

Sheriff Jimmy Wechsler had lost his life in the same manner. He had twenty-eight ax wounds, but he also had the puncture wound to his left chest that was caused by an unknown weapon. Whatever had caused the wound had clipped the aorta. With any luck, he had died before the ax attack had begun.

Mitchell Groves was the surprise. Other than

the damage caused to his body where his ribs had been hacked from his spinal cord, splayed open, and his lungs removed and hung on the broken ribs, Mitchell suffered only two stab wounds to his chest. Dr. Parkinson found evidence of recent drug use, and his bodily fluids and hair samples were sent to the State Crime Lab for a tox screen.

Buck stood up and stretched as the orderlies went about the task of sewing up the last Y incision. Dr. Parkinson had retired to the doctor's lounge to get some sleep before transcribing his autopsy notes. It had been a long night, and Buck felt like he had seen enough death to last him a while. He was also stiff as a board and thought that maybe he was getting too old for this shit.

He walked over to the counter, put all the evidence bags and samples into a large banker's box, sealed it with evidence tape and signed the tape at both ends. He threw out the four empty bottles of Coke that sat on the counter and grabbed his backpack and the banker's box. He walked the box to the front desk at the hospital entrance and handed it over to the secure courier who would take the box to the State Crime Lab in Pueblo, Colorado.

Buck stepped out into the cool, early morning air and took a deep breath. He looked at his watch. He needed two things: food and a shower. He walked across the parking lot, slid into his Jeep and headed for his house. He had just pulled into his driveway when his phone rang. He saw the name and smiled.

"Hiya, Max," he said.

He waited for the same greeting she always started her conversation with. "Buck Taylor. How's my favorite cop?" This morning it didn't happen.

"Don't sound so chipper this early in the morning, Buck Taylor. You could have warned me in your email what to expect when I opened the pictures. For God's sake, Buck, I just finished breakfast."

Buck laughed. "Sorry, Max. It was a long night, and I uploaded them and hit send. Didn't even think about it."

"What the hell have you gotten yourself involved with this time, Buck?" she asked.

Dr. Maxine Clinton was the director of the State Crime Lab and one of Buck's oldest and dearest friends. She was a matronly woman in her late sixties, about five foot five, with short gray hair. She thought she carried around an extra fifteen pounds she didn't need, but she was still a handsome woman. Married for forty years, Max had four children, eleven grandchildren and six great-grandchildren. She lived in a one-hundred-fifty-year-old farmhouse in Pueblo, where she liked to tend her garden and sit on her porch and drink iced tea. She was also a bourbon girl and could drink most people under the table. She was loud and outspoken, but she knew her job.

Max had received her PhD in biology from the University of Colorado and worked as a biology professor for twenty years before joining CBI. She was the head of the State Crime Lab, which she thoroughly enjoyed. She was a tough taskmaster, but she had a belief system that didn't allow for defeat. Her goal was to give the crime investigator, no matter which department or municipality they worked for, all the information they would need to solve any crime. She held that as a sacred obligation to the victims. She was dedicated to her job and her staff, and the team at the lab practically worshipped her.

Buck would have been included in that group. Many times, during a challenging investigation, it was Max and her team that lit the spark that led to a breakthrough. Max was one of Buck's favorite people, and she felt the same way about him.

Buck gave Max a debrief about the case and the four bodies. He explained that he was looking for any information she might be able to find on the weapons that caused the wounds. Buck was confident that if Max couldn't get the answer from someone on her staff, she would have an outside source that would know.

The people Buck worked with always joked that there wasn't anyone in Colorado that Buck didn't know. But the truth was, Max was way ahead of him in that department. She had contacts all around the world, and she never failed to get him the answers he needed.

During one recent case, Buck was looking for information on infrasound weapons and what effect they would have on the body. Within a couple of hours, Buck was on the phone with a colleague of Max's who was an expert in those types of weapons.

Max told him she would reach out and see what she could find, and Buck thanked her. She ended the call the way she always did. "You're a good man, Buck Taylor; God will watch over you."

Buck wasn't much of a religious man. He hadn't been to church in forty years. He had been raised Catholic but left the church right after confirmation. He always had too many questions about the teachings and too many people telling him that he had to have faith. That wasn't the answer he was looking for. He had a lot of friends, Max among them, who had always offered up a prayer when Lucy was dying. He never once rejected any of those offers, often smiling and thanking them for their kind thoughts.

Buck had realized long ago that it wasn't God and faith that he had a problem with; it was organized religion. In his many years in law enforcement, he had seen too many times the aftereffects of someone's religious beliefs. It amazed him that so many people of faith could cause so much hatred and crime. But then nonbelievers created just as much havoc.

Buck always believed there was probably a higher power out there, but he didn't believe that whatever that power was, it cared about one individual over another. His football coach always offered up a prayer before each game, asking for help in defeating the other team. He always suspected the other team's coach was doing the same thing. So how did God decide which team should win?

He knew a lot of people who said a lot of prayers for Lucy over the five years she was sick, but in the end, she still died. And she was the last person who should have gotten cancer. But Buck didn't carry any hatred. Who could he possibly get mad at? Who could he blame?

Buck believed that there were spirits or a force all around us, and he always thanked them for allowing him to enjoy the hike, or for allowing him to catch fish, or see the sunrise and the sunset. It wasn't religion. It was something deeper. Something Buck didn't understand. He just accepted it. But no matter what, he always appreciated it when Max told him that God was watching over him. After all, what could it hurt?

CHAPTER SIXTEEN

Bax and Paul met for breakfast at a little mom-and-pop restaurant in the middle of town called the Daytripper. He had arrived after Buck had left. He spent most of the evening inventorying the evidence from the two crime scenes and logging it into the investigation file.

Paul was over six foot four with a muscular physique. He had joined CBI five years earlier after spending ten years with the Dallas, Texas, police department. His last post had been as a homicide detective. Paul may have seemed like a giant, but those who knew him knew he was a pussycat. He was one of the most soft-spoken men Buck had ever met.

Bax had her laptop open on the table, and she noticed that Buck had entered the autopsy pictures. She clicked on the first one and then closed the lid as several customers sat down in the booth next to them. These were not photos to enjoy with your breakfast.

The waitress came by and set the scrambled

egg and bacon platter in front of her. The second plate she carried contained Paul's Belgian waffles. She stepped away and returned to fill their coffee mugs before moving on to the new customers.

Bax loved little restaurants like this one, and she had fond memories of spending a lot of time sitting with Buck and running through a case while enjoying a big meal. This morning it would be her and Paul running through the case. But first, they dug into their meals.

They finished their meals and sat back. "What's the first thing on our agenda this morning?" asked Bax.

Paul thought for a minute. "I'd like to head over to Mitchell Groves's house. I have this feeling we missed something. I'm not sure what. I also need to follow up on any CCTV video of the sheriff's SUV. The new sheriff and his deputies are so far in the weeds they will never get to it. I'll grab a couple of the troopers to help."

"What are you thinking?" she asked.

"I'm not sure. Something is off. There was a complete drug lab in the room where Groves died, yet you guys found no drugs on the property. If he was manufacturing, then there must be a supply someplace."

"Makes sense," said Bax. "Couldn't hurt to put a fresh set of eyes on the house and see if there's anything hidden."

"What are you gonna do?" asked Paul.

"I'm gonna head up to the Conway Hiker's Resort. Both Jenny and Rachel Carrollton worked at the resort, and I'd like to find out more about them. Maybe talk to some of their coworkers and see who they might party with or have a problem with."

She closed her laptop and put it into her backpack as her phone rang. She checked the name and pushed the green phone button.

"Hey, Buck. Did you get any sleep?"

"Hey, Bax. No, not much. We didn't finish until sunrise. Did you guys send off the evidence to the lab yet?"

"Paul gave it to the secure courier about an hour ago. Why? What's up?"

"We found a wound on the sheriff we couldn't explain, and I was wondering if the techs found anything out of the ordinary at either scene."

Bax pushed her phone towards Paul, clicked on the speaker button, and turned the volume down. They both leaned in.

"Can you describe what you're looking for?" asked Paul.

"Oh, hi, Paul. Yeah. It's something that would leave a square hole, and it would have to be hard enough to pierce a ballistic vest. It could be an arrow. Whatever it was, it went through the sheriff's vest and continued eight inches into his chest. Dr. Parkinson has never seen anything like it."

"It doesn't sound like anything I inventoried this morning, but I'll look at the pictures from the inventory and see if anything jumps out at me. What about Max? Did you send it to her?"

Buck laughed. "Yeah, along with some of the wound pictures to see if we can get a line on the ax-like weapon. The problem was, I didn't tell her I included the wound pictures, and she opened the email right after breakfast. She was not pleased."

"I can imagine," said Bax.

"Any luck with tracking down the sheriff's SUV?" Buck asked.

Bax filled him in on the lack of progress by the sheriff and his team and told him the plan for the morning. Buck agreed with the plan and told them he was running home to grab a shower and would be there in a couple of hours.

They disconnected the call, and Bax and Paul left a couple of twenties on the table, finished off the last of their coffees, grabbed their backpacks and headed for their Jeeps.

Paul pulled out of the parking lot and

headed for the sheriff's office three blocks east on Highway 114. He would go through the inventory photos before heading to the second crime scene.

Bax pulled out behind him and turned west on Highway 114. She traveled three miles out of Silver City and then turned onto County Road 4, following the signs for the Conway Hiker's Resort. She followed the winding road for another three miles, passing several hikers heading towards Silver City.

The entrance gate to the Conway Hiker's Resort was made up of two massive logs, twelve feet tall and four feet around, topped by a massive twenty-five-foot-long log. It was an impressive structure, and Bax admired it as she passed under it.

She followed the road for another mile and drove towards a large parking lot. She knew something was wrong as soon as she pulled into the lot. Five U.S. Forest Service pickup trucks were parked in front of the main lodge. She grabbed her backpack, slid out of the Jeep and headed for the front door.

The sign over the front door noted that the lodge was on the National Register of Historic Places and had been built in 1929. Bax pulled open the massive door and stepped into one of the largest log buildings she had ever seen. The logs that made up the walls were huge, and the ceiling was all post and beam construction.

There was a large restaurant and bar off to the left, and on the right was the front desk and registration area. She headed that way until she spotted a knot of Forest Service rangers standing on a patio at the back of the space. She walked across the lobby, passed through a large sliding glass door and approached the group.

Holding up her credentials, she said, "Gentlemen, can I be of assistance?"

Standing in the middle of the group was a large man, mostly bald, and he wore jeans and a flannel shirt and a Carhartt insulated vest. He was talking to one of the rangers while everyone else listened. He stopped talking and looked at Bax and then the badge.

"CBI," he said. "How did you guys find out? We haven't called anyone yet."

She looked at the nameplate on his chest. "Mr. Conway. I'm Ashley Baxter. Perhaps you should start at the beginning."

"You're here about the missing hikers, right?" said the ranger standing next to Conway. He shook Bax's hand and introduced himself as Chief Ranger Kellan Martin.

"I'm here regarding the murders in Silver City, but why don't you tell me about the missing hikers."

"We heard about the murders," said Ranger Martin. Everyone shook their heads. "Tragic. Do you think they're related to the missing hikers?" She could see the concerned look in their eyes.

"Why don't you fill me in, and we can see where we are," she said.

CHAPTER SEVENTEEN

R anger Martin pulled a notebook from his back pocket. He flipped it open to a page held by a thin rubber band. "Two hours ago, Fred"—he looked at Mr. Conway—"received a call from James Talbot. He called to see if his daughter and son-in-law, McKenzie and Mark Kearney, had arrived at the resort yesterday evening. He had not heard from them since Friday night, and their GPS signal hadn't moved in a couple of days."

Bax looked at Fred Conway. "Did they have a reservation?"

"I checked the book, and they had reserved one of our regular guest rooms here in the lodge for two nights starting last night," said Fred.

Ranger Martin continued. "According to the father, the couple were on their honeymoon and had planned to spend five nights on the trail and two nights in the lodge. They were in contact through one of those GPS transmitters and had sent out a prerecorded message each night, but nothing on Saturday night."

"Any idea why he waited two nights to report them missing?" asked Bax.

"He thought maybe they found a great spot and decided to spend an extra day or two on the trail. He wasn't concerned when they didn't check in the first night. He made it sound like his daughter wasn't thrilled with having to check in every night. It was the son-in-law's idea. I guess he is not much of an outdoorsman, whereas the daughter, on the other hand, is all about adventure."

"The father," said Fred Conway, "gave us the last GPS coordinates he received from them. We were just discussing sending out a search party when you walked up."

Bax thought for a minute. "Mr. Conway, does this happen often? Hikers not showing up as scheduled?"

Fred Conway laughed. "If you only knew. Most people hit the CDT with a predetermined game plan. What happens is, once they get on the trail, reality sets in. Most people overestimate how far they can travel with a thirty-pound pack over rough terrain. They don't realize this isn't Disneyland. There are some well-defined trails and trail markers, but some are not so well defined. People get lost. They get hurt, sick, tired or just plain overwhelmed. My family built this resort, and over the years, we've seen it all."

"How far from the resort were the last GPS coordinates?" asked Bax.

One of the other rangers handed Ranger Martin an iPad, and he opened it to a section map of the trail. "We're here at the resort. The last coordinates are here." He pointed to both locations. "They are about twelve miles from here if they are still in that same spot. It's also possible that the GPS failed, or the batteries died, and they could come walking in any minute."

"What's your typical procedure for a situation like this?" asked Bax.

"Since we have a GPS location to start with, our first step would be to send two rangers to the area and see if they can find them there. If we don't have any luck, we can organize a ground search. I asked the father to send us pictures of the bride and groom, and we will start asking the hikers here at the resort if they remember seeing them."

"How long to get the two rangers to the GPS location?" asked Bax.

"On one of Fred's ATVs, we could be there in a couple of hours."

"Okay," said Bax. "Get your team headed to the location. Circulate the pictures of the missing couple and let's see if anyone saw them in the last two days.

"While you're doing that, I need to speak with Fred about a couple of his employees. Please let me know when your team gets on-site."

Bax asked Fred Conway if there was someplace they could speak in private, and he led her through the main lobby to a series of offices behind the registration desk. He pushed open the door to a large, comfortable-looking office and pointed to a leather wingback chair in front of a beautiful live edge desk. Fred Conway sat behind the desk.

"What's this about, Agent Baxter?"

"Do you know Jenny and Rachel Carrollton?"

Fred tented his fingers together, and sadness filled his eyes. "Oh my god, we heard two young women were killed. It's them, isn't it?"

Bax was about to respond when the door opened, and a heavyset woman, about Fred's age, with long gray hair and wearing identical clothes to Fred, walked in. "Oh, sorry. I didn't realize you were in a meeting." She started to back out when Fred stopped her.

"Billie, those women in town that were killed. It was Rachel and Jenny." Tears filled his eyes.

The woman at the door stared in disbelief. She made the sign of the cross, walked in and closed the door. She looked at Bax.

"Are you sure?" she asked.

Bax nodded. "Yes, ma'am. No doubt."

The woman looked like her legs were going to go out from under her, so Bax jumped up, took her by the arm and guided her to the other chair opposite the desk. She handed her a box of tissues that sat on the corner of the desk.

"We've known those girls since they were born," said Billie Conway between sobs. "Was it an accident? I've told Rachel not to drive so fast on these back roads. Jimmy must be devastated. He hasn't had a death in the county since he became sheriff. Their poor parents."

Bax took a deep breath. She had assumed that in a small county like this, everyone would have already heard about the murders.

"I hate to be the one to tell you, but Rachel and Jenny were murdered over the weekend, along with Sheriff Wechsler and another man, Mitchell Groves."

Both Fred and Billie stared at Bax in disbelief, not comprehending what she had just told them.

"How is that possible?" asked Fred. "They were here for their shift on Saturday night."

Billie was too stunned to speak, and tears flowed down her cheeks.

"Mr. Conway," said Bax. "I know this is hard, but when was the last time you saw them Saturday night?"

Fred Conway wiped his eyes on his sleeves. "They worked the early evening shift, so they would have left here around seven p.m."

"Did they have any problems that night or in the days leading up to that night? Problems with guests or coworkers. Anything out of the ordinary?"

Fred looked at Billie, and they both shook their heads. "Everyone adored them," said Billie. "They've been working in the restaurant since they were fifteen years old, during high school and college breaks. I just can't believe this. So many murders in our community. My god."

"If it's all right with you," said Bax. "I'd like to talk to some of their coworkers."

Fred Conway nodded. "I'll take you over to the restaurant. This is just awful."

He stood up, walked over to Billie, gave her a hug and headed towards the door. Bax followed, leaving Billie Conway crying in the office.

Bax followed Fred into the restaurant/bar, and she could tell from the crying that the coworkers already knew what had happened. They were all gathered at the bar, trying to look busy but not doing a very good job. They all stopped and wiped their eyes as Bax and Fred Conway approached.

It was a good thing Fred Conway was a large

man because everyone crowded around him in one big hug. Bax stood back to let them have their moment.

Fred stayed with the group for a few minutes, and then he peeled everyone off. He explained what Bax had told him and then introduced her to the workers.

"Agent Baxter is going to ask you guys some questions. Please give her your complete cooperation so we can find out who would do such a thing."

Bax stepped up to the group. "Like Mr. Conway said. I am going to speak with you individually. This is completely informal and just between us. If you have anything to tell me that might be relevant, please do so at this time, so we do not lose time on this investigation. You are under no obligation to talk to me, and anyone who feels uncomfortable or wants a lawyer or a family member present, just let me know, and we will make other arrangements."

She tapped the closest young woman on the shoulder and asked her to follow her to a table in the corner, where Bax set up her laptop and her phone with the recording app open.

So began a long afternoon of tears and discoveries.

CHAPTER EIGHTEEN

B uck stepped out of the shower to the smell of bacon cooking. He got dressed and walked into the kitchen to find his son, David, making breakfast.

"Thought you might sleep all morning," said David.

"Just came home for a catnap," said Buck. "Slept through the damn alarm on my phone. What are you doing?"

David tilted the frying pan full of scrambled eggs and laughed. "What's it look like? Breakfast."

"Yeah, I can see that. Why?" asked Buck.

"Saw you leave the hospital as I made my final rounds of the neighborhood. Figured you'd been up all night, and besides, I was hungry."

David spooned the eggs onto two plates and set them on the table next to a plate of bacon. He had set a bottle of Coke on the table for Buck and poured himself a big mug of coffee. He moved his gun belt from the back of the chair, set it on the counter and sat down.

"What did Dr. Parkinson have to say? You guys put in a long night."

"Looks like we're dealing with some kind of ax murderer."

Buck filled David in on what they learned from the autopsy and about the various victims. It was good to have a sounding board, and since David was in the business, he often offered a different perspective but, more importantly, knew when to keep his mouth shut.

"The frenzy was incredible. Each victim had multiple ax and knife wounds, and the sheriff had a square hole in his chest. Whatever did it went through his vest," said Buck.

"Frenzy like you're describing usually means it was personal. Anything point to this not being some random killer?"

"Nothing so far, but we're looking into friends and enemies of the victims. My gut tells me the sheriff was unplanned. Maybe wrong place, wrong time. He was killed with the same frenzy, but it just felt different. The young women were raped first and then killed. The fourth victim, I have no idea at this point. That one was ritualistic."

"You sure it's the same killer?" asked David.

"I think so. The last victim had two ax wounds

on his upper chest and shoulder. It looked like the killer hit him first to incapacitate him, then dragged him into the bedroom and tied him to the table. Garrett thinks the same weapon was used to chop away his ribs."

David looked at Buck over his coffee mug. "Sounds like you're thinking there had to be more than one killer."

"That's the one thing I feel certain about. One person couldn't do this alone. When it comes to the two women, I'm not sure two people could have done it. The ax blows were similar in depth, so that could have been one person, but how do you control one woman while raping the other. And at some point, they were interrupted by the sheriff, who barely had time to pull his weapon before he was hit with whatever penetrated his vest. No. There were definitely multiple people involved."

"Any gang violence in the area?" asked David.

"We'll need to look into that, but I didn't notice any gang graffiti on anything. It seems like a nice, quiet little town."

"How about the drug dealer? Could he have been the target, and the others were just collateral damage?"

"I've asked the temporary sheriff to run background on all the victims. I can't see a connection, but anything's possible. With luck,

DNA will give us some answers. The killers left sperm in the two women, so we'll see where that leads."

"You got the pictures of the molds on your phone?" asked David.

Buck unclipped his phone from his belt, flipped through the pictures till he found what he was looking for and handed the phone to David. David studied the pictures for several minutes, flipping back and forth. He held up the picture of the paraffin mold from the square hole.

"Could be an arrow. Nothing like I've seen before. What type of arrow goes through ballistic armor?" asked David.

David knew a lot about arrows. Unlike Buck, who was an avid fly fisherman and hunted during rifle season, David loved the thrill of a bow hunt. He learned to use a bow and arrow when he was ten years old and never missed a hunting season. Since Buck had never hunted with a bow, David had turned to his grandfather Fernando to teach him.

"No idea," said Buck. "Didn't know an arrow could go through a vest. With any luck, Max will have a contact out in the world who can shed some light on it and the ax."

David flipped through a couple more pictures and landed on the picture of the body of Mitchell

Groves. "Glad I was finished with breakfast. Who could do something like that? There must have been blood everywhere."

Buck shook his head. "I wish I knew who could do something like that."

David closed the gallery and handed the phone back to Buck. "What's your next step?"

"First and foremost, we need to find the sheriff's SUV. If we find the car, we find the killer or killers. At least that's what always happens on TV."

They both laughed, and David cleared the table and washed the plates and silverware. Buck gave him a rundown on where he hoped to take the investigation next.

"Do you think there's a drug angle here?" asked David.

"At this point, anything's possible. I'm just not sure. What I can't figure out is, if our victim was manufacturing drugs, which it looked like he was, where are the drugs? We found just a few pills."

David shook his head. "Well, since I can't help you with that, I need to sleep. Good luck and stay safe."

He slung his gun belt over his shoulder, hugged Buck and headed out the kitchen door.

Buck enjoyed spending time with David.

Unfortunately, they didn't see much of each other since David worked nights and Buck was always running off to some far-flung corner of Colorado. He used to use Lucy as a sounding board, but since she passed, he relied more and more on the kids, especially his daughter, Cassie.

Cassie was the middle child, and she was every bit a middle child. In high school, she played soccer, ran track and played volleyball. She lettered in all three sports. She was also the one who got in trouble for violating curfew, drinking and whatever other mischief she could find. Buck was surprised when she was accepted to the University of Arizona with a full scholarship for volleyball. He was even more surprised when she was accepted into law school. Cassie was never much for regimented education.

Four years ago, she'd dropped out of law school, and her career path took a different track. She joined the Forest Service and was working as a wildland firefighter with the Helena Hotshots. The Helena Hotshots were one of the country's elite firefighting teams and were based out of Helena, Montana. Buck was not surprised. He never saw her sitting behind a desk as a lawyer. She loved the outdoors, and she was as tough as they come. Lucy wasn't pleased that she quit school without any discussion, and she constantly worried whenever Cassie was called out to a fire, but she also knew her daughter, and if this was where she was happy, then so was her mom.

Buck picked up his phone and speed-dialed her number. He hadn't spoken to her in a couple of days and figured she was on a fire line someplace. The phone went to voice mail.

"Hey, kiddo. It's Dad. Just checking in. I'm working a case not far from home, but I didn't want you to worry if you didn't hear from me. Love ya."

He ended the call, dialed a second number and got another voice mail. He left the same message for his youngest son, Jason.

Jason was an architect, and he lived in Boulder with his wife, Kate, and their three children. Of all of Buck's kids, Jason was the one who had continued to follow Catholicism, just like his mom, and seemed to get more involved in his church after Lucy died. Jason was also the most sensitive of the three kids. He worried when Buck was on a case, so Buck had to be careful how much he told him about what he was working on.

Buck clicked off his phone, clipped his badge and gun to his belt, grabbed his backpack and headed out the kitchen door, locking it behind him.

Buck threw his backpack on the passenger

seat and slid into the Jeep. He pulled out of his driveway and headed back towards Silver City. He was still tired. The nap had done little to make up for his lost sleep. The big breakfast wasn't helping either. He opened another bottle of Coke and took a big swig. Maybe the caffeine would keep him awake.

CHAPTER NINETEEN

Paul parked along the curb in front of the sheriff's office, grabbed his backpack and slid out of his Jeep. He pushed open the door to the office and was greeted by the bell clanging over the door. An older woman sat behind the counter reading a novel.

She put down the book. "Hi. Can I help you?"

Paul held up his credentials and leaned on the counter. "Paul Webber, CBI. First, my condolences for the loss of your sheriff; secondly, I need a place to set up my laptop."

She reached out her hand. "Thank you. We're all a little unnerved around here. Never been anything like this in our town before. Margaret Gillam, nice to meet you, Paul." Paul shook her hand.

Margaret Gillam was heavyset, with long, light gray hair, and she wore a Carhartt vest over a flowery yellow shirt. Paul was surprised by how firm her grip was.

"Are you the only one around?" asked Paul.

"Yeas, sir," she said. "Marvin and the boys are grabbing a couple of hours of shut-eye. So I told them I'd cover the desk for them. I'm part time and work a couple of hours a week, but with the tragedy in town, it's all hands on deck."

She stood up and lifted her cane off the back of the chair. She told Paul to follow her, and she stepped over to the desk by the window that Bax had used.

"You're welcome to set up here, Paul. Is there anything I can get you? There's a small kitchen in the back. Maybe not a kitchen, but there's a microwave and a small refrigerator. Help yourself to whatever you find."

"Thanks, Margaret. There is one thing I'm looking for. The sheriff was going to see if they could find anyone who might have a video in the area of Mitchell Groves's house to see if we can figure out where the sheriff's SUV went after it left the house. You don't know if they had a chance to get to that?"

She walked over to the counter and picked up a piece of paper. She walked back and handed it to Paul.

"Mike, Deputy Tortelli, left this note for Agent Taylor." She handed it to Paul.

Paul frowned as he tried to read the handwriting on the note. He was used to reading Buck's chicken scratch, but if this were a competition, Deputy Tortelli would have won for worst handwriting.

Margaret reached out and took the note. "Here. Let me. He wrote that he found two cameras so far. One on a residence and one on the grocery store at the end of Main Street. It was too late, and he didn't want to wake the owners, so he was going to follow up today."

She pulled a pen out of her hair and rewrote the addresses so Paul could read them. He read them and thanked her. He set the note on the desk next to his laptop and sat down.

Margaret headed back to her novel and told Paul to yell if he needed anything else.

Paul opened the investigation file and pulled up the inventory of items sent to the State Crime Lab. Then, he pulled up the pictures and compared them to Buck's pictures of the paraffin molds. Nothing he saw came anywhere close to matching the pictures of the paraffin molds of the wounds. He felt frustrated.

The first picture was, without a doubt, some kind of ax head, but the second picture was a challenge. It looked like an arrowhead or a spear point, which seemed out of place.

He sat back in his chair and thought about the crime scene pictures and the autopsy reports. He wondered to himself why someone would have chosen an ax. It seemed like an odd, clunky weapon to use.

If you were trying to make a statement, an ax would certainly do that. It made a mess of the bodies, and ax murderers had been the evil monsters hiding in the closet when he was growing up. Everyone knew the story of Lizzie Borden.

What he couldn't wrap his head around was the brutality of the attacks. Dr. Parkinson had said that any of the wounds could have proven fatal, and he could not say with certainty which wound was first and which one killed each victim. So why the savagery, or was that the point? Was someone out to scare the people of the town? To what end?

The other thing he couldn't understand was the drug dealer and what part he played in all this. The sheriff, he thought, might have stumbled on the crime in progress, but what was the deal with the drug dealer?

He pulled up the interview with the young women's parents. Deputy Jefferson had done a decent job under trying circumstances.

Paul remembered the first time he did a death notification and what it was like trying to interview a grieving widow. It was one of the most uncomfortable experiences of his rookie year in Dallas. Luckily, the new widow held it together through most of his questions, and the detectives working the case were able to come back a few days later and fill in the missing pieces.

He read through the report, and one comment jumped out at him. The father talked about being gone for the weekend, leaving his two college-age daughters home by themselves.

Father: "I wasn't the least bit concerned because I knew the sheriff would stop by and check on them at the end of his shift. Jimmy told me he would make sure they were safe and sound. If I hadn't asked Jimmy to check on them, he might still be alive today."

That comment reinforced Paul's theory that the father might be right and that the sheriff stumbled onto a crime in progress.

The parents had gone on to say that neither daughter did drugs, and they rarely used alcohol. They also mentioned that they were both scheduled to work the entire weekend at Conway's, so they planned to stay home and watch a bunch of movies.

The deputy asked them if either daughter had a boyfriend or, being politically correct, a girlfriend, and the parents responded that they didn't have anyone serious in their lives.

Paul added in his mind. At least none they were aware of. Both women were in college, out of state, and both, based on their most recent photos, were pretty, one with long blond hair and one with short red hair.

He understood from dealing with his younger sister that what goes on at college stays at college, and the parents are the last to know. He made a note to contact the colleges and see if he could locate some of their friends.

He made a note to do a follow-up interview with the parents. Mr. Carrollton was a big player in state Republican politics, so maybe there was a political element to the crimes. However, the more he read through the autopsy reports, the more he was convinced that these were crimes of passion.

He pulled out his phone and sent Bax a text asking her to check with the other employees at the resort and see if the women had any wanted or unwanted romantic entanglements.

He pulled up the sheriff's autopsy report. The brutality was the same, but he couldn't figure out a passion angle. Both women had been raped, but the sheriff, although unclothed, showed there was no sexual assault angle. He read the forensics report. The sheriff had been found lying next to the door leading into the game room.

Paul ran a scenario through his head. The sheriff drove up to the house to check on the women before heading home for the evening.

Something about the house caught his attention. The first responder report noted that the front door was unlocked, all the curtains were drawn, and loud noises were coming from the house.

He entered the house and called out for the women. Hearing no response, he did the next logical thing and followed the noise to the media room. He must have walked in on either the rapes or the murders in progress, but what happened next? Did he freeze? Did he yell for the killers to stop? Or could he have been ambushed as soon as he entered the room?

Since his gun was not in his holster, Paul felt that the last choice didn't make sense. He pulled up the autopsy report. Dr. Parkinson felt confident that the arrow, or whatever it was, was the first wound, and it would have been fatal, having nicked the heart. Of all the wounds on the sheriff, only three had bled profusely, suggesting that his heart had stopped beating by the third ax blow.

If the sheriff was dead by the time the third blow was struck, then why continue attacking him? The killers had taken off his vest and continued to chop at him: no passion that Paul could see, just frenzy.

Paul's head was hurting, so he closed the investigation report and shut down his laptop. He put it in his backpack, picked up the list that

Margaret had given him with the addresses on it and headed for the door. He told Margaret where he was heading, asked her for directions to the residence with the doorbell camera and headed for his Jeep.

CHAPTER TWENTY

Buck slid his Jeep to the curb just down the street from the sheriff's office. He was about to grab his backpack when the phone rang. He looked at the number and hit the green button.

"Hey, George. What's up?"

George Peterman and Melanie Hart were the CBI cybersecurity team based out of Grand Junction, Colorado, and they couldn't be more different.

George Peterman had joined CBI after retiring from the navy, where he'd spent his entire career working in cybersecurity. As far as Buck was concerned, George and his partner, Melanie, were two of the best computer people he knew. Paul Webber was good. Ashley Baxter was better, but these two were world-class.

Melanie was about five foot two, with shoulder-length black hair; she always wore black jeans and dark gray hoodies, and she had several piercings. Anyone meeting her for the first time would think she was a high school kid, but she had received her doctorate in computer science from MIT about a dozen years before. She'd joined CBI right out of college.

George Peterman could have passed for her father. George was about the same height as Buck, a shade under six foot, but where Buck still weighed what he'd weighed when he played football in high school, George had added a few pounds over the years.

"Hey, Buck. Wow, what a mess. I looked at the pictures in the investigation file. A lot of brutality there. Looks like a massacre. Any luck researching the weapons?"

"Not yet. I sent the pictures to Max. Hopefully she knows someone who can identify them. What's going on?"

"Franklin dropped off several cell phones and four laptops," said George. "What are we looking for?"

"Can you access any of the phones?" asked Buck.

"Yeah. He got passwords for three of the four phones. We don't have a password for the phone that belonged to Mitchell Groves. Same thing with the laptops."

"That should help, George. Have Mel get subpoenas to access everything. Let's see if we can get call and text history from the phone companies. Also, run deep background on everyone. The two women, Rachel and Jennifer, are both in college. Let's see if they had problems with anyone."

"How deep do you want to go on the sheriff?" asked George.

Buck thought for a minute. He hated investigations that involved law enforcement officers. He never wanted to sully the victim's name, but he needed to go wherever the evidence took him.

"Go deep," said Buck. "My first impression of the crime scene is that he was in the wrong place at the wrong time, but we need to make sure he wasn't targeted."

"Okay," said George. "Anything else?"

"Yeah. Can we request a warrant to look at all the cell phones connected to a single cell tower on the night of the murder?"

"What are you thinking?" asked George.

"This is a small town," said Buck. "It would be interesting to see whose phones were out and about during the period of the murder."

"Hey, Buck. It's Mel."

"Hiya, Mel. What's up?"

"Because of the short time frame and the

need established by an ongoing investigation, we don't need a warrant to get that information from the cell tower company. The problem is that since it is a small town and very few people turn off their phones at night, just about the entire town will show up as being connected to the tower. We can request a tower dump and get those records without a warrant. The CSLI, cell site location information, can help us pinpoint what phone was in a particular area at a specific time. We will need a warrant to get more detail on those individual phones."

Buck was quiet for a minute. "Sounds like a lot of work. Do you think it can help us?"

"It can help us if the killer or killers had their phones on. If they disabled their phones or left them home, not so much. What do you want to do?" asked Mel.

"Go ahead and request the tower dump. Who knows, maybe we'll get lucky," said Buck.

George laughed. "Or we might find out some embarrassing details about small-town life, like who wasn't where they were supposed to be."

"Don't mind George; his mind is always in the gutter," said Mel. "We'll get cracking on everything and let you know when we have something."

Buck thanked them and disconnected the call. He grabbed his backpack and walked down the street to the sheriff's office. He spotted several people along the street that were openly carrying either a pistol or a rifle, or both. Everyone looked on edge, and he was worried that a simple situation could turn deadly in a heartbeat.

He was also grateful to see two state police cars patrolling Main Street. He hoped that might help calm down the fears of the residents. One of the troopers came to a stop next to him, and he stepped into the street and walked up to the open passenger window.

"Trooper," said Buck. "All quiet?"

"Mornin', Agent Taylor. Yeah, so far." He looked across the street at two guys carrying AR-15 style rifles. "Lot of guns in town. Makes me a little nervous, know what I mean?"

Buck knew what he meant, having just had that same thought.

"Well, Trooper. Let's hope we nail this guy soon before something stupid happens. Just keep an eye on things and try to keep the peace."

Buck tapped his palm on the window opening and stood up. He told the trooper to stay safe, turned and walked towards the door. He pushed open the door and listened to the clanging of the little bell.

Marvin Willets was talking to a heavyset woman who sat behind the counter. He introduced Buck to Margaret Gillam, and they spent a few minutes talking about the state of the town.

"Sounds like you have the same concerns I do," said Marvin. "All these guns make me nervous."

Buck noticed that Marvin Willets now had a gun holster around his waist and a badge clipped to his shirt. He still looked nervous as a cat in a room full of rocking chairs, but he now looked the part compared to the man Buck met yesterday.

Marvin led Buck over to the desk in the corner with a brass sign on the edge that said sheriff, james wechsler. He sat down, and Buck set his backpack on the floor and pulled up the chair from the desk in front of the sheriff's.

Marvin filled him in on the video search that his two deputies were still on. "So, besides the addresses Margaret gave to Paul Webber, the deputies think they have found four more. They're on their way back, and I called Paul and let him know. He's on his way as well."

Buck filled him in on the work his team was doing on the phones and laptops and gave him a rundown on the autopsies. Buck could see the details made Marvin a little queasy, so he held back some of the more graphic information.

Buck pulled his laptop out of his backpack, set it on the desk and powered it up. He opened the investigation file and located the pictures of the two paraffin molds. He turned the computer to face Marvin.

"Have you ever seen anything that looks like this in town?" Buck flipped the pictures.

Marvin took off his glasses and got close to the screen. Buck felt right at home because he often did the same thing. He gave Marvin a minute to look at each picture. Marvin raised his head.

"Doesn't look like anything I've ever seen, but then I'm not much into weapons." He rested his hand on the gun in his holster. "Used to belong to my dad before he passed. He was the outdoorsman in the family, along with my older brother. Not sure I could hit anything with it if I had to."

That made Buck nervous. There was nothing worse than an amateur carrying a gun that he didn't know how to shoot. He made a mental note to take Marvin out to the forest and give him a lesson.

He turned his laptop around and was about to close it when the two deputies came through the front door. They walked up to the desk and handed Buck a USB drive, which he plugged into the side of his laptop. While he pulled up the information on the drive, he asked them to look at the pictures of the paraffin molds.

They took turns looking at the pictures, but

neither one had seen anything that looked like the molds. Buck opened the first video.

Buck ran the video while all eyes were on the screen. They thought they caught a glimpse of the back end of a black SUV, but they couldn't be sure. Buck pulled up the second video and saw which direction the sheriff's SUV traveled after leaving Mitchell Groves's house.

Buck was pulling up the third video when he heard the bell clang over the door. He looked up as Paul walked into the office. He walked over and joined the little group surrounding Buck's laptop.

Buck was halfway through the video when Tortelli said, "Stop." He asked Buck to back up a frame or two. The video had captured the sheriff's SUV, but just for a second.

"Where's this video from?" asked Buck.

Deputy Tortelli stepped away from the desk and returned with a large, framed map of the town. He set it on the desk next to the laptop and focused on getting his bearings.

He pointed to a gray square indicating a house. "This is Groves's house," he said. He ran his figure over two blocks and pointed to another square. "This is where the video came from."

Paul leaned over the desk. "If the house is here, then the video shows the SUV traveling in this direction." The direction Paul indicated would take the car out of town in the opposite direction from the market, where he had spent the better part of the morning going over their videos.

Buck pulled up the fourth video and ran it. This video was from a house four blocks along the expected travel route of the SUV. The video was poor quality, but it looked like they had captured the SUV in a couple of frames.

"Paul, anything on the videos you followed up on this morning?"

Paul shook his head. "Nothing, but those locations are in the opposite direction."

Buck asked for a local highway map, and Margaret walked over with an old, neatly folded map that looked like it had been in a desk for a decade or more. He opened the map and laid it on the desk.

"Where does that direction take us?" he asked.

Marvin Willets placed his hand on the desk. "Unless they grabbed a Forest Service road, and there are only two in this direction, just outside the town limits, they would have to get back on 114. Since it didn't show up on the market video, then they headed east, and that would take them to Saguache."

"That's not bad. Marvin, why don't you and the deputies head towards Saguache and check any side roads, farm roads, basically anyplace you could hide an SUV. One of you take the two Forest Service roads Marvin mentioned. Let's meet back here in a couple of hours and see what you found. Paul and I are heading back to the Groves house to give it another look."

Everyone grabbed their gear and headed out. Buck loaded up his laptop. "Let's go see if we can figure out what got Mitchell Groves killed."

Paul nodded, and they grabbed their backpacks and headed for their Jeeps. Buck wasn't unhappy with their progress. At the very least, they had a line on where the sheriff's SUV might have headed. He was optimistic, but he was also a realist. With all the side roads and cabins between Silver City and Saguache, they would have to get incredibly lucky to find the SUV, but stranger things had happened.

CHAPTER TWENTY-ONE

Bax leaned back in the wooden chair and stretched. So far, she had interviewed about half of Rachel and Jennifer's coworkers, and the story was mostly the same.

Both Rachel and Jennifer had worked at the resort since they were fifteen. Everyone, including the guests, loved them. They were hard workers and reliable. No one could remember a time when they missed a shift or came in late.

As far as anyone knew, they didn't drink, and they didn't do drugs, not even marijuana. If anyone needed a shift covered, one of them was always willing to help.

She closed her eyes to gather her thoughts, and when she reopened them, her next interviewee was standing next to her chair. Bax pointed towards the opposite chair.

"Hi. What's your name?" asked Bax.

The young woman was pretty with a turned-up nose and fair complexion. Her smile was huge, and it covered half her face. Bax could tell that she hadn't yet dressed for work because she wore baggy black pants and a black hoodie covering her shoulder-length blond hair. She wore black military-style boots, with her pants tucked into them, and around her neck she wore a silver necklace with a Celtic cross pendant hanging from it.

The girl shook Bax's hand, and Bax could feel more strength in her grip than she expected. The young woman was stronger than she appeared. She had calloused hands. All in all, there was nothing feminine about this woman. She was the opposite of both Rachel and Jennifer, yet Bax had been told by everyone that she was Rachel's closest friend.

"I'm VJ," said the young woman.

"Last name?" asked Bax.

"Sorry. VJ Florence. Everyone is really broken up with what happened to Jen and Rach."

Bax noticed that the woman spent most of the time looking at her hands, never looking Bax in the eye when she answered. Bax noted this in her notebook, along with the fact that the woman kept wringing her hands like she was nervous.

"Okay, good, VJ. Can you remove your hood? I like to see who I'm talking to."

The young woman reluctantly pushed her

hood back and looked back down at her hands.

"Thanks, VJ. Are you willing to talk to me without a lawyer present?"

"Yeah, I guess so."

"Great. What does VJ stand for?"

"Victoria Jean. I was named after my two grandmothers."

"I understand from talking to some of the others that you were Rachel's best friend. Would that be accurate?"

VJ wiped a tear from her eye. "I guess you could say that."

"Well, how would you describe your friendship?" asked Bax.

VJ was silent for a few seconds. "I guess we're good friends. Never thought of her as anything other than Rach."

"How long have you known Rach?"

"We went all through school together and stayed in contact when she left for college." More hand wringing.

"VJ, you seem nervous. Are you okay?"

VJ moved her hands to her sides and forced a smile. "I'm okay. Just sad about Rach. Everyone is scared."

"I want you to know that we are doing

everything we can to find out who did this. Why don't you tell me a little about Rachel and Jennifer?"

VJ sat, thinking. After a minute, she spoke; her voice was low. "I don't know what to say. We were friends, and we worked together. When we weren't working, we hung out together. That's about it."

"What did you do when you hung out together?"

More silence and hand-wringing. "We listen to music, play video games, you know, stuff like that."

"VJ, did Rachel have a boyfriend or a girlfriend?"

VJ perked up. "We weren't like that. She was just my friend."

"I'm sorry," said Bax. "I didn't mean with you. Was there someone at school she was seeing? Or maybe someone here at the resort. Someone besides you that she was close to."

"I know she went on dates at school, but I don't think she was serious with anyone. She was very focused on doing good in college."

"What about here at the resort?" asked Bax.

"No," said VJ. Too quickly for Bax's liking.

"Where were you between seven p.m.

Saturday night and, say, seven a.m. Sunday morning?"

VJ didn't say anything for several moments, just looked at her hands, which were back on the table. "Rach and I worked the early shift, so we left here around seven. Rach drove, so she dropped me off at home, and then she headed home."

"VJ. You may have been the last person to see her alive. Now I need you to think. Was Rachel being bothered by anyone, a guest, a hiker or a neighbor? Anything that might have seemed out of place?"

VJ closed her eyes. "Everyone liked Rach. I never saw anyone hassle her."

More fidgeting. "What did you do after Rachel dropped you off?"

"Rach said she was staying home, so that was the last time I saw her." She wiped more tears from her eyes.

"What did you do next?" asked Bax.

"Had dinner at home and then headed to a gaming tournament in Saguache?"

"Were you alone at this tournament?" asked Bax.

"Well, the place was full of people playing."

"What was the name of the place that held the

tournament?"

"The Fishbowl."

Bax was getting frustrated with the short answers and the lack of eye contact.

"What time did you leave the tournament?"

"Around four."

"Did you win?"

"No. Some guy from Denver won. Supposed to be a real hot shit when it comes to gaming."

Bax spent the next fifteen minutes trying to get VJ to engage. She tried to engage her about gaming and about the game she'd played at the tournament, but by the time she finished, she wasn't sure if she had anything to work with or not. She tried to blame it on the shock of VJ finding out that her best friend was murdered, but it wasn't working for her.

VJ looked Bax in the eyes. "Can I go now? I have to get ready for the lunch shift."

Bax nodded. "Go ahead but stick around town. We may want to talk to you some more to get some background on Rach."

VJ stood up, put her hood back over her hair and turned to leave.

"VJ. One last question. You never mentioned Jennifer. Were you two friends?"

VJ turned and faced Bax. "Jennifer didn't like

me, never did." She turned and headed for the kitchen.

Bax took a break and grabbed lunch in the restaurant before she interviewed the next person. Fred Conway stopped at the table to see if there was anything she needed, and Bax invited him to sit for a minute. Fred sat opposite her and poured himself a cup of coffee from the carafe.

"Mr. Conway, tell me about VJ and Rachel. From everything I've heard so far today, they seem like an odd match. What am I missing?"

Fred Conway looked at her with suspicion. "You don't think VJ had anything to do with the murders? She's odd, but she's a good worker. I don't see her as a murderer."

"Right now, we're just talking to anyone who knew the victims," said Bax. "I was just curious."

That seemed to bring Fred Conway back around. "VJ and Rachel have known each other since grade school. I guess Rachel was always kind of protecting VJ. She's quiet and keeps to herself, except around Rachel. VJ can be moody and sullen one minute, and then Rachel shows up, and she changes dramatically."

"VJ mentioned she was into gaming. What do you know about that?" asked Bax.

"That's her favorite thing. I've watched her play in the break room. She really gets into the game. Total focus. And from what I've seen, the more violent, the more she focuses, but it's never interfered with her doing her job."

"Who else were Rachel and VJ close to?"

Fred Conway laughed. "Rachel was friends with everyone. As far as VJ, I know she hung around with some of the staff, but she never seemed close to anyone else."

Fred Conway stood up and headed for the front door to seat a couple of guests. Bax finished her meal, lost in thought. She called the server and asked her for the check. When the server returned, she handed her a twenty and told her to keep the change. The server smiled, and Bax gathered up her laptop and notebook, placed them in her backpack and headed for the door. She needed to take a break and get some air.

As she reached the door, Ranger Martin pushed through and almost ran her down. He looked frazzled. "Shit, Agent Baxter, I'm so sorry." He caught his breath. "We may need your help. The two rangers I sent to look for those missing hikers think they may have found blood. A lot of it."

Bax nodded and followed Ranger Martin to an ATV sitting at the curb. She threw her backpack in the back of the ATV, slid into the passenger seat and buckled in. She was in for a bumpy ride.

CHAPTER TWENTY-TWO

B uck and Paul pulled their Jeeps to the curb in front of Mitchell Groves's house, grabbed their backpacks and ducked under the crime scene tape that was wrapped around the front porch. They stepped onto the porch, and Buck unlocked the door with the key he got from Marvin Willets.

They stepped inside, and Buck left the door open. The coppery smell of death and the unmistakable smell of decomp filled the sealed house. Paul opened several windows and the back door to get some cross-ventilation going.

They walked back to the rear bedroom, where the stench was the most noticeable. The state police hazmat team had removed all the chemicals and drug paraphernalia from the bedroom, so all that was left was the desk the lab had been set up on and the table where Mitchell Groves died in a grotesque manner.

Buck looked around. There were some of those lavender pills on the floor, but other than that, the room was empty. Paul stepped up behind him, holding up his phone, and played the video Buck had made when he first entered the room. He wasn't sure what he was looking for, but other than the missing chemicals and stuff, the room looked the same as it did in the video.

"If this guy was manufacturing, where is everything, or did the killers take the drugs after killing him?" asked Paul.

"Maybe that's why the killers took the sheriff's SUV. Maybe they needed more room for the drugs. The only problem with that is there was no place in this room to store drugs. He could have stored the drugs in the other bedroom, but you would think we'd find shelving or boxes. Something that says, here is where we were stored."

"What about attic space or a basement?" asked Paul.

Buck shook his head. "Franklin and his team covered the attic and didn't find anything. There is no basement. Maybe he had a storage unit someplace?"

Paul told Buck he was going to walk around the outside of the house and check the small, detached garage. Buck walked around and started tapping on walls and stomping on the floor. Everything sounded solid. Buck was perplexed.

He checked the rest of the house with no luck

and headed back towards the front door. He'd just stepped out onto the front porch to get a breath of fresh air when a black Chevy Suburban with government plates pulled to the curb. Buck wondered what government agency was stopping by to get in his way when the driver's side door opened, and Jess Gonzales slid out of the driver's seat and waved to Buck. She waited at the curb until another woman climbed down from the passenger side and walked around the SUV and joined Jess.

Jess and the other woman stepped up to the crime scene tape and stopped. "Hey, Buck. Okay to come across?"

Buck nodded, and the two women slid under the tape and walked up the steps to the front porch.

Jessica Gonzales was a deputy director of the Drug Enforcement Agency, working out of the Grand Junction field office, and oversaw DEA operation in a seven-state region that spanned the western United States from the Canadian border to the Mexican border. She was also one of Buck's dearest friends.

"Jesus, Buck, what the fuck are you into now?" she asked as she walked up the steps and gave him a big hug.

That was one of the things Buck liked so much about Jess Gonzales. She was not afraid to tell it as she saw it, and you never knew what to expect. He was also constantly surprised by her appearance. Most of the time, Jess wore black tactical boots, black jeans and a black T-shirt that was tight enough to show off some impressive curves. Her hair was gray, short, and spiked, and she looked more like a college girl than her position would typically require. Today her T-shirt was covered by a black nylon jacket with dea in large letters on the left side.

Jess was only about five foot five, but her body was tight. She prided herself on her less than twenty percent body fat, and even in her new position, she still managed to work out at the gym for two or three hours a day. She was also an expert in several martial arts disciplines. Jess was one tough woman, and she wasn't someone you would want to mess with.

Jess had been the special agent in charge of the DEA's Grand Junction office a couple of years back when Buck called looking for her help. She had joined Buck and several other local and federal law enforcement teams on a raid on a Mexican drug cartel warehouse and trucking operation in the small mountain town of Durango, Colorado. The raid resulted in one of the largest drug busts in history. They confiscated hundreds of millions of dollars in cash, drugs and weapons that had been bound for the southwest and Mexico and put a serious dent in the cartel's operations. They also saved over three dozen young Mexicans who had been brought to the United States against their will and forced to work manufacturing the drugs. During that investigation, she also saved Buck's life during a shoot-out in his hotel parking lot.

Before heading to Durango, Buck had been involved in a triple murder investigation in Teller County. During a lull in the investigation, while waiting on DNA and ballistics results, he had been sent to Durango. The two prime suspects in the triple murder followed Buck to Durango and attempted to ambush him as he walked through his hotel parking lot. Jess had arrived on the scene as the shooting started, and she killed one of the suspects after Buck killed the other. For her heroism during the shoot-out and her exemplary work on the drug investigation, she was promoted to deputy director.

Buck considered Jess to be one of his closest friends, and she had been instrumental in helping him get through those terrible days following his wife's death. Jess was one of the first people to arrive at Buck's house the morning Buck's wife, Lucy, died. She helped him make all the final arrangements and stuck around a couple of days to ensure he was all right.

A few months back, Jess had helped Buck save several deputy U.S. Marshals who came under attack in the courthouse parking garage in downtown Denver. Buck and Jess were there giving testimony against a survivalist Buck had arrested during an investigation into an arson fire. At the close of the trial, several survivalists tried to rescue their brother by ambushing the Marshals' transport van.

The survivalists failed in their attempt and died in the process, also killing the guy they tried to rescue. Buck had been made a deputy U.S. Marshal as a reward for his courage, and he was allowed to keep his job with the Colorado Bureau of Investigation.

Jess introduced Special Agent Angie Montoya, and Buck shook her hand. At six feet tall, she towered over Jess and could look Buck straight in the eye. She had long, curly black hair and a cream complexion, and she wore jeans and Adidas cross-trainers.

"Jess, what are you doing here?" asked Buck.

"Those pill pictures you sent me got my attention. I needed to see the setup for myself."

"I take it you've seen those pills before. What are they?"

Jess hesitated a moment before answering. "That's the problem, Buck. We haven't seen them before. At least not in this country."

Buck waited for more of an explanation, but he didn't have to wait long.

"In Europe, they call them lavender because of the color. No one knows where they came from or how they got into the major distribution networks, but Europe is flooded with them, which has our friends overseas worried. Until you sent me those pictures, we had no record of them being in the U.S., but it looks like that's all changed."

"What's got everyone so worried?" asked Buck.

"We're not sure how they work," said Jess. "Scotland Yard has their lab working overtime to figure out the ingredients. Most of which are common chemicals, but they must be combined with something that enhances all the ingredients; we just don't know what."

Agent Montoya stepped into the conversation. "The various European drug agencies have told us that the person taking the drug loses all inhibition. Supposedly they act out based on a trigger of some sort. We don't yet know what that trigger is. The user can be in a mild state of euphoria one minute and then get triggered into an act of craziness and, in several cases, incredible violence.

"What has the agencies in Europe worried is that most users are not aware that the effects of the drug seem to be cumulative. The more times you use the drug, the stronger the impulses become. England, where the drug first appeared, has had several deaths amongst users, and there have been numerous violent crimes attributed to the drug. One Scotland Yard investigator told me that after several uses, the user's violence becomes out of control."

"Almost like a frenzy?" asked Buck.

"Yeah. That's a good way to describe it," said Agent Montoya.

Jess took over. "Once the drug wears off, there's no hangover or residual effect of any kind. It's like nothing happened."

Jess noticed the seriousness in Buck's eyes. "What's going on, Buck?"

Buck pulled out his phone and opened the crime scene photos in his gallery. He flipped through until he found what he was looking for and handed his phone to Jess. With Agent Montoya looking over her shoulder, Jess flipped through the photos. They both looked stunned. Jess handed back the phone.

"Holy shit, Buck. This is what you're here investigating? My god."

Buck put away his phone. "Those are four victims from this past weekend. The drug dealer, who lived in this house, is the one lying on the table."

"Can we look inside?" asked Agent Montoya, still shaken by the pictures she had just viewed.

Buck nodded and led the way.

CHAPTER TWENTY-THREE

They walked into the house, and Agent Montoya pulled a tissue from her front pocket and held it up to cover her nose. Even with the windows and doors open, the smell was still horrendous.

Buck led them down the hallway and stepped into the back bedroom where the lab had been located. He stepped aside so they could enter the room. Jess gave him a look when she saw the bloodstained table and carpet.

He pointed to the table along the one wall. "This is where the lab was set up. The chemicals were lined up along that shelf, and there was some other equipment under the table." He pulled out his phone, found the video and handed it to Jess.

Jess watched the video several times and then handed it to Agent Montoya, who also watched it a couple of times.

"This looks like a typical meth lab. I don't see any of the chemicals that we were told were used in the manufacturing of lavender."

Agent Montoya agreed. Buck flipped screens and showed her the picture of the pile of lavender-colored pills that were lying on the floor under the table.

"It sure looks like the same pills," said Jess. "But where are they being manufactured? Not here, so where did they come from?"

Jess walked over to the bloodstained table on the other side of the room. She looked at the remnants of the ropes that were tied to the table legs. She looked at Buck.

"This guy was alive when someone carved him up?"

"That's what the pathologist thinks, and the ropes tied to the table legs would seem to back that up," said Buck

"Good god. How fucked up can people be?"

At that point, Agent Montoya had seen enough, and she raced out the door and down the hall to the front porch, almost knocking over Paul, who had just come in from outside. He looked around to see who that person might be when he saw Jess.

"Hey, Jess. Long time." He pointed over his shoulder. "She one of yours?"

Jess nodded. "Good to see you again, Paul. It has been a while." They shook hands. "Yeah. Paul, that flash you saw was Angie Montoya, DEA."

"Ever seen anything like this before?" he asked her.

"No. And I never want to see anything like this again. You guys get sucked into the strangest shit."

Paul laughed. He looked at Buck. "Might want to follow me. I think I might have found something, but I'm gonna need some help."

Buck and Jess followed Paul through the kitchen, out the back door, and across the yard. The yard was a lot deeper than Buck realized. Paul kept walking till he came to a small, partially collapsed fence that separated Groves's yard from the neighbor behind. He placed one hand on the fence and stepped over. Buck and Jess followed until they came to an old, rusted garden tractor standing in a pile of weeds and tree branches.

Paul stopped. "I think there's a hatch under this thing, but I can't move it. Not sure if it's heavier than it looks, or it's bolted down."

Buck and Jess walked around the tractor in opposite directions, looking at the base. Buck tried to pull a couple of the branches out of the way, but they too were held fast. Buck wasn't sure what to do next when Jess called to him.

She pointed to a latch hidden under the

tractor's wheel. "I think I found a way in."

Buck reached in and flipped the latch, and they heard a loud clunk, and the front of the tractor raised off the ground. Jess and Paul reached under what felt like a metal lip and lifted, and the entire tractor and debris pile rose. Buck noticed it was hinged at the back. He also noticed there were stairs leading down.

Buck pulled his pistol from his holster and a flashlight out of his back pocket and shined it down the stairs. About ten feet below, he could see a floor. He looked at Paul.

"We'd better talk to the owner before we go barging into his root cellar."

"No need. As I walked around the yard, I looked for anything out of place. When I saw the broken fence and what looked like a trail leading into this yard, I called Margaret Gillam at the sheriff's office and asked her to check the tax rolls and see who owned this property. It's owned by a corporation, and it appears to be empty."

"You've got to be kidding. Could Mitchell Groves be that corporation and own two houses back-to-back?" asked Buck.

"Yep," said Paul. "We may have been looking in the wrong house all along."

Buck raised his pistol, held his flashlight against his gun and started down the stairs.

Buck hated these kinds of places. The last time he'd descended into a dark hole in the ground, he uncovered fifteen mummified bodies from an ancient serial killer. That find started a young woman on a trail of death and destruction that continued until her death in Aspen.

Buck stopped at the bottom of the stairs and shined his light around until he spotted a light switch on the wall. He turned on the lights and started down a short tunnel that led to a hole in the basement wall. Stepping into the basement, Buck had a minute to look around until Paul and Jess followed him.

In front of him were several tables containing lab equipment and more boxes and containers of chemicals. Buck looked around and whistled.

Jess pulled out her phone, asked Agent Montoya to join them and explained where to go. Paul stepped around Buck and walked along the shelves that lined one wall. The shelves contained hundreds of plastic packets of various pills and powders.

Jess walked up to Buck. "I think your drug dealer was pretty smart. I'd bet money that the lab in the other house was a decoy." She waved her hand around. "This is where all the magic happened."

Agent Montoya stepped through the hole and holstered her pistol. "Wow. Looks like we hit the mother lode. Whose house is this?"

Paul told her what he had told Buck and Jess. Jess turned back to Buck.

"We need to clear the rest of the house, but let's be careful not to contaminate the scene."

Buck nodded and headed for the stairs. He asked Paul to remain behind. Jess and Agent Montoya followed him to the stairs leading to the house. Once again, they all pulled their pistols and followed Buck up the stairs.

At the top of the stairs, Buck stopped and placed his ear next to the door. Not hearing anything from the other side of the door, he pushed open the door and stepped to the right, his pistol leading the way. Jess came up behind him and went left, and Agent Montoya stayed at the top of the stairs, her gun in the low ready position.

The house was unfurnished, and clearing it took a matter of minutes. They holstered their weapons and returned to the basement.

"Okay, Jess. This is your area of expertise. What do you want to do?" asked Buck.

"Before you call the state police hazmat team, we need to inventory everything here and mark it all as evidence—no telling who else might be involved. I'm gonna call Hank Clancy and see if he can send out an FBI Evidence Response

Team. Then, I'm gonna call my team and start a full-blown investigation. Angie and I will stay here to preserve the scene until I can get some agents here. By noon tomorrow, this town will be crawling with DEA agents."

She pulled out her phone as Agent Montoya stepped up, holding a small bag of lavender pills. She handed the bag to Jess.

"There must be hundreds of these baggies in a box on the shelf, but I took a quick look, and the chemicals aren't here. He must have been bringing these in from somewhere else and just distributing them." She took the baggie back from Jess and placed it back in the box.

Jess turned back to Paul and Buck. "Do you think this may be related to your murders?"

Buck shook his head. "I wish I knew. I can see his murder, but why the other three, unless there's a lot more going on around here than meets the eye?"

Jess started dialing her phone, and Agent Montoya was doing the same. Buck turned to Paul.

"Let's head back to the other house and lock the place down and then I'm gonna call Franklin and have him bring the forensic team back out here. I want them to go through the whole upstairs. Let's find out if any of our victims have ever been here."

Buck made his call while they walked back to the first house. He was about to put his phone away when it rang. He looked at the number and pushed the green button.

"Hey, Bax. What's going on?"

The sound of her voice made it obvious that this was going to be a long night.

CHAPTER TWENTY-FOUR

B ax and Ranger Martin made good time reaching the last known coordinates of the lost hikers. The trip had been crazy as they flew along trails that were made for people and horses and not for four-wheeled ATVs. There was little time to talk as they drove. The noise from the ATV was making it impossible to hear anything above the sound of the engine.

Bax held on as best she could, but she hoped the drive would be over soon. She was sore from her head to her toes from the bumpy trail. The scenery, what she could see of it, was beautiful, and she made a mental note to call her dad once this was all over and see if he'd like to spend a couple of days hiking this section of the trail.

Ranger Martin steered through the trees and came to a small field. The wildflowers were just starting to bloom at this elevation, and the ground was covered in brightly colored flowers. He pulled up next to the other ATV and shut off the engine. It took a minute for their hearing to return to normal and their bodies to stop shaking. Bax slid out of the passenger seat and grabbed her backpack.

Ranger Martin spotted the trail his guys had mentioned, and they headed off, following the trail through a small section of woods to a larger clearing with a view of the valley below. The other rangers, Jones and Simpson, were standing off to the side, looking at the view. They skirted the clearing and walked up to Ranger Martin.

Jones pointed towards the edge of the forest on the opposite side of the clearing. "We found the initial blood, or at least that's what it looks like, just this side of the forest. It's possible it's blood from an animal kill. That's what we thought until we spotted a larger patch near what looks like an open firepit."

"What makes you think that the larger patch isn't the same thing, an animal kill?" asked Bax.

Bax followed him as he skirted the clearing and approached the firepit, following his own tracks. He pointed to the pit.

Bax noted that the pit was little more than a burned spot on the ground, but she also noted several decent-sized rocks that covered a small area of the clearing. It looked like someone had removed the rocks from the firepit, hoping that no one would notice the burned area.

Jones used a small stick to push some of the dirt away from the firepit. He touched something green with burned edges. Bax kneeled and leaned in closer.

"That looks like green fabric that didn't quite burn all the way." He scraped the loose dirt a foot or so from the pit. The ground under the dust had a reddish tint to it. Bax couldn't help but notice how large an area the loose soil covered.

"And then there's this." He used the stick to push one of the rocks aside, and Bax stared at what was under the rock.

"That's a finger," she said.

"Yeah," said Jones. "Looks like it might have been chopped off. Once we found that, we stopped thinking this might be an animal gut pile that a poacher tried to clean up."

Bax pointed and followed Jones along the same path back to the others.

"What do you think, Agent Baxter? Are they right?"

"I think they might be. I want to define the area. Fan out and see if you can find any indication that this wasn't just a terrible accident, and the person who lost the finger isn't in a hospital. While you guys do that, I will see if I can get a print off the finger and test the soil to see if it's human blood. Watch your step and yell out if you see something."

Bax set her backpack on the ground and pulled

out a pair of blue nitrile gloves. She pulled out a fine brush and a small trowel, retraced her steps and kneeled next to the possible blood spot. She used the brush to clear some loose soil away from the spot. The more she brushed, the more stained area became visible.

Like an archeologist digging up an Egyptian burial chamber, she worked methodically until she cleared an area of about three feet square. She picked up the trowel and removed the surface layer of dirt until she exposed an area that had not been contaminated by the dirt someone had used to cover the spot.

She reached into her backpack, pulled out a small forensics kit, opened it and removed a Rapid Stain Identification (RSID) Blood Field Kit and a small test tube. She put some of the dirt into the test tube, added a few drops of water and shook up the test tube. She dropped a few drops of the water onto the test strip, set it aside and waited. She would have the results in about an hour.

Next, she took a pair of tweezers out of her kit and picked up the finger. She opened a fingerprint app on her phone and pushed the finger onto the screen. She filled out a data form within the app and hit send.

She knew the app could take a while if she got a result at all. This was the real world and not

TV, where the cops would get a match before the next commercial. If the person had never been fingerprinted, she would never get a match. It was all a waiting game.

She put the finger in an evidence bag she pulled from her backpack. She backtracked the way she came and walked to the edge of the forest. She stood there for a minute and just looked at the area. She felt something bad had happened here. She wasn't sure what, but a shiver ran up her spine.

Bax noticed a flattened area at the edge of the forest, and she circumvented the field and stopped at the location. The grass in the area looked flatter than the grass surrounding the area, but with everything so dry, it was hard to tell. She spotted something, kneeled and ran her hand over a small hole. She picked up a stick and pushed it into the hole. The stick slid in about six inches. She looked closer and spotted several more holes.

"Tent pegs," she said out loud to no one.

Ranger Martin saw her studying the ground and walked over. "Agent Baxter, what do you see?"

She stuck the stick into the hole. "There was a tent here," she said.

"Over here," came a yell from one of the rangers. Bax stood up, and they headed in the direction of the yell.

Ranger Simpson stood looking at a shrub that sat just off a game trail.

"What have you got?" asked Ranger Martin.

He raised the branch with his gloved hand. "Looks like blood. There's more heading off in that direction." He pointed to a rock outcropping about twenty yards away. "Didn't follow it all the way. Figured I'd wait for you all."

Bax looked at the blood on the leaf. "Let's follow the blood trail and see where it takes us."

They walked carefully, making sure not to step on any evidence they might need later, until they reached the rocks. Bax stopped short when she saw the bloodstain.

She pulled out her phone, opened the camera and started a video as she walked forward. The bloodstain wasn't huge, but there was enough to make it obvious once you knew where to look. She climbed up on the rock pile, careful to avoid the blood, and stopped at the top.

In front of her was a cavity formed by several large boulders. She pulled a flashlight out of her back pocket and shined the light into the hole. The sides of the rocks were slick with blood, and below her, about eight feet down, was a pile of something. It looked like a brown piece of fabric surrounding something.

Not wanting to smear the blood on the rocks, she zoomed her camera as much as it would go, turned on the light and filmed the pile. She stopped filming, climbed off the rocks and played back the video. Ranger Simpson, who was standing behind her, asked her to stop the video. He pointed over her shoulder at the screen.

"Is that a hand?" he asked.

Bax used the digital zoom feature and enlarged the picture, which also blurred it, but she saw what he saw.

Ranger Simpson said, "Shit, sure looks like a hand to me."

Bax looked at Ranger Martin. "Please recall Ranger Jones. This entire area is now a crime scene. We need to go back to the ATVs the way we came and disturb as little as possible."

Ranger Martin used his radio to call Jones and told him to head back to the clearing. He made his way back to the group.

"What's going on?" he asked. "I was following some broken branches. Looks like someone headed north from here and wasn't being careful. Didn't find any footprints, but I only followed the branches a little ways."

"We found a body stuffed in a pile of boulders. We need to call in a forensic team."

"A human body?" Jones asked. They all

nodded.

Bax led them back to the ATVs. "Can your rangers secure the area until I can get a team up here?" she asked.

Ranger Martin nodded, gave instructions to Jones and Simpson and they nodded. "I'll have my other guys grab some gear from their trucks and head up here as soon as possible. These guys are all trained in search and rescue, so once the gear gets here, we'll be ready to pull out the body. They'll wait for the pathologist." He looked at Jones and Simpson.

Bax had walked back and picked up her backpack, the finger and the test strip. She held up the strip. "Test is positive for human blood." She placed both items into her backpack and placed it in the back of the ATV.

Ranger Martin looked at the two other rangers. "Be careful. We don't know the whole story here, but if this has anything to do with the murders in town, the bad guy could still be out here."

They both nodded, and Bax and Ranger Martin climbed onto the ATV and headed back to the resort. Since it was hard to hear over the engine noise and since cell service was spotty at best, she'd wait until they were back at the resort to call Buck.

Ranger Martin parked in front of the resort and headed over to talk to the other two rangers.

Bax pulled out her phone and hit a speed dial button.

"Hey, Bax. What's going on?" asked Buck.

She filled him in on what they found in the clearing, and about the body, and he told her he'd be there as soon as he could. She headed into the restaurant to finish her interviews.

CHAPTER TWENTY-FIVE

B uck and Paul walked back to the original crime scene and locked up the house. This investigation had taken a strange turn, and he was grateful that Jess and her team were taking over the drug investigation. That still left the murders in town and now another body on the trail. Bax hadn't given him all the details, but he relayed what he had to Paul.

"How did she end up on the Continental Divide Trail? I thought she was interviewing friends of the victims at the resort?" asked Paul.

"Not sure, but I need to call the pathologist and get him headed this way. Call Franklin and have him and his team meet us at the resort."

Buck pulled out his phone and dialed.

"Buck. I'm guessing this isn't a social call?" asked Dr. Parkinson.

"Sorry, Garrett. We found another body up on the trail. The Forest Service called their search and rescue guys, so it will be a bit before they can retrieve the body. I'm gonna see if I can get some

ATVs. The site is not easy to get to."

Dr. Parkinson said he would get his gear and head out, and Buck gave him directions to the resort. He clipped his phone back on his belt and started towards his Jeep when his phone rang. He looked at the number but didn't recognize it.

"Buck Taylor."

"Agent Taylor. My name is Larsen, Dr. Nils Larsen, and I'm calling about a call I received earlier today from Maxine Clinton. Do you have a few minutes to speak?"

His English was perfect, but Buck noticed an accent he couldn't place. It sounded like it was from one of the Scandinavian countries. He hoped this call might shed some light on the murders.

"Yes, Doctor. Thanks for calling. How can I help you?"

"Well, Agent Taylor. Hopefully, I can help you. Maxine sent me some photos of the molds you took of two wounds that I understand came from some rather gruesome murders. I believe I can identify the weapons that made those wounds but let me give you a little background on myself."

Buck clicked on the speaker and held the phone out so Paul could hear.

"Go ahead, Doctor."

"First, I want you to understand that I am a professor, not a medical doctor. I am currently employed at the U.S. Military Academy at West Point, and I am a professor of the history of the Middle Ages. I am also considered to be an expert on the weapons of the Middle Ages, although I dislike the word expert. Are you familiar with the Middle Ages, Agent Taylor?"

Buck thought back to his high school history classes. Classes he had skipped out of as often as he could. If he knew there was going to be a test, he would have studied harder.

"If I'm not mistaken, Doctor, isn't that during the Crusades and such?" he said.

"Correct, Agent Taylor. It was the period from around 500 AD to roughly 1500 AD, and as you said, it was during the Crusades and the appearance of many new religions. However, it also contained the age of the Vikings. This is the period that our conversation will revolve around.

"The first weapon is called a Skeggox or a bearded ax. This was typically carried by every Viking, man and woman. It was lightweight and easy to conceal, but more importantly, it was a versatile weapon. This was not a chopping ax for felling trees or chopping firewood. This was a killing weapon, small, sharp and deadly. The tail on the bottom of the ax head was for gripping your opponent's shield, weapon or arm, during battle. Many Vikings carried two of these, and they were masters in their use."

"Doctor," said Buck. "Would this weapon be used to inflict multiple wounds on an opponent? Our victims were hit multiple times."

"Absolutely, Agent Taylor. Frenzy killings and mutilations were not uncommon during a Viking siege. The savagery was what most people of the period feared about a Viking encounter."

"What about the second weapon, Doctor? Any luck identifying that one?"

"Yes, Agent Taylor. That square hole was made by a bodkin point arrowhead. This was another weapon used extensively during the Middle Ages. It was a simple steel arrowhead, square and tapered down to look like a punch. It was designed to penetrate armor and chain mail but testing of early arrows did not show significant penetration.

"Now, my understanding from Maxine and the photos is that the gentleman who had this wound was wearing a ballistic vest. Is that correct?"

"That's correct, Doctor, and according to the pathologist, the wound penetrated almost eight inches into his chest. Is that possible with a bodkin point arrowhead?"

"Yes, Agent Taylor, it is possible, but I don't

think you are looking for an arrow. I believe this person was killed by someone using a modern-day compound crossbow—something with a lot of power and at a short distance. Tests have been conducted on bodkins made of high carbon steel and hardened, and they have penetrated various types of ballistic armor. With penetration as deep as your pathologist described. The weapon would have had to have been fired within twenty feet of the victim."

Buck was silent for a minute.

"Doctor, did Max send you the picture of what we think might be a ritualistic killing?"

"She did, Agent Taylor. In all its gruesome detail. It is a ritualistic killing, but unlike your weapons, it was not something used by the Vikings of old. It is a modern interpretation of something that might have been used in the Middle Ages, but it was created by Hollywood. Let me explain.

"It is called the Viking blood eagle. There are only two vague references to something similar in all the historical documentation. There is also an old wood carving in a museum in Norway that depicts what might be this ritualistic killing, but it is not a definitive depiction.

"The killing you saw was first portrayed in a popular television show depicting Viking life during the Middle Ages. It is also a popular element in several Viking-inspired video games. My guess is that whoever your killer or killers are, they are video gamers, copying something horrendous they saw in a game."

"Doctor, this has been very helpful, and you've given us a lot to think about. Thank you for taking the time."

"You are quite welcome, Agent Taylor, and please thank Maxine for thinking of me. This added a little excitement to my day. Have a good evening, Agent Taylor."

Buck hung up, and Paul handed him his phone with a picture of a Skeggox on the screen.

"That's what it looks like. Pretty deadly looking."

Buck spent a few minutes studying the picture. "You would think this would be an easy murder weapon to find. How many of these can there be in Pine County or the surrounding area?"

"Not many," said Paul. "A crossbow might be easier to track down since there are a lot of hunters in the area, but there is no way to get a ballistics match unless we find the type of arrow the professor described."

Buck nodded, and he was about to say something when he stopped. He looked at Paul. "Let's stop at the Carrollton house. The first deputy on the scene said he turned off a video game that was playing on the big screen. I wonder if it was a Viking-themed game?"

Buck called Bax to let her know what they were going to do before heading to the resort. He disconnected the call, and they headed for their Jeeps.

The bug in his brain was jumping up and down, and it felt like it was wearing a spiked helmet.

CHAPTER TWENTY-SIX

Marvin Willets, the acting sheriff of Pine County, crossed off the last Forest Service road on his map. He was parked on the Pine County–Saguache County line, and he felt like he had driven five hundred miles. Trying to find the missing sheriff's department SUV was like looking for a needle in a huge haystack, and so far, luck was not on his side.

He picked up the radio and called Deputies Tortelli and Jefferson, and they sounded as frustrated as he felt. No one had had any luck. He thought about how hard it was to find a truck in a small county. It should not have been this difficult. He checked his map one more time and noticed an old, abandoned logging road that ran along the county border.

With the sun setting low in the western sky, he thought about calling it quits and saving it for tomorrow, but he didn't feel right leaving any stone unturned. CBI and the state troopers were working their tails off trying to find the murderer or murderers, and the least he could do was finish the task he had been assigned.

He picked up the radio, let his deputies know where he was heading and declined the request for backup. The road wasn't that far away, and he figured it would be overgrown with weeds and impassable, so it shouldn't take long.

He pulled onto the highway and looked for the unmarked turn he'd missed on the first two passes. He spotted the hidden drive between the trees and turned down the road, if you could call it that. The dirt path was overgrown with weeds and small trees and shrubs, but it was passable so far, so he continued.

A half of a mile from the highway, the road entered an open field, and he spotted a green metal gate that was part of a barbed-wire fence that disappeared in both directions. He pulled up to the gate, slid out of the SUV and looked around. It was quiet and didn't look like the road had been used in years, until he stepped over the gate.

Lying on the ground to the side of the gate was a rusty chain and padlock. He kneeled and picked up the chain and looked at the end where it had been cut. The metal was shiny. Someone had been through here recently. The hairs on the back of his neck stood up, and he walked back to his SUV, scanning the area as he went.

He pulled the radio from its holder on the dashboard. "Hey, guys. You still out there?"

"This is Mike, Marvin. What's up?"

Marvin Willets filled him in on what he'd found and suggested they both head his way. He knew his limitations, and with no formal training as a law enforcement officer, he decided to err on the side of caution and wait for backup.

He'd just settled into the driver's seat to wait when he heard a truck coming up the road. He knew his deputies couldn't have gotten there that fast, so he pulled his pistol and ensured the safety was off before placing it back in his holster. He stepped out of the SUV just as an old beat-up Dodge Ram pickup truck slid to a stop behind him. He didn't recognize the young man behind the wheel, and he stood watching as the man slid out of the truck and walked up to him.

"Afternoon, Officer," the young man said. "You need some help or something?"

He was tall and thin and wore black jeans and a black sweatshirt. The hood was pulled over his head and blocked a good portion of his face.

Marvin Willets rested his hand on his pistol. "I'm good. Routine patrol, just waiting for my deputies to arrive. You have business around here?"

The young man smiled under his hoodie. "No.

No business. Saw you turn down the road, and when you didn't pull back out, I thought I'd better check, what with all the murders going on. Just doing my civic duty."

The young man backed up and then turned and walked back to his truck. He slid in, hit the starter and waved through the windshield. Then, he backed across the road and headed towards the highway.

Marvin Willets wiped the sweat from his brow. Something didn't feel right about the encounter, but he wasn't sure what that something was. All he knew was that his hands were shaking. He was glad he didn't have to pull his weapon because he was sure he would have dropped it.

He sat in his SUV and tried not to think about it. This was a small county, and he knew just about everyone in it, but he had never seen that man or that truck before. That surprised him. He also wondered what the man was doing on this nothing of a road.

He heard a truck coming up the road, and he slid out of his SUV and pulled his gun out of his holster. He wasn't taking any chances, but he could barely keep the gun from shaking as he held it next to his leg.

He was relieved when he saw another sheriff's department SUV coming down the road. It pulled in behind him, and Deputy Tortelli slid out of the driver's seat.

Deputy Tortelli watched Marvin put the gun back in his holster and lean back on the bumper. His face was as white as a sheet.

"You okay, Marvin?" Deputy Tortelli asked.

Marvin told him about the encounter he'd had with the young man.

"Shit, Marvin. The murders have everyone a little jumpy. I just came from town, and I didn't pass any old pickup trucks heading back towards town. Must have headed towards Saguache."

He walked over to the gate, and Marvin pointed to the chain. Deputy Tortelli picked up the chain and looked at the end.

"Someone's been by here recently," he said. "Any idea what's down this road?"

Marvin shook his head. He had lived his whole life in Silver City, but he did not know this road existed. Deputy Tortelli pushed open the gate and looked at the ground on the other side. It hadn't rained in several days, and the dirt was dry and baked to a hard crust. There were no tire tracks in the dirt.

The third sheriff's department SUV came over the slight rise and pulled up behind the other two. Deputy Jefferson slid out of the seat and walked over to Marvin and Tortelli.

Deputy Tortelli handed him the cut chain, and Deputy Jefferson examined the cut end. He noticed the open gate and the old dirt road that disappeared into the trees on the other side of the field.

"If we're gonna check this out, we need to get a move on; we're burning daylight." He handed the chain back to Deputy Tortelli.

Marvin Willets nodded, and they slid into their SUVs and drove past the gate and into the forest. They had no idea what awaited them at the other end of the road.

CHAPTER TWENTY-SEVEN

B uck unlocked the door to the Carrollton home and stepped into the living room. The smell in the house was terrible, and Buck wasn't sure if it would ever be okay to move back into. His gut told him that the Carrolltons were going to need a new place to live. Their two daughters, having been slaughtered in the house, made that a certainty.

Buck and Paul walked through the kitchen to the media room, and Paul headed for the closet that housed all the media equipment. This was not Buck's area of expertise. He would call one of his grandkids when he needed to update his computer or phone. Trying to find a channel to watch on television, now that he had agreed to get rid of cable and use streaming services, meant that his TV watching was almost nonexistent since he could never find his favorite shows.

Paul found the game console and noted that the game was still in place. He used the remote to turn on the big-screen TV and then hit play on the gaming console. The screen jumped to life, and Buck watched as the Vikings attacked the small seaside village. He had a hard time believing this was all computer-generated. The characters and scenery were so lifelike.

Paul hit the back button, ran the game back to the beginning and then hit play. He picked up one of the handheld controllers, sat down and started playing. Buck watched Paul's fingers on the controller and had trouble comprehending the speed with which he moved the various buttons.

Paul continued to advance the game until they came to the attack on the village. They watched as the Vikings tore the village apart and used their Skeggoxs to slaughter the inhabitants. The weapons were efficient and deadly, and even though he knew this was a game, Buck felt his adrenaline spike. He could see how someone could get into this game, but he wasn't sure how it could turn real people into killers.

The violence continued until the only survivor left was the village leader, who was being held between two huge fur-clad Vikings. They tied him between two posts and stripped off his tunic. The Viking chieftain then stepped up and began hacking away at his back using both a long knife and the Skeggoxs. The village leader never screamed because if he screamed, he would not be allowed to enter Valhalla. When he was finished, the chieftain spread apart the ribs, then pulled the lungs out and hung them over the broken ribs to look like eagle wings.

Paul had seen enough; he turned off the game and sat for a minute. They both knew this was a computer game but seeing the end result in real life made the game just as gruesome and horrendous. Buck hoped that Mitchell Groves had died quickly.

Paul walked back to the console, pulled the game cartridge and placed it in an evidence bag he pulled from his backpack.

"That explains a lot," said Paul.

Buck shook his head. "So, let's think about this for a minute. We have these lavender pills that can make you crazy. Is a video game enough to trigger a frenzy?"

"I don't know how you felt during the game," said Paul, "but I know my adrenaline was way up the chart. I can see how a game could trigger a person's raw emotion and lead someone into a frenzy."

Buck thought for a minute. "So, if we're right, we have at least two people using these pills, they come over here and put on the video game, and after playing for a bit, their adrenaline sets them into a frenzy, and they take it out on the two sisters."

"The sisters knew their killers. This wasn't random," said Paul.

Buck looked towards the door that had led them to the media room. "So, the sheriff comes by to check on the girls, as a favor to their parents, hears the noise blasting from this room and walks through that door. His senses are under attack from the game's lights and sounds, and at the same time, he is witnessing a brutal attack, both on the screen and in front of him. Not sure what to do, he might have yelled to get their attention, or he could have walked deeper into the room. We know his gun was lying on the floor when Tortelli arrived on the scene."

Paul looked at Buck. "There was a third person in the room. Someone who wasn't part of the frenzy."

"The person with the crossbow, and Wechsler was so focused on the frenzy, he never saw the third person until it was too late."

Buck turned and scanned the room. "This is gonna sound crazy, but knowing how people are today, do you think the third person could have been filming the frenzy?"

"Fuck, Buck. I hope no one is that sick, but we've seen some sick sons of bitches over the years. I guess nothing is impossible."

"We need to talk to Mr. and Mrs. Carrollton," said Buck. "We need to look at the daughter's friends and find out whose game this is."

Buck pulled out his phone and speed-dialed a number.

"Hey, Buck," said Mel. "We haven't finished with the victim's computer or phones, so I don't have an update for you. We were going to start on social media next. What else can we help you with?"

"We just had a crazy thought and figured you guys might know where to look. There was a video game playing during the killings." Paul handed him the evidence bag with the game in it. "The game is called *Viking Warrior*. We wondered if someone might have been filming the attack."

"And you want to see if they posted it online?" asked Mel.

"Is it possible to track something like that?"

"Sure, Buck. Since we know the name of the game, we'll run a search algorithm." Mel stopped in mid-sentence. "Sorry, Buck." She laughed. "Forgot who I was talking to. We can run a search for the name of the game, and if the killers referenced the game, we should be able to find it."

Paul and Buck both laughed. "Thanks for dumbing it down, Mel," said Buck. "Go ahead and run your search and see if anything pops up."

Buck thanked Mel and disconnected the call. "Now, let's go see the Carrolltons and see if they can shed some light on who might be playing video games with their daughters."

Paul placed the game back into his backpack, and they headed for the door. They would get to the resort as soon as possible, but Buck was feeling good about their theory. Now to see if they could turn it into facts.

CHAPTER TWENTY-EIGHT

Buck pulled out his phone and dialed a number from memory. Michael Torres answered the phone.

"Hey, Buck."

"Hi, Michael. What's going on?"

Michael Torres was Buck's brother-in-law and Lucy's younger brother. He had also been a defensive tackle on the Gunnison High School Cowboys football team and played varsity football with Buck and Hardy Braxton.

Buck and Hardy were called the Wrecking Crew during their senior year in high school, where they broke almost every state defensive football record there was. Some of those records stood to this day.

Michael Torres had worked as a hunting and fishing guide in his father's company until Fernando died from a heart attack a few years back. Upon his father's death, Michael took over the small ranch and guide service just outside of the Gunnison city limits. He was a skilled guide, and his services were in high demand. He was very good at what he did, and his calendar was always booked full.

"Staying busy," said Michael. "What's up?"

"Are any of your ATVs available for the next couple of days?"

"You're lucky, Buck. I just got back from a trip and don't have another one until next weekend. Why?"

Buck explained what he could about the case he was working on and told Michael he would need as many ATVs as he could get together.

"I've got four of them on the trailer right now. Where do you need me?"

Buck gave him the address of the Conway Hiker's Resort and asked him if he could haul them there before dark.

"No problem," said Michael. "I just need to gas them up, and I'll head right out. I'll see you in a couple of hours."

Buck thanked Michael and disconnected the call. He then dialed Bax and left a voice message, letting her know that he had four ATVs on the way that they could use for a couple of days.

Buck disconnected the call and slid out of his Jeep, grabbing his backpack as he went. Paul was standing in front of an open hotel room door and was talking with Lenny Carrollton. Buck walked up, introduced himself and offered his condolences. They shook hands.

Buck asked how Mrs. Carrollton was holding up, and Lenny Carrollton told him that she was in bed asleep. That the doctor had given her a sedative.

"I don't know how she's going to hold it together. We have so much to do, and I'm trying to pick up the slack, but it's hard." Tears filled his eyes.

"We understand, sir, and we hate to intrude, but the first forty-eight hours are critical in a murder investigation."

Mr. Carrollton wiped his eyes. "I understand, and we will help all we can."

"Thank you, sir," said Buck. "When you arrived home yesterday and walked into the media room, was there a video game playing on the big TV?"

Mr. Carrollton thought for a minute. Tears streamed down his face. "I'm sorry," he said as he pulled himself together.

He wiped his face. "Yes. There was something on the TV. The noise was horrendous, and I couldn't believe my daughters could stand the noise, but I guess it didn't matter."

"Sir," said Paul. "Did you recognize the game? Was it something your daughters played often?"

"What?" said Mr. Carrollton, trying to focus. "No. I didn't recognize the game. It was some warrior game, I think." He closed his eyes, trying to recall.

"Were your daughters into video games?"

Mr. Carrollton focused on Buck's voice. "Rachel would play occasionally, but I don't think Jenny ever played."

"So that was your gaming console in the media room?" asked Buck.

"Yes, we bought it a few years back. Jenny and her friends were into kid's games. Nothing like the violence that was on the screen."

Paul pulled the evidence bag out of his backpack and showed Mr. Carrollton the game cartridge. He looked at it and then at Paul. "No, I've never seen that before. I don't know where it came from."

"Sir," asked Buck. "Do you know which of her friends she would play video games with?"

Mr. Carrollton thought for a minute. "Yeah, she used to play with her best friend, VJ. VJ Florence. Her father is one of the other county commissioners. I don't think they've played much lately. VJ got kind of dark as she got older."

"How so, sir?" asked Paul.

"You know kids, she outgrew the kid games and started into those Warcraft games, with all the death and destruction. She also started dressing in dark clothes, like those—what do you call them? Gothics."

"Goths," said Paul. Mr. Carrollton nodded his head.

"Do you remember anyone else they might have played with?" asked Buck.

"Not really. A lot of the kids were friends of VJ's. I'm not sure how close Rachel and VJ were lately, especially with Rachel away at college most of the year."

Buck asked for VJ's address, and he wrote it down in his notebook. Then he handed Mr. Carrollton his business card and asked him to call if he or Mrs. Carrollton might have anything to add.

"When will we be able to bury our daughters, Agent Taylor?"

"I'll make a call, sir, and let you know as soon as we can release the bodies. Again, sir, we are very sorry for your loss, and we will do everything we can to find the person or persons responsible."

Buck and Paul stepped away and heard the door close behind them. They stood next to Buck's Jeep.

"So, as far as he knows, the video game was not his daughter's? That means the killers brought it with them."

"That's one possibility," said Buck. "The other is that they brought over the game to have some fun, a couple of them took the lavender, and the game triggered the events that followed."

Paul thought for a minute. "That makes sense, Buck. This whole thing could have started as fun, but—"

Buck cut him off. "Except two people had the Skeggoxs, and one person brought a crossbow. Not something you would need for a night of video gaming."

"That's what I was going to say."

Buck smiled. "Don't you just hate it when you blow up your own theory?"

"Okay," said Paul. "Sounds like we need to pay a visit to this VJ."

"Just what I was thinking," said Buck.

Buck pulled out his phone and called Dr. Parkinson. "Hi, Buck, we just got to the resort. What's up?"

Buck asked him when he would be ready to release the bodies, and Dr. Parkinson told him that the families could arrange to have the bodies picked up any time after noon tomorrow. Buck thanked him and told him he would see him in a little while.

Paul and Buck slid into their Jeeps, entered the address of the Florence home in their GPS and pulled out of the parking lot. Buck had decided he would give Mr. Carrollton some time to calm down before giving him the word about the bodies. The man was under tremendous stress, and Buck didn't want to add to it today. Tomorrow would be soon enough.

CHAPTER TWENTY-NINE

B ax sat back in the chair in the corner of the restaurant. She didn't seem to be getting anywhere with interviewing the staff, which was frustrating. She looked at the list Mr. Conway had given her of the employees and saw she had only four people left. She went in search of the last server on the list.

Holly Woods was rolling silverware in white napkins in the corner of the kitchen. She was older than most of the other staff, tall with platinum hair. She looked up as Bax approached. She also hadn't been amongst the staff when Bax and Mr. Conway first spoke with them.

"Holly, I'm Ashley Baxter with CBI." She held up her credentials. "I need a few minutes of your time; Mr. Conway is okay with you stepping away for a few minutes."

"What's this about?"

"I'm interviewing the staff about two of your coworkers. It will only take a minute."

Bax waited while Holly rolled the last napkin

and placed it in the basket on the table. She followed Bax into the dining room, and Bax pointed to the seat on the other side of the table. Holly sat down.

Holly looked confused, like she couldn't figure out why she was being questioned by a state cop. Bax clicked the audio recorder program on her phone and set it on the table.

"How well do you know Jenny and Rachel Carrollton?"

"Why do you ask?"

Bax smiled. "Holly, this will go a lot faster if you answer my questions and not ask yours."

Holly looked down at her shoes and then back at Bax. "Sorry, I'm not used to being questioned by the police."

"That's okay," said Bax. "Can you answer my question?"

"I had been working here for a couple of years when they both started. They were still in high school. You may have noticed I'm older than most of the staff, so we never interacted outside of work."

"When was the last time you spoke with either of them?"

Holly thought for a minute. "I guess it was Thursday night. We were busy, so we didn't talk much, but they were both here."

"So, you didn't work with them either Friday or Saturday?" asked Bax.

"No. I worked the breakfast shift Friday; they both worked the dinner shift. I was gone by then. What's this all about?"

"Did you see them on Saturday?" asked Bax.

"No. I was off Saturday and Sunday. We just got back into town about an hour ago. So, I came straight here."

"Where were you?"

Holly looked nervous. "We were in Denver for the weekend. It was my dad's eightieth birthday. We headed over Friday after work and just got back. It was kind of a family reunion. Why?"

"You keep saying we. Who were you with?"

"I was with my wife, Bridgette, and our daughter, Stephanie." She fidgeted in the chair and started to say something, but Bax held up her hand.

"Were you aware that Rachel and Jenny were murdered on Saturday night?"

Holly looked stunned. "Oh my god. Did he kill them?" She covered her mouth, but it was too late, and the comment was already on the table.

Bax looked at her. "Did who kill them?"

Holly stood up. "I've said too much already."

Bax reached out and placed her hand on top

of Holly's. "Holly, if you know something about these murders, you need to tell me. We've got four dead bodies. Anything you can tell me, no matter how insignificant you think it might be, could help."

Holly sat back down. "Four murders. You said Rachel and Jenny. Who else got murdered?"

Bax filled her in about the deaths of Sheriff Wechsler and Mitchell Groves. While Bax talked, Holly grew noticeably more upset.

"Jimmy's dead?"

Bax nodded her head. "So, you see why we need any information you might have."

Holly wiped the tears from her eyes, but it was a losing battle as the gusher hit. She covered her face with her hands and let the tears flow. Bax gave her a minute to console herself.

"Holly, you seem very upset about the sheriff. You want to tell me why?"

Holly took a couple of paper napkins off the table, wiped her eyes and shook her head. Bax decided to take a chance.

"How long have you been sleeping with him?" she asked.

Holly looked stunned as she looked around the room to make sure no one had overheard the question. Her voice quivered.

"Wha . . . what are you talking about? I wasn't sleeping with Jimmy."

"Then why don't you tell me what's going on. I'm trying to solve his murder."

Holly thought for a minute before answering in a voice so low that Bax needed to lean across the table to hear her.

"We've been seeing each other for a couple of months. It wasn't like he was going to leave his wife or his daughters. Those kids were his whole world, and I love my wife and daughter. It was just a part-time thing. Nothing more."

Bax could see that it was more than a part-time thing, but she decided to allow Holly some dignity and not go into any details. What did surprise her was that Holly had mentioned that she had a wife. Bax wondered if her wife was aware of the affair. Something like that could put her in the frame as a potential murderer, so she asked the question that needed to be asked.

"Holly, was your wife aware of the affair?"

Holly looked at her through bloodshot eyes. "You can't believe that Bridgette could have killed Jimmy and three other people because we slept together? Well, let me tell you. She knew all about it, and she wasn't concerned in the least. We have an open relationship, and sometimes I like to sleep with a man. She has that same option. So, it works for us, okay?"

Bax held up her hands. "No problem, Holly, but now I need to know what you meant when you asked me if her boyfriend did it? Everyone I've talked to told me that neither Rachel nor Jenny had a boyfriend."

"That's bullshit. Do you believe that two attractive young women in college don't have any boyfriends? I bet you had plenty," said Holly.

"Why would no one admit to knowing that?"

"They're all trying to protect Rachel and Jenny's reputations. Their parents are in the dark or in denial, or both. Ask that bitch VJ. She knows all about it. The guy Rachel has been seeing is one of her gamer friends. They were all at a bar in Saguache on Saturday night playing in a gaming contest. When Rachel's around them, she's a different person."

"I take it you don't like VJ much?"

"That girl is nothing but trouble. She got herself thrown out of the University of New Mexico because she manipulated two male students into doing some stupid stunts, and one of them died. She may come across as meek and mild, with that whole Goth or Celtic thing going on, but she is a major psycho."

Holly looked around and noticed that the dining room was filling up. "I've got to go to work."

She stood and walked away from the table, leaving Bax bewildered. Bax turned off the recording app on her phone, placed her laptop in her backpack and pushed back from the table. She headed for the kitchen in search of VJ.

VJ was nowhere in sight, and she spotted a harried-looking Mrs. Conway wiping the lines indicating server stations off a plastic floor plan hanging on the wall and mumbling to herself.

"Mrs. Conway, have you seen VJ? I need to talk to her again."

Mrs. Conway turned and looked at Bax with fire in her eyes. "If you find her, you can tell her she's fired. She can't just walk out at the start of her shift without telling anyone she's leaving. Left me shorthanded."

"VJ left?" asked Bax. "When did this happen?"

"I have no idea. Someone told me that she watched you and Holly having a long discussion, and she just grabbed her backpack and left. What's going on, Agent Baxter?"

"I don't know, Mrs. Conway, But you can be damn sure I will find out."

CHAPTER THIRTY

Sheriff Willets led their small caravan down the dirt road and across the small clearing. The road wasn't much of a road, and it looked like it hadn't been used in years, but they all knew differently. This was the mountains, and no one cuts another person's lock unless they're looking to trespass onto someone else's land.

They were all on high alert as they headed into the trees, and the road climbed up the side of a ridge. They had to back up several times to make the hairpin turns until they reached the top of the small hill.

From the top, the road dropped into a small clearing with what looked like the remains of an old mining cabin visible in the distance. Sheriff Willets stopped his SUV, and the deputies stopped behind him.

Deputy Tortelli pulled a pair of binoculars out of the glove box and slid out of his SUV. He walked up to the side of Willet's SUV and scanned the area.

"Looks abandoned," he said. He looked at Willets. "What do you want to do?"

"Why don't you stay here and keep an eye out, and Tommy and I will drive down there and take a look."

He waved to Deputy Jefferson, and they continued down what was now little more than two tracks in the dirt, towards the old building. They stopped about twenty-five feet away and slid out of their SUVs, pulling their pistols as they moved.

They both stopped for a minute and looked around.

"Did you know this place was here?" asked Sheriff Willets.

Deputy Jefferson shook his head. "Didn't even know this road existed until today. I wonder who used to live here?"

They left the relative safety of their SUVs and approached the cabin on foot, leading with their pistols, neither one saying a word.

At the door to the cabin, Sheriff Willets pushed aside a plastic shower curtain and stepped inside, scanning the one-room structure with his pistol. Jefferson came in behind him and looked at the shower curtain covering the entrance. "Looks new," he said. "Someone's been living here."

The sheriff kicked a sleeping bag that was lying on a blue insulated pad. "Yeah, but who, and how did they find this place?"

"Let's look around the area and see if there is any other evidence of habitation," said Sheriff Willets.

They stepped back through the shower curtain door, and Sheriff Willets waved for Deputy Tortelli to come down from the hill. They waited until he arrived and then worked out a plan. Since the front of the cabin faced the clearing, they decided to check out the woods behind the cabin.

The sheriff would head straight back from the rear of the cabin, while Tortelli would go left, and Jefferson would go right. Once they were out about fifty yards, they would turn and return to the cabin. Fearing that the young man in the old pickup truck might be in the area, they each drew their pistols and moved into the woods.

They weren't sure why they were concerned with the young man. His driving up on the sheriff might have been just what it appeared, a friendly gesture, but they all felt that something about the encounter was off. Finding the sleeping bag in the old cabin didn't change that opinion, so they proceeded with caution.

They each returned to the cabin with nothing to report. Maybe they were mistaken. The cabin was only a mile and a half from the Continental Divide Trail. Perhaps the sleeping bag belonged to a lone hiker.

They were walking back to their SUVs when something caught Tortelli's eye. It was a momentary flash of light about twenty yards from the cabin just inside the tree line. They stopped as he walked towards where he thought he saw the flash.

He reached the location and looked around. There was nothing obvious that could have caused the flash, and he wondered if his mind was playing tricks on him. On a whim, he kicked the leaves and pine needles that covered the ground.

He was about to give up when his foot hit something hard. He kicked away more of the debris, and there, next to his foot, was a padlock, but it wasn't just lying on the ground. This was a shiny new padlock, and it was hooked through a hasp, which did not belong under the debris on the forest floor. He swept more debris away and revealed the front edge of a hatch.

He'd just turned to call over the sheriff and Jefferson when the first bullet hit the ground right where his hand had been. He jumped up and sprinted for the cover of a fallen tree as Sheriff Willets and Deputy Jefferson ran for the cabin and dove through the door.

They stayed below the one window as bullets slammed into the side of the cabin, causing dust and debris to fall from the rafters. The sound was deafening as a second rifle opened up, alternating between the back wall of the cabin and Deputy Tortelli's position behind the fallen tree.

Several times they heard what they believed was Tortelli shooting back into the woods. They had no way of knowing if he could see the shooters or if he was shooting towards the sounds, but they felt helpless sitting on the dirt floor inside the cabin.

There was a momentary lull in the shooting as one of the shooters stopped to reload. When he started shooting again, they heard windows exploding and tires blowing out, and they knew that the shooter's focus had shifted to the SUVs. They took that opportunity to rise, look out the window and shoot back. They did not know what they were shooting at, but they needed to do something.

Jefferson stopped to reload and pulled his radio from his utility belt.

"Margaret, this is Jefferson. Do you copy, over? Margaret, can you hear me? This is Jefferson, over."

"Tommy, what's all that noise in the background? I can barely hear you."

"Margaret, we're under attack. There's an old fire road two miles east of the edge of town on the right side. It's hard to find. Send help."

Sheriff Willets was firing back, as was Tortelli from behind the tree. Jefferson repeated his request when Margaret responded that she couldn't understand him for all the noise. He tried again, and this time she seemed to understand. Bullets were hitting the cabin at a furious pace, and Sheriff Willets had no doubt that they were all going to die, and he didn't know why. He reloaded and opened fire again.

Jefferson nodded as Margaret responded that help was on the way, and he rejoined the fight, shooting at anything that looked like it didn't belong.

Just as suddenly as it started, the shooting ended. The sudden quiet was eerier than the shooting, and the sheriff wondered if the shooters were changing locations and moving closer. They each slapped a new magazine into their pistols and waited.

After five minutes, they heard the first sirens coming over the hill, and they breathed a sigh of relief when they saw the first state trooper crest the hill.

Behind the trooper came Buck Taylor's Jeep, followed by a gray Jeep with flashing lights. The sheriff and Jefferson stood up and stepped out of the cabin, looking in every direction before walking out to meet the cavalry. They were thrilled to see Tortelli emerge from the woods unscathed.

Holding an assault rifle, the trooper scanned the area from behind his SUV. When he felt sure the threat was gone, he stepped out and walked to the cabin.

Buck and Paul, with pistols in their hands, followed the trooper. Seeing that everyone was okay, everyone holstered their weapons.

"Marvin. What the hell happened?" Buck asked as he pulled aside the shower curtain door and looked at all the wood chips and debris that littered the cabin.

"We don't know. This was the last road we had to check, and when we got here, someone opened fire on us."

"Sounded like two rifles," said Tortelli.

"Whoever they were, they had us pinned down pretty good, and they just kept shooting," said Jefferson.

"Whose cabin is this?" asked Paul as he stepped through the door. "There's a sleeping bag on the floor."

"We don't know," said Tortelli. "But I also found what I think might be a root cellar with a new lock on it."

He led the team over to the root cellar and pointed towards the lock. Buck kneeled, raised the lock and pulled a small brown case out of his vest pocket. He pulled two lockpicks out of the case and, within seconds, had the lock unlocked.

Sheriff Willets watched as Buck picked the lock and put away his tools. "Do I want to know why you have a lockpick set?" he asked.

Buck looked up and smiled. "In case I lose my house keys."

The rest of the team helped clear away the debris that covered the hatch, and then, with pistols drawn, Buck raised it. He pulled a flashlight from his belt and shined it down into the darkness. They all stood and stared at what the light revealed.

"I guess we found the missing drugs from Mitchell Groves's house," said Paul.

"Yeah," said Buck. "But did Groves hide them here, or is this someone else's stash?"

Buck closed the hatch and relocked the lock. "We need to search this area before it gets dark and see if we can find the sheriff's SUV. Stay within shouting distance of each other, keep your heads on a swivel and let's fan out. Trooper, I'd like you to stay here and watch the scene."

While the others headed out in the directions that the sheriff and the deputies hadn't covered before, Buck unclipped his phone from his belt and speed-dialed a number.

"What's up?" asked Jess Gonzales when she answered the call.

Buck filled her in on the details of the firefight and about the drug stash they'd found in the root cellar. He sent her the GPS coordinates, and she said she'd have agents there in a heartbeat, along with the FBI Evidence Response Team that was wrapping up at the drug lab.

Buck had just hung up when his phone rang.

"Hey, Bax, we're still trying to get there."

Bax cut him off and explained why she was calling. She told him about the information she had received about VJ Florence and that she had taken off from work without telling anyone she was leaving. Buck listened until she took a breath.

"We were on our way to the Florence house to interview this VJ and her parents when we got an emergency call," he said.

He explained about the shoot-out and the new drug stash.

"Was anyone hurt?" she asked.

"Just an old cabin and a couple of SUVs that belonged to the sheriff's department. Jess is sending some of her people over to take over the scene. Right now, we're trying to find the sheriff's missing SUV. Then I'll go talk to VJ Florence. You wait for Dr. Parkinson, and let's see if the body in the rocks is related to the murders in town."

Buck disconnected the call. This case was getting more and more interesting with every hour that passed. He clipped his phone back on his belt and headed into the woods, following the others. It was going to be a long night.

CHAPTER THIRTY-ONE

D r. Parkinson pulled into the parking lot outside the lodge and slid out of his SUV. He saw Bax talking with Michael Torres while he unloaded the fourth ATV from the trailer behind his pickup. He walked up and shook hands all around.

"Agent Baxter is this our transport to the body?" he asked.

Bax nodded. "Search and rescue have already headed out. They should have the body out by the time we get there."

Dr. Parkinson, with a scowl on his face, was about to say something when she held up her hand. "I know it's not procedure to move the body before you have a look, but this time we have no choice. The body's wedged between two boulders, about an eight-foot drop with little room to move. Thought it would be best to pull the body out first."

He nodded and loaded his gear bag in the back of one of the ATVs. They waited as the two EMTs from the ambulance loaded what they thought they might need into the same SUV and climbed into the seats.

Michael Torres nodded to Bax. "Tell Buck I'd like these back in one piece, if possible." He laughed, climbed into his truck and pulled out of the lot.

Bax told the doctor to follow Ranger Martin, who was once again driving one of the resort's ATVs. She told them she was going to wait for the forensic team. The two ATVs pulled out and headed down the trail.

Bax pulled an emergency bag from the back of her Jeep and placed it in the back of one of the other ATVs. She had no idea how long this investigation would take or how long she might need to stay on the scene, so she needed to be ready. She headed back into the resort and ran into Fred Conway, pushing a cart with a large cooler towards the front doors.

"Thought you guys might like some food, so I had the kitchen prepare some sandwiches and drinks. You let me know if you need more, and I'll make sure to keep you guys fed."

Bax followed him over to one of the other ATVs and helped him load the cooler into the cargo space in the back.

"I heard about VJ disappearing," he said. "Billie is not happy. You don't think she had anything to do with the murders, do you? I mean, she's a little strange, but she and Rachel go way back."

"I wish I knew, Mr. Conway. I guess anything is possible. All I know right now is that she said nothing to me about leaving during our interview. Seems strange that she would just pick up and leave."

Bax knew the old adage about guilty people running, and even though she had seen it herself, she didn't believe that was always the case. She'd been involved in several investigations where the guilty party ingratiated themself into the investigation instead of running. Still, she had to admit that the way VJ took off, and the fact that she lied about Rachel having a boyfriend, gave her a bad feeling.

Bax held the door so Mr. Conway could return the cart to the kitchen and returned to the ATV in time to see a white van with state plates drive under the entry gate and pull up to the curb next to Bax.

April Wang climbed out of the driver's seat and walked up to Bax. She gave her a big hug. "My god, Bax. How long has it been? You look great."

Bax smiled and hugged her back. "Hey, April. Been a while, huh? Thanks for getting here so quickly."

April Wang was the senior evidence tech based out of the State Crime Lab in Pueblo,

Colorado. She was a short Asian woman with long black hair pulled up in a bun.

"Hey, you know our motto. We go where the crime is. From the looks of the ATVs, we must be going on a journey?"

Bax nodded and gave her the *Reader's Digest* version of the events that had unfolded. When she finished, April gathered the three techs who had also arrived in the van and gave them their marching orders. Like a well-oiled machine, they started pulling gear from the van and loading it into the other ATV.

Once they were loaded up, Bax climbed into the ATV with the cooler in the back and headed across the parking lot to the old fire road that was the shortcut to the trail. April and her team followed close behind her.

An hour and a half later, they pulled into the clearing that was now crowded with ATVs and people. She spotted the search and rescue team standing on top of the boulders and followed by April, headed that way.

Dr. Parkinson was standing on top of the rocks, next to Ranger Martin, who was feeding a rope through the winch they had secured to a tree. Although he felt the need to be involved, he stood by and let the professionals do their jobs. His time would come once the body was released from the crevasse between the boulders.

Bax and April climbed onto the boulders, and Bax introduced April to Ranger Martin and Dr. Parkinson. She stepped over to the crevasse and looked down. One of the rangers was suspended on a rope halfway down, while a second ranger was hanging upside down, feeding web straps around the body. He connected the straps to a carabiner and signaled that he was ready.

The first ranger climbed out of the crevasse, and then the team hoisted the upside-down ranger out. His face was bright red, and he was drenched in sweat. Everyone stood back as the rangers began winching the body out of the hole.

Once the body was free of the crevasse, the rangers swung it over the boulders and slid it down until it settled on a clean drop cloth one of the forensic techs had laid out on the ground. One of the techs unhooked the strapping and removed it from the body.

Even before anyone opened the sleeping bag the body was wrapped in, they knew it would not be a pleasant sight. The sleeping bag, which had originally been some shade of green, was drenched in blood and body fluids, giving it a reddish-brown hue.

Dr. Parkinson and April Wang, now wearing Tyvek suits, nitrile gloves and glasses, kneeled next to the body, and April unzipped the sleeping bag. She folded back the top portion of the bag, revealing the same brutality seen on the other victims.

Dr. Parkinson leaned in for a closer look at the wounds and opened what was left of the shirt the person had been wearing. The tearing sound as the shirt, stiff and sticky, pulled away from the flesh made several of the rangers gag. April uncovered the rest of the body and stood back, giving the doctor room to work.

Dr. Parkinson stood up and looked at Bax. "No doubt about it," he said. "Definitely the same killer or killers as the sheriff and the others. Must be twenty or thirty ax wounds under all that blood."

April photographed the body from every angle while her team examined the body and the sleeping bag, looking for any evidence they could salvage from the blood. By the time they were done, they had recovered a few stray hairs, but that was about all.

Dr. Parkinson called over the two EMTs and asked them to bring out a body bag so they could transport the corpse. While they grabbed the bag, April quickly searched the body. There was a wedding band on the left hand and a smartwatch on the left wrist with a shattered screen. His right thumb was missing. The victim had a wallet in his left rear pocket. April handed the wallet to Bax.

Bax, wearing blue nitrile gloves, opened the wallet, which was no easy task considering it was welded closed by the victim's blood. The wallet contained several hundred dollars in cash and several credit cards, which April photographed as Bax pulled them free. Each item was placed in an evidence bag. Bax noted to herself that robbery did not appear to be a motive.

She found a Michigan driver's license and compared the name on the license to those on the credit cards. They were a match. Bax placed the license into the evidence bag, sealed it and signed the flap. She handed it to April.

Ranger Martin stepped over. "Well, what do you think? This is some pretty brutal stuff."

"Yeah. Sometime during the last few nights, Mark Kearney ran into the same person or persons who killed the Carrollton girls, Sheriff Wechsler, and Mitchell Groves," said Bax. "This is now a crime scene. April, please have your team rope off the entire area."

April looked at the sky. "Gonna be dark soon. We're gonna need some lights."

Ranger Martin signaled his rangers, and they ran back to the ATVs and returned with a portable generator and several work lights on stands.

"You just tell us where you want them, and

we'll get them all set up," he said to April, who headed off with the rangers to locate the lights. He spotted Bax looking out over the clearing towards the mountains beyond. He walked up behind her.

"I guess you're not looking at the scenery, are you?" he asked.

She looked up at him, the concern in her eyes speaking volumes.

"No. Although it is beautiful, no, I'm wondering where his wife is and if she's safe and hiding, or are we going to find her dead, and how many more bodies are we going to find before this is all over?"

"Shit," he said. "With everything that's been going on, I forgot he was married. We're gonna need to start searching at first light. Do you think we are going to find more bodies?"

"At this point," said Bax, "anyone on this trail is in danger. So, make sure all your people are armed, and let's set up an overnight watch schedule."

Ranger Martin nodded and headed back towards the rest of the group. Dr. Parkinson walked up to let her know he was heading back with the body and that he'd let Buck know when the autopsy was scheduled for. He noticed the faraway look in her eyes.

"You're looking for more bodies, aren't you?" he asked.

Bax nodded and kept looking into the distance as the doctor walked off.

"Where are you, McKenzie?"

She pulled the sat phone out of her backpack that she had retrieved from her Jeep and dialed Buck.

"Hey, Buck. Bad news."

CHAPTER THIRTY-TWO

The shout came from off in the distance, and Buck headed towards the voice. About a hundred yards from the cabin was another fire road, and lying on its side, in a small ravine, was the sheriff's missing SUV. Or what was left of it.

The fire had turned the SUV into a blackened shell, nothing left but twisted and melted metal. Whoever torched it had done a thorough job. There wasn't any sense calling the forensic team since there would be no evidence to find.

Buck slid down into the ravine and walked around the wreck. He used his flashlight to look under the frame and in all the small crevasses. He saw nothing that would be useful.

Another shout, this time from Deputy Tortelli, led them to a pile of spent ammo, some of the hundreds of rounds that had been fired at the cabin. The pile was next to the dirt road that disappeared into a thicker area of trees. It looked like whoever was staying in the cabin had found another way out.

Once again, the ground was too dry and hard for tire tracks or footprints, which left Buck frustrated. The lack of evidence in these cases was overwhelming.

Buck led the group back towards the cabin. They were losing light fast, and he wanted to talk to VJ Florence before it got too late.

The area around the cabin was filling up fast, and besides his Jeep, Paul's Jeep, and the trooper's SUV, there were now several black government Suburbans and the FBI van belonging to the Evidence Response Team. Jess Gonzales was standing next to the open hatch at the root cellar.

"You sure know how to show a lady a good time, Buck." She laughed.

"What do you think, Jess?"

"What I think is that this town is hiding a major drug manufacturing and distribution network, and what pisses me off is we didn't even have it on our radar."

Buck stood quietly for a minute. "Do you think all these murders could be related to the drugs?"

"It would be nice to know who's financing this venture before answering that question. But let me ask you this. Why now? The basement lab tells us that the manufacturing has been going on for a long time, so what changed in the last week that led to these killings?" she asked.

Buck didn't have an answer. What he had were more questions. They were missing something, but he didn't know the right questions to ask. He hoped he might find some answers once he interviewed VJ Florence, but first they had to find her, and if Bax was correct and she was running, she could be anywhere.

Buck looked at Paul. "We need to head to the Florence home and see if VJ is there."

Paul nodded and had started heading towards his Jeep when he heard Buck's phone ring. He walked back over to Buck and watched Buck pull out his phone. The words private number appeared on the screen, and Buck frowned. He pushed the green button.

"Taylor."

"You've got a Russian problem," said the gruff voice on the other end. Buck knew the voice, and he knew that this investigation was about to take an interesting turn if this person was calling him.

Buck hadn't seen Frank DiNardo in almost twenty years, but he had files dating back that far, and DiNardo's name was all over them. He thought back to that first time he'd arrested him.

Frank DiNardo was the "godfather" of the western United States. He had his fingers in everything—drugs, prostitution, gambling, and protection—that went on in Colorado and a good chunk of Utah and Wyoming. He was a cousin of Vincent Scapelli, the mafia boss who controlled everything from Kansas City to Reno, a guy who ruled his kingdom with an iron fist.

When Buck had first joined CBI, he was assigned to a task force investigating the Scapelli crime family. It was a region-wide federal and local task force whose sole purpose was to break up the family. They never succeeded. Buck never got all the details, but one day they were running an investigation; the next, they were told to clear out their desks and leave all the evidence and documents with the FBI. He wasn't sure what changed, but he never heard another word about the investigation. As far as he knew, no one associated with the Scapelli family ever went to jail because of that investigation.

Over the years, he'd encountered Frank DiNardo during several investigations, but there was never enough evidence to make a case stick. Which, frustrating as it was, helped Buck. Frank DiNardo could be as charming as he was ruthless, and for some reason Buck never understood, Frank had taken a liking to him. He was never a confidential informant, but over the years, Frank had reached out to Buck with information about potential crimes that were occurring around Colorado.

Buck had also reached out to Frank when he needed information he couldn't get from another source. They were never friends, more like adversaries with a vested interest. Frank DiNardo knew enough about Buck that he understood that if Buck ever found enough evidence, he would arrest him in an instant. Still, Frank also knew that it was good business to pass along information to Buck that might get one of his rivals arrested.

Buck would have liked nothing better than to put Frank DiNardo in jail and throw away the key, and he always vowed he would. As far as Buck was concerned, this guy was as dirty and ruthless as they come, but he was also careful.

Buck walked away from the group. "Can you elaborate?"

"Yeah. I hear you're working on a couple of murders in a little town in Pine County. I heard there might also be some missing drugs. I also heard that a very nasty tourist is on the way to that little piece of paradise to find those missing drugs and the people who took them."

"Do you have a name for me?" asked Buck.

Frank let out a growling laugh. "You know I don't deal in names, but this name is one you've heard of, Victor Poroshenko. This guy is a ghost, and he is incredibly dangerous."

"Why are you telling me this? What's in it for you?"

Buck knew there had to be an angle he hadn't seen yet but that Frank DiNardo was all over. Frank never did anything out of the goodness of his heart.

Frank was quiet, and Buck thought he had hung up. "Let's just say that I dislike these folks and leave it at that."

"Any idea how soon I can expect him?"

"You'll know when he gets there. More bodies will start to stack up." The line went dead, and Buck stood there looking at his phone. He didn't like what he had just heard, and he didn't need any more uninvited guests at this party. He clipped his phone back on his belt and walked back to where Jess and Paul were chatting.

Jess smiled. "Was that your Italian guardian angel?"

"Yeah. He said we're about to get an uninvited guest. A guy whose clients are not happy about their missing drugs."

"Big guy with a thick accent and lots of tattoos?" asked Paul.

Buck shook his head. "Victor Poroshenko."

Jess looked at them both. "Fuck, Buck. Do you know how dangerous that guy is? He's wanted all over the world. No one even knows what he looks like. Can you trust your friend's information?"

"He has never given me bad information. I

don't know what it is, but there's something in this for him, or he wouldn't have called. Jess, you'd better put your folks on high alert."

"I'm also gonna call Denver and get more help up here. Maybe we can stop whatever's coming before this town turns into Dodge City on a Saturday night." She pulled out her phone and walked towards the cabin. Buck called Sheriff Willets and the two deputies over and filled them in.

Marvin Willits's face turned white as a ghost. "A Russian killer in our town? Holy shit. What are we going to do?"

Buck could see the panic rising in his face. "I don't think I'm cut out for this," said Sheriff Willets.

Buck put his hand on his shoulder. "You survived a firefight with multiple shooters on your first day on the job. There are very few people in law enforcement who can make that claim, but right now, I need you to go home and get some sleep. Tomorrow you're on duty while the rest of us get some sleep. While you're sleeping, the DEA will be bringing in reinforcements. By morning this will be the best-protected town in the entire United States. Today, you and the deputies did good, but tomorrow is a new day."

Buck didn't see much relief in Marvin

Willetts's face, but he hoped his little speech was enough to calm him down. He pointed them towards his Jeep, and he stepped back to talk to Jess, who was disconnecting her call. He gave her a questioning look.

"That was one of my guys on the inside. Victor Poroshenko is definitely in the United States. This town must be important to them. They only send Poroshenko when big things are involved. I've got twelve more agents on the way. Maybe he'll see all the DEA jackets and decide to turn around and leave."

Buck nodded. "Okay. I'm taking the sheriff and the deputies back to town so they can get some rest. There is a pile of shell casing behind the cabin, about fifty yards down another dirt trail. See if they can lift any prints. Paul and I still have a couple of murders to investigate and a missing person of interest to find. Keep me posted and watch your six."

Jess hugged Buck, and he headed for his Jeep. He had just put his hand on the handle when his phone jingled again. He pulled it from his belt and looked at the number. He clicked the green button.

"Hey, Buck. Bad news," said Bax.

CHAPTER THIRTY-THREE

"**A**re you sure it's the husband?" asked Buck.

Bax had finished filling him in on the body in the crevasse and that the wounds were consistent with the wounds on the other victims. She told him that Dr. Parkinson was certain it was the same killer or killers. She also told him she had asked George and Mel to locate his relatives in Michigan and ask the locals to do a death notification.

"Any sign of the wife?" asked Buck.

"We haven't had time to start searching, and it's getting dark. I don't want anyone searching after dark if these psychos are running around out here."

She was about to say something else when Buck heard a voice in the background. "Agent Baxter, there's more debris in the bottom of the crevasse. It was under the body."

"Buck, I need to go see what else they found. I'll call you in a bit. The body is on the way back to the resort."

Bax headed towards the ranger, standing on top of the boulders. She climbed up, and he shined his light into the crevasse. She could see what looked like a sleeping bag and a metal tent pole. She stood back and yelled for April, who was supervising her team, as they searched the sleeping bag for evidence. She climbed to the top of the boulders.

"Looks like we have more personal effects in the bottom of the crevasse," said Bax. "There's no room to work down there, so I would like to have the rangers bring up whatever they find."

"I agree," said April. "It's not the best solution, but like the body, I don't think we have any choice. I hope there isn't a woman's body under all that debris."

The two rangers descended back into the space, the lead ranger once again upside down. He loaded the items into several large evidence bags that April had one of her techs bring over from their ATV. He passed each bag to the ranger above him, who passed them up to April.

After several minutes he called up, letting everyone know that there were no other human remains in the space. The two rangers made their way out of the crevasse while Bax and April carried the bags to the tent that her team had set up near the ATVs.

Bax put on a pair of blue nitrile gloves and opened the first bag. As she removed each item, April photographed it. When she finished emptying the last bag, she walked back to the front of the line of items and looked at each piece. The items consisted of two backpacks, a second sleeping bag, a two-person tent, and miscellaneous other camping items.

She picked up a cell phone–sized item and looked at it. She showed it to April and Ranger Martin, who had walked up a minute earlier.

"Here's their GPS tracker. This explains why it hasn't moved in a couple of days." She placed it back on the table and lifted another item. Her expression got dark as she looked at the item in question.

"This bra was cut off." She pointed to the sliced material between the cups. She picked up another piece of sliced clothing. "As were these jeans," she said.

Ranger Martin got a serious look on his face. "You think the woman was raped?" he asked.

"That would be my guess based on this." She put the jeans down and pushed some of the other items around. "What I don't see is a shirt of any kind or a pair of hiking boots. The husband had his clothes on."

She stopped talking for a minute and looked at the items on the table. "I think the husband was killed as soon as the attackers hit the camp or shortly after that. They dragged him out of the tent and killed him in his sleeping bag. They stripped the woman and raped her. April, have your folks check the other sleeping bag for semen. At some point after the rape, I think she grabbed a shirt and her boots and escaped. The question is, did they let her go, or did they follow her? And which way did she head?"

"Well, we're not going to find her tonight," said Ranger Martin. "I suggest we set up a couple of tents and make ourselves as comfortable as possible. Let's get everyone fed, and then we can figure out a plan for tomorrow."

Bax was frustrated, but she knew Ranger Martin was correct. With a psycho killer or killers running around, it was best not to be in the woods after dark. At least at their makeshift camp, they were a larger force, and they were all armed.

She spent the better part of the next couple of hours working with April and her team, looking for any evidence that might lead them to a suspect. She took a break after dark, sat on her jacket next to the campfire one of the rangers had built and enjoyed her first cup of coffee of the day. She stared into the flames, again wondering where McKenzie was and if she was still alive.

Her thoughts were interrupted by what

sounded like footsteps in the woods behind the ATVs. Several of the rangers had heard the same noises and were on their feet with their weapons drawn and their flashlights scanning the area. It was a good bet that no one would get any sleep tonight.

Bax hoped the noise was a bear or a mountain lion. Those would be easier to face than some crazed human with an ax. She settled back down to her coffee when she received a text message on her sat phone.

She opened the text app and found a message from Mel that the Mackinaw City police had made the notification to Mark Kearney's parents. She didn't elaborate.

The silence was broken by the sound of someone or something running in the woods not far from camp. Two of the rangers headed into the woods with guns drawn. She decided to do the same thing; only she headed in the direction the sounds had already come from, hoping that the rangers might force whoever it was back towards her.

She moved as quietly as she could without snapping dead branches below her feet, stopping every so often to crouch down and listen. With no moon to light the way, she moved cautiously from one tree to the next. Her reflexes and senses were on high alert as she moved through the woods. She stopped and got as low as she could behind a downed tree and waited.

Someone cried out that they'd been hit, followed by several shots. She stayed hidden behind the log and waited until she heard footsteps heading away from the rangers and coming towards her. She steadied her breathing and, at what she felt was the right moment, stood up in a Weaver stance, pointing her gun towards the sound.

Someone yelled, "Shit," and she spotted one dark two-legged shadow running away from her location. She jumped over the fallen tree and heard something whiz by and slam into the tree trunk. She spotted two shadows standing behind another fallen tree, and she could see that one of the shadows was bending over and pulling something upwards.

The shadow stood up, and Bax could see that it held a compound crossbow, which was pointed at her. Bax fired a round and dove to her right as a second crossbow bolt slammed into the fallen tree. She heard a grunt come from the pair, and she saw one of the shadows running, bent over as they disappeared into the woods.

Bax heard footsteps behind her as Ranger Martin yelled, "Coming in, Agent Baxter." He appeared behind the fallen tree and stopped short. Bax stood up and looked where he was looking. Embedded in the trunk of the fallen tree about four inches apart were two crossbow bolts.

Bax brushed herself off. "Brazen fuckers," she said. "I think I hit one. Someone cried out."

"One of the rangers, Toledo, got hit in the shoulder with a bolt. He should be okay," said Ranger Martin. "We'll bandage him up tonight and get him to the hospital first thing in the morning. That was nuts, you coming out here on your own." He looked at the two bolts sticking out of the tree and shook his head.

"Yeah, but it gave us a better idea of who we are dealing with. Besides the footsteps running from where I think your rangers were, there were two distinct shadows twenty yards away, and only one had a crossbow. That gives us three people. And we know they're still out here."

"Okay," said Ranger Martin. "So, what do we do with that information?"

Bax looked at him. "Tomorrow, we go hunting."

CHAPTER THIRTY-FOUR

B uck asked the waitress for a table in the corner, and she showed him and Paul to the table next to the kitchen door. Buck thanked her, and they sat down and ordered drinks: a Coke for Buck and coffee for Paul. Buck was trying to remember when he ate last. It had been a busy day, and they still had a lot to do. He looked around the restaurant and wondered if one of the people sitting at the other tables or the counter was the Russian enforcer, Poroshenko.

The waitress walked up to the table, set down their drinks and asked them what they would have. Buck ordered the cheeseburger deluxe, and Paul ordered the meatloaf and mashed potatoes. She thanked them and left with their orders.

"What's our next move if this VJ isn't home?" asked Paul.

"We might get something out of the visit anyway if her parents will let us see her room without a warrant. All we know about her is what Bax found out during the interviews at the resort. We need to understand why she lied to

Bax." He stopped talking, picked up his glass and drank half the Coke.

"Once we're done with VJ, I'd like you to head for that bar in Saguache and see if she was there Saturday night and if they know who she was with. Maybe they have CCTV, which would be huge."

Buck thought of something, pulled out his phone and dialed a number he didn't use all that often.

"Good evening, Deputy Taylor," said the female voice on the other end, with a slight Southern accent. "How may I help you?"

"I need to know if there are any outstanding warrants for a Victor Poroshenko. He's a Russian national, and he might be operating in the U.S." Buck could hear computer keys clicking in the background. A few minutes went by.

"There are no warrants for his arrest in this country, but I found several from other counties. He is wanted for murder, extortion and assault. He seems like a nice guy. What's your interest?"

Buck explained the information he had received from Frank DiNardo, without naming names, and that he might be in or on his way to Colorado.

He could hear more keys clicking, and then his phone buzzed with an incoming message.

"I just sent you his Interpol file. There's not much there, but from what I can see, this man is dangerous. I also included copies of several international arrest warrants. Do you need backup, Deputy?"

"Not right now," said Buck. "We're not even sure if the information we have is real."

"I have a team on standby, so all you need to do is yell, and they'll be there. Be careful, Deputy. Call if you need anything else."

Buck disconnected the call, looked at the file and the warrants and slid his phone over to Paul, who laid it face down on the table as the server set their plates in place. Once she left, he read through the file and the warrants and handed it back.

"Pretty thin file considering his reputation. Hopefully, he'll see all the alphabet soup jackets in town and stay away."

They both dug into their food and kept the conversation to a minimum while they ate, enjoying the quiet. Buck looked around the cafe and noticed that there were a lot of people carrying guns. Everyone in town was on edge.

Their meals finished, they each left a twenty on the table and headed for the door. They never noticed the gray-haired man sitting by the front window eating his pie and drinking coffee. He looked like everyone else in town, dressed in jeans, a blue button-down shirt and a gray fleece vest. They didn't notice him, but he noticed them as they left the cafe. Once again, anonymity proved to be his friend.

He looked at the picture of their faces on the camera on his phone and implanted them in his memory. He wasn't sure who they were, but he knew they could be a problem. He would need to keep an eye on them.

Buck pulled to the curb in front of the address he had been given for the Florences. He could see that the lights were on through the opening between the front drapes. He was about to get out of the Jeep when he received a text message. The message came from Mel, letting him know that the cops in Michigan had informed the Kearney family of their son's death. He clipped his phone to his belt, grabbed his backpack and slid out of the Jeep.

Paul was standing by the front door with his backpack slung over his shoulder. He rang the bell as Buck approached. They stood for a minute, and then he rang the bell again. Still no response. The third time he used his fist in a classic cop knock, which shook the entire door.

Buck stepped off the front step and walked around to the driveway on the side of the house.

At the end of the driveway was a two-car garage. He looked through the window in the side door and saw two cars. He walked around to the back door and knocked hard. Still no answer.

Paul came around and stood behind him. "Doesn't look like they're home," he said.

"There are two cars in the garage. They could be avoiding us."

Buck pulled out his phone and checked his messages. He found the one with Mr. Florence's number and dialed the number. They could hear the phone ringing somewhere in the house.

Buck tried the knob and found it unlocked. He looked at Paul, who pulled his pistol and held it down by his leg. Buck unsnapped the backstrap on his holster and pulled his pistol. He held the gun at low ready and pushed open the door. With his pistol now raised, he entered the kitchen.

"Hello," he said at the top of his voice. "Mr. Florence, Mrs. Florence, police. Anyone home?"

Buck stepped into the living room, and Paul headed up the short flight of stairs to the right. The home was an immaculate side-by-side tri-level. With Paul checking upstairs, Buck descended into what he assumed was the family room. The room was covered in dark wood paneling, and there was a large wood-burning fireplace on one wall. There was an oversized leather couch that was pushed to the side and looked out of place in the room. What he saw in its original place stopped him cold.

The two wood kitchen armchairs sat side by side in the center of the room. As he stepped closer, he noticed a film on the arm of the chairs. He touched the film, and it felt sticky. He saw the same film on the front legs of the chair. Paul came down and told him that the upstairs was clear, and then he stopped and looked at what Buck was looking at.

"That doesn't look good," said Paul.

"It sure as shit don't," said Buck.

He noticed a wet spot on the left chair, and without touching the chair, he kneeled and sniffed the spot. "Urine," he said.

Paul pointed at something under the right chair, almost hidden by the leg. "I think I've got blood."

Buck stepped away from the chairs. "What the fuck happened here?" he asked, not expecting an answer. It was too early to speculate, but they both knew what it looked like. Two people had been tortured here.

Buck pulled out his phone and dialed.

"Hey, Buck," said Franklin. "We're just wrapping up at Mitchell Groves's second house and heading to the hotel. What's up?"

Buck explained what they were looking at,

and he asked Franklin to head over as soon as possible. When he disconnected the call, he texted Franklin the address. His next call was to George and Mel. George answered the phone.

"Hey, Buck. We were just going to call you. What's up?"

"George, I need you to run deep background on Steven Florence and his wife, Elizabeth. Look at everything—social media, finances, anything you can find." Buck gave him a short version of what they'd found at the house.

"Fuck, Buck. What's going on in that town? If these people are missing and presumed dead, that makes six bodies."

"Seven," said Buck, "and maybe a few more. Bax found a missing hiker who had been hacked to death, and his wife is missing."

"That's right, I forgot about the hiker. Mel made the notification arrangement with the local police. Damn. We are up to our hips in dead bodies."

George didn't know how right he was, and what was worse, the night wasn't over yet.

CHAPTER THIRTY-FIVE

"Okay, Buck," said George. "Couple of things. We have the cell site location data. I loaded it into the investigation file. There were three phones that caught our attention because they were in the area of both murder sites. We also found the same three phones on the resort tower, but we lost them in the mountains."

"Who are the lucky winners?" asked Buck.

"One phone belongs to Victoria Jean Florence; one belongs to Gerald Nelson, and the third is a burner."

"Can you trace the burner?" asked Paul, standing next to Buck.

"It's a New York number, but Mel is trying to trace it. We'll let you know."

"What else?" asked Buck.

"We hit the jackpot on social media for Ms. Florence. She has a private page that requires an invitation to enter. Her persona is that of a Viking queen named Sheera. Lots of Viking lore and rituals, but here's the best part. She had a link on the page that, for twenty dollars, gave you access to a private page. Whoever set it up for her is good but not as good as Mel. She was able to hack into it in no time. The page takes you to some pretty dark places and includes several Viking death scenes. They could be faked, but if they're real, then these are brutal snuff films. We're looking closer to see if we can identify any of the victims."

"George, how many people are plugged into this pay-per-view page?" asked Buck.

"The most recent scenes from Saturday night had ten thousand views each. This girl is raking in some money."

"Is there any way to identify her helpers as the guys with the phones?"

"No. Everyone has on a heavy fur coat and a mask. They act like they are Vikings. If it's any consolation, Ms. Florence isn't seen in any of the clips taking part in the murders. She must be the one with the camera."

"Can you do an emergency locate on all three phones?" asked Buck.

"Yeah, hold on a sec."

The line went dead, and Buck turned to Paul. "I'll wait here for Franklin. Why don't you head to Saguache and see if you can find out who was with VJ Florence on Saturday night? Maybe someone has video."

As if reading his mind, Mel came on the line. "Hey, Buck. We scrubbed her normal social media posts, and VJ Florence was not alone at the Saturday night gamers tournament like she told Bax. There were plenty of posts with her and several people, one of whom we identified as Rachel Carrollton. I uploaded some of the videos for you."

George joined the conversation. "Buck, all three phones pinged off the resort cell tower. Florence's phone was there for a couple of hours this afternoon, then about three hours ago, it was joined by the other two. We lost them after that. They're out of range, or they've turned them off."

Paul tapped Buck on the shoulder and indicated he was heading out. Buck nodded. He watched as Franklin's SUV pulled up to the curb, and the team began dressing in new Tyvek suits and booties.

Buck went back to his call. "Last thing, Buck. We ran all the victims' financials," said George. "The sheriff looks clean. He has no mortgage, no car payment, and about three thousand in a 401(k). Nothing weird in his bank accounts. His wife collects a fifty-thousand-dollar payout from his city life insurance policy.

"Mitchell Groves has a small savings account and an overdrawn checking account. We did find a cryptocurrency account, but that one is tougher to get into. His name appears on his home mortgage, but the home behind his house is mortgage free, and the deed is for a corporation in the Cayman Islands. Mel's working on tracking that.

"The Florences are interesting. Three months ago, Steven and Elizabeth Florence paid off the remaining balance on their mortgage, ten years ahead of schedule.

"They have several high-interest savings accounts with about one point five million in cash. They deposit a hundred grand each month. Both their cars are paid off, and they had a student loan. The amount is only a couple of grand, probably covered one year. They have no credit card debt.

"Victoria Jean has a checking account, and she makes a regular deposit of two fifty each week, most likely her paycheck. She has no debts that I could find, but something doesn't add up."

"What's that?" asked Buck.

"She buys a lot of stuff online, several grand a month, but none of the purchases show up on her checking account. I think she has a hidden account. We're still looking for it."

"What do Steven and Elizabeth Florence do for

a living?" asked Buck. "I doubt he accumulated that much money being a county commissioner in one of the smallest counties in the state, and where does the hundred grand a month come from?"

"Funny you should ask," said Mel. "We wondered the same thing. He owns a small delivery service, delivering products that folks purchase online. He covers areas that the bigger delivery companies don't want to handle. We pulled his business tax return for last year, and he claimed about sixty-five thousand in personal income. The business made a little over two hundred grand, and, according to his itemized deductions, he pays three drivers. One of those drivers is Gerald Nelson."

"There's no way," said George, "that Florence could stash that much cash from what his company makes. We couldn't find any inheritance or old family money for either him or Mrs. Florence. Mrs. Florence does not appear to work, and she has a checking account with about two hundred dollars in it. She deposits five grand each month, and that goes right out again for groceries and other common household bills."

"Makes me think he might be doing more with his delivery company than delivering packages," said Buck.

"Yeah," said George. "Makes you wonder."

"Okay, thanks, guys. Great work. See what you can find out about Gerald Nelson and the mystery player. I'll check in later."

Buck disconnected the call and met Franklin as they reached the front door. They pulled up their masks and stepped inside. Buck directed them to the family room and stepped back outside. He pulled out his phone and speed-dialed the director.

CHAPTER THIRTY-SIX

Bax slid off the ATV seat, where she had spent most of the night watching the camp. She stretched out the kinks and walked over to the firepit, where the rangers had fresh coffee brewing. She found a foam coffee cup in the box of goodies Mr. Conway had supplied the day before and sat on a tree trunk someone had dragged over during the night.

She rummaged through the box, looking for something to eat, when she heard an ATV approaching. Mr. Conway, good to his word, had sent up breakfast, and everyone in camp dug into the assortment of pastries and juices. It tasted like a feast, and it brightened the spirits of the entire team.

Once they were filled up on pastries and coffee, their first task of the day was to get Ranger Toledo back to the resort so they could get him to the hospital and check his wound. The crossbow bolt had passed through the fleshy part of his shoulder, and other than a hole that was now plugged with a tampon, he was in good spirits. They loaded him onto one of the ATVs, and another ranger slid onto the seat and headed out. They were fortunate he was the only person injured during the raid, if you will, on the camp.

The second thing Bax wanted to do was to go back to where she believed she had shot the intruder and see if there was a blood trail. Ranger Martin offered to walk with her, and they headed off towards the downed tree with the two bolts sticking out of it.

April and her team packed up all the evidence they had collected and all the personal gear they had found in the crevasse and loaded up one of the ATVs.

Bax and Ranger Martin searched the area where Bax believed the two shadows had been standing, but they couldn't find any blood. Or any evidence for that matter. Using her knife, she dug the two bolts out of the fallen tree and carried them back to camp, where she handed them to April.

"See if you can get some useable prints off these. I'd like to know who tried to kill me," said Bax.

April placed the bolts into a long bag, sealed and signed it and placed it in the ATV. She told Bax to keep an eye out and to stay safe, then she and her team slid onto the ATV and headed back to the resort. Bax hoped she wouldn't need them again, but she knew deep inside that that would not be the case. McKenzie Kearney was still out there, possibly injured, but more likely dead, and it was Bax's job to find her.

Bax and the remaining rangers gathered around one of the ATVs, and Ranger Martin pulled a wrinkled old map out of his backpack and spread it out on the hood. He oriented the map and pointed to a spot.

"This is our location." He pointed to a second location. "And this is the resort. That's about twelve miles. I'm guessing if she escaped, she would head towards the resort. She knew she would find people there who could help her. I think we should concentrate on the main trail. It's the fastest way back."

"I don't believe she would have headed in that direction," said a voice coming from the trees.

Everyone stopped and placed their hands on their weapons.

"Permission to enter the camp?" asked the voice, a silky-smooth British accent that Bax recognized. But there was no way it could be. The person the voice belonged to, whom she knew, was a long distance away.

She stood astonished when the odd man stepped out of the trees and approached the group, and everyone looked at the strangely dressed man, wondering who this fellow could be.

PIS had lived in Aspen for the past twenty-some years and was considered one of its most colorful characters in a city filled with colorful characters. Everyone in Aspen had either heard of or knew PIS, except that no one knew much about him. He was tall, about six foot two, and gangly, as folks used to say. He couldn't have weighed over one hundred fifty pounds soaking wet. He had long gray hair pulled back in a ponytail, piercing gray eyes, and a three-day growth of stubble on his face. The odd thing was, no matter what day or time you encountered PIS, his stubble was always the same. It never seemed to grow out or look untidy.

Unlike most homeless characters in Aspen, PIS never smelled like a homeless person. He wore the same clothes every day but never looked dirty or unkempt. His outfit hadn't changed in over twenty years. He wore calf-height brown leather lace-up moccasin-style boots, light gray tuxedo pants with a dark gray stripe down each leg and a worn white dress shirt, frayed and yellow with age. Around his waist, he wore a bright red cummerbund, and around his neck, he wore a bright red ascot.

No matter what time of year or what the temperature was, PIS always wore the same tattered brown linen coat and black beret. He looked rather elegant for a homeless person. His only other possession was a well-worn leather backpack that looked like it had traveled the world. The initials p.i.s. were stamped on the flap, and since no one knew his name, everyone called him PIS, which he never seemed to mind. His demeanor was always cheerful and friendly, and no one ever complained about feeling threatened by his presence. Most striking was his British accent. Not the harsh Cockney accent you associate with street people, but a silky-smooth accent that exuded sophistication.

No one ever saw him panhandling for money, yet he always seemed to have enough to visit one of the local pubs for his nightly glass of brandy. As it turned out, PIS also had an incredible talent, which helped him generate some income on a regular basis. PIS was an amazing tracker. There wasn't anything he couldn't find, whether it be an animal or a missing child, and his abilities had come to the attention of many of the local hunting guides, who paid him a fee to help them find game for their out-of-town clients. PIS's tracking skills had also come to the attention of the local police and sheriff, and over the years, he had been involved in finding many lost hikers or missing persons in the rugged mountains surrounding Aspen.

Early on, when he'd first arrived in Aspen, many people tried to engage him in conversation to determine his real name or his background.

It was rumored that several times, people had tried to follow him as he left the downtown area and headed for the forest at the end of the day. No one was ever successful. Within minutes of entering the forest, PIS would disappear, leaving his followers bewildered. No one had any idea where he went at night or where he slept, but every morning he was right back downtown walking the alleys between East Hopkins Avenue and East Hyman Avenue, rummaging through trash dumpsters. If you asked people to guess PIS's age, you would get answers from forty to eighty. He truly was a mystery.

The sheriff had run his fingerprints once when an overzealous deputy tried to arrest PIS for vagrancy. His prints came back as flagged, meaning some government agency had restricted access to his information. PIS had become furious at the intrusion into his privacy, and ever since, there had been a truce between local law enforcement and PIS. He would provide his tracking services for free to any agency that needed such services; in exchange, local law enforcement would no longer try to determine his identity. That truce had lasted almost twenty years.

Bax was speechless. PIS was the last person she would expect to find this far from Aspen. She stuttered her words as she spoke.

"PIS, what are you doing here?" she asked.

"I heard you and Agent Taylor could use some help, and since it was a beautiful day for a walk, I decided to head here and see if I might be of some use in your expedition."

She could stand and listen to his voice all day long, but she pulled herself together and walked over and hugged him.

She pushed him away and looked at him. "How did you get here? It's got to be close to a hundred miles from Aspen."

"I have my ways, Agent Baxter," he said with a smile. "Now, if you could introduce me to your friends, we can get going. We have a lot of ground to cover."

CHAPTER THIRTY-SEVEN

"Hi, Buck," said Director Jackson. "How are things going?"

Buck told Director Jackson about the shoot-out that the sheriff and his deputies were involved in, the drug stash they found in the root cellar, and the disappearance and possible torture of Steven and Elizabeth Florence.

"Shit, Buck. All that, coupled with the body Bax found up on the trail, makes it sound like there's a war going on in Pine County. Do you think the Russian, Poroshenko, is responsible for the disappearance of the Florences?"

"I do, sir, but since we know very little about this guy's MO, we can't say for sure. Franklin pulled a bunch of prints, and we'll need to run those first, but I doubt anyone has this guy's prints on file."

"Do you think they're still alive?" asked Director Jackson.

"I don't think so, sir. If even half the rumors

are true, the Russian doesn't leave many people he encounters alive."

"Why focus on these two?" asked Director Jackson.

Buck explained the working theory that their daughter was involved in the killings and the theft of the drugs. "The daughter skipped out on her shift at the resort, and her phone and those of two of her friends were near all the crime scenes on Saturday night."

"No idea where the girl is?" asked Director Jackson.

"No, sir. We lost the cell signal heading east of the resort, so she's most likely somewhere up on the trail. I let Bax know to keep alert."

Buck stopped listening as he watched an old blue Ford Bronco pull to the curb. Marvin Willets and Deputy Tortelli slid out of the SUV and headed up the walk.

Buck told the director that he would follow up with him as he got more information and thanked him for the offer of more help. He disconnected the call and clipped his phone to his belt.

"Thought you guys were getting some rest?"

Marvin Willets shook his head. "Heard there might be a problem here, so we thought we'd come check it out. We didn't wake Tommy, so at least one of us will be rested in the morning."

Buck gave them a quick debrief and watched as they both looked stunned. "My god," said Marvin Willets. "How much more can one little town take? People are already nervous. This will drive them over the edge."

Buck wasn't sure how to respond, but he didn't have to, as Franklin stepped out onto the porch and gave Buck the all clear. Buck, Marvin Willets and Deputy Tortelli walked through the front door and followed him to the family room. The chairs were still in the same position they were in when Buck had first entered the room. Franklin kneeled next to the chair.

"Lab results will say for sure, but my guess is that the residue on the chairs is duct tape," said Franklin. "The blood is human, as is the urine. From the temperature of the urine, whatever happened here happened in the past two or three hours. We've pulled prints from this room and the kitchen. The team is now upstairs going through what appears to be the daughter's room."

Tortelli, who had stepped away from the group and was looking at pictures on the wall, called Buck. "You're gonna want to see this," he said.

Buck walked over to the pictures Tortelli was looking at and scanned the wall. He stopped when he saw the picture that had attracted his attention. The picture showed a camo-clad VJ Florence and her dad, Steven, kneeling next to a large elk. That was not an unusual sight in this part of the country, but what attracted their attention was the compound crossbow that VJ held in her hand.

"You think that's one of our murder weapons?" asked Marvin Willets, who had walked up behind them.

"I wouldn't bet against it," said Buck.

They were still looking at the pictures when Paul walked into the house. They all turned expectantly.

"VJ Florence was at the bar on Saturday night for the video game tournament, and the guy who owns the bar said she's a regular, and she wasn't alone like she told Bax. According to the game master, she was with Rachel Carrollton, Gerald Nelson and Stefan Kolchenko, her boyfriend. They were there until around eight p.m., and then they were asked to leave by the owner. He said they were getting rowdy and belligerent."

Buck pulled a small notebook out of his back pocket, flipped it open and wrote their names. He looked at Marvin Willets and Deputy Tortelli. "Do you know either of these guys?"

Sheriff Willets responded first. "Yeah, we know both. Gerald has lived here all his life;

his parents own the grocery store at the end of town. He's a driver for Steven Florence's delivery company. Kolchenko we don't know as well. Only arrived in town a month or so back. Not sure if he has a job or not."

"Why don't you see if you can find these guys. It's late enough; maybe they're at home. Let me know if you find them. Paul and I are heading for the resort."

The little bug in Buck's brain was working overtime. He felt they were onto something critical. He didn't know how right he was.

CHAPTER THIRTY-EIGHT

Bax gathered everyone around the map that Ranger Martin had placed on the hood of the ATV. PIS stood next to her and looked at the map with the eyes of a skilled tracker. She didn't know anyone better at tracking, either animals or people. All of that was important, but more important was that Buck trusted him without question.

She hadn't known PIS as long as Buck had, but she knew that he and Buck had worked some big investigations together, and she also knew that PIS had saved his life on more than one occasion.

Ranger Martin signaled for her to follow him as he walked a couple of feet from the ATV.

"Are you sure about this guy?" he asked. "He looks like some doper from the sixties. He's got to be eighty years old. Do you think he can keep up with us?"

Bax laughed. "That old doper, as you called him, can run circles around you and me. He's one of the fittest people I've ever met, and once he gets on the trail, he doesn't know how to stop. You would be wise to watch and learn. I know I have over the years."

Bax stepped away, pulled out the sat phone, dialed Buck and told him what had happened during the night and so far that day.

She stepped back to the group.

"Agent Baxter, would you be so kind as to show me where you think the attack took place?" asked PIS.

Bax led him into the clearing at the edge of the forest. "From what we can tell," she said, stopping at the area still roped off with crime scene tape, "we think the tent was here. The husband's body was found in a crevasse in that cluster of boulders."

PIS examined the campsite like a bloodhound sniffing out a prisoner on the run. Several times he got down on all fours and put his face close to the ground and looked off into the distance. Bax knew from experience that he was looking for minuscule trail signs that might show up in the morning dew.

He walked over and climbed up on the boulders. Bax looked at Ranger Martin, and he nodded his head. She smiled.

PIS stood on top of the boulders and scanned the area. Then he bounced back down the boulders, like a mountain goat, and walked back to the campsite.

"Agent Baxter, I am certain that the young woman headed off in that direction." He pointed to the northeast. "Allow me a few moments to confirm my suspicions." She nodded, and PIS stepped off into the forest. She had seen the next part several times. PIS would walk out about twenty yards and circle the campsite, looking for trail signs.

Ranger Martin and the other rangers joined her, and they watched and waited. "What's he doing now?" asked one of the rangers, still not sure if this guy was for real or not. Bax explained the process and told them that once he found the trail, he might do this several more times if he were to lose the trail.

PIS circumvented the camp area twice, stopping and examining several locations. He then stepped off another twenty yards and repeated the process. After completing the last circle, he walked back to the group.

"She headed off to the northeast," he said. "We should get moving. She wasn't alone."

Ranger Martin looked at the map he had brought with him. "But that would take her away from the fastest route to the resort. I don't think she would go that way. I still think the trail is the best bet."

PIS smiled and asked them to follow him. They started down a slight incline and came to some low shrubs. He stopped at the first shrub and pointed to several broken stems and brown spots on several leaves.

"The brown spots are blood." He looked back up the trail. "You estimated that the husband was killed sometime Saturday night. There was no moon on Saturday night, so the darkness would have been total. We assume the wife was raped repeatedly, so she was most likely disoriented, exhausted from the ordeal and in shock from watching her husband being brutally attacked. If Agent Baxter is correct about her escaping with just her panties and a T-shirt, she was also cold. She wasn't thinking of anything but escaping. She figured she could make the fastest time by going downhill, getting as much separation as possible between her and her captors."

Ranger Martin looked at PIS. "How do you have all this information? We speculated about her escape in the early hours of the morning before you arrived. When did you get here?"

PIS ignored the question and stepped ten feet from where he was standing. He pointed to some matted undergrowth at the edge of the shrubs. "Several people came through here. Note the fur on the ends of the branches. The fur is fake. I believe it came from a heavy cloak. There is also evidence on the main trail that someone headed towards the resort, most likely one of her attackers, attempting to cut her off. We'll follow this trail," he said, and he headed off into the woods.

Bax looked at the rangers. "Grab your gear and let's go before we lose him."

She pulled her GPS tracker off her belt and marked the first waypoint at the camp location, and then marked the second waypoint for the start of the trail. She pushed through the shrubs and entered the thickest part of the woods. She caught up with PIS a hundred yards ahead. He was looking at something in the undergrowth.

He pointed to the ground. "You can see the small footprint in the moist undergrowth. There are several more just up ahead. You can also see two boot prints, one overlaying the barefoot print. From the size and the depth of the prints, she was being pursued by two men, and from the spacing on the barefoot prints, she was running for her life. She was also off her track, no longer heading northeast, but still heading downhill."

The group followed PIS as he headed through the trees. He stopped, kneeled and waved over the team. "Looks like she tripped here. You can see the impressions where her knees hit the ground. There is also blood on this tree trunk. I believe she hit the tree. There's a lot of blood spatter, so I think this is a head wound."

PIS turned farther to the east. "She seems to be more disoriented after hitting her head. She moved in several directions, trying to get her bearings, and then headed this way."

Ranger Martin tapped Bax on the shoulder. "You were right. This fella may look odd, but he has some mad skills. There's no way I would have caught even half these signs."

Bax nodded and moved on. PIS was down the mountain another couple of hundred yards when he stopped and sat on a downed tree. The others joined him.

"She fell here again and hit this tree. There is a torn piece of white fabric stuck to this broken branch. I think she is now seriously hurt." He looked at the sky between the branches. "Let's break here for a bit. We will need sustenance if we are to continue."

Bax opened her backpack and handed each person one of the leftover sandwiches from the night before. They all pulled out water bottles and drank their fill. They rested for twenty minutes, and then PIS was back looking for a trail sign. He rejoined the group.

"She went back uphill from here. Her attackers are still behind her."

"Night vision goggles?" asked one of the

rangers.

"Good deduction, my young friend. That would explain a lot."

PIS turned and started uphill, the trail getting rougher and the trees and shrubs much denser. "She must have had a hell of a time navigating this slope in the dark." He stopped several times and pointed out locations where she fell, several more places where she had lost blood and more bare footprints. The woman had made a valiant effort to escape her pursuers, but to what end?

After another hour of moving in an erratic pattern, going both up and downhill, they came to the edge of the forest and the start of the scrub oak field. PIS stopped. As the group gathered behind him, they all had the same opinion. "There's no way she could have gone through there."

PIS found more blood, more footprints, and more fabric pieces. He also found a couple of spots where there appeared to be skin on the broken branches. They continued to push through, experiencing what McKenzie Kearney must have experienced, only she was doing it in the dark. It was hard enough to navigate in the sunlight. By this point, she must have given up hope of finding someone to help her.

PIS moved ahead of the group, following the broken trail. Bax and the rangers caught up to him about a hundred yards ahead. He had stopped and was looking ahead. He held up his hand for them to stop.

Bax stepped up next to him. They had reached the edge of the scrub oak. She looked at him as he stared ahead. He raised a finger to his lips. He was telling her to stand quietly and listen.

Bax concentrated, and then she heard it. The sound of ravens, dozens of them, chattering away. She scanned the field in front of her and spotted a pile of rocks, left from the last ice age, a dozen yards down the slope. PIS looked around and found a rock. He threw the rock, and it bounced off the pile. Dozens of birds scattered, circled back around and landed back behind the pile.

Ranger Martin joined them and stopped next to PIS.

"What's going on?"

PIS pointed to the pile of rocks. He looked at Bax and then at Ranger Martin. Bax could see the sadness in his eyes.

"I believe we have found the wife," he said.

CHAPTER THIRTY-NINE

Buck had made it back to his motel room in the wee hours of the morning, but he was too wound up to sleep. He had left a message for Bax to watch herself and hadn't heard anything back from her, so he hoped she was getting some sleep. He spent an hour uploading information into the investigation file and crashed at four a.m.

His phone rang at six a.m., and it took him a few seconds to figure out where he was. He answered the phone and took a big gulp of warm Coke from the bottle next to the bed.

"Hey, Buck. Hope I didn't wake you," said Bax.

Buck looked at his watch and rubbed his eyes. "No, I'm good. What's up?"

"Your voice mail was appreciated, but we were right in the middle of an attack when you rang."

Buck was now wide awake. "What happened?"

Bax filled him in on the attack and that they believed there were at least three people in the woods. She told him about the one ranger being injured by a crossbow bolt and the belief that she had hit one of the assailants when she fired at the person with the crossbow. She didn't mention anything about the two crossbow bolts they'd dug out of the fallen tree next to where she was concealed.

"How badly was the ranger injured?" he asked.

"We patched him up. It went clean through the fleshy part of his shoulder. He's on the way back to the resort. I also wanted to tell you that PIS is here."

"What?" said Buck. "When did that happen, and what's he doing there?" It was easy to hear the surprise in Buck's voice.

"He showed up about twenty minutes ago and offered to help us search for the missing hiker. I don't know how he got here or how he knew where to find us, but you know PIS. He has a way of turning up at just the right time."

To say that Buck was stunned would be an understatement. He hadn't seen PIS since his father's funeral. At least he thought that was PIS standing off in the distance dressed in a gray three-piece suit with a red cummerbund. He never approached the service, and he was gone before Buck knew it, but he sensed that that was him.

They had just finished the hunt for Alicia Hawkins, a serial killer from Aspen, Colorado, who killed fourteen young women and one young man on her quest to fulfill a promise she had made to her grandfather, a man who had killed fifteen women in Aspen during the sixties and seventies and would have continued had it not been for an accident that left him paralyzed.

Alicia had learned the story of her grandfather's exploits and chose to follow in his footsteps. She had, by accident, located the woman who was supposed to be his sixteenth victim but had survived because of the accident. She decided to honor his memory by killing that same woman on the anniversary of his death. A death she wrongfully blamed on Buck. She had almost succeeded.

During her return to Aspen, she had decided to hurt Buck for taking away her grandfather, who had passed away soon after the investigation. She had located PIS, a close friend of Buck's, and stabbed him in an alley near downtown, but PIS survived because of an oddity of birth.

By the time Buck and the FBI arrived at her hideout in the mountains near Aspen, they found the victim alive and Alicia dead from a stab wound, a red ascot tied around her neck. Even though the FBI was still pursuing the case of her death, believing that one of her acolytes had killed her, Buck knew, deep in his soul, that PIS was responsible for ending her reign of terror. He never pursued that feeling.

Buck had learned a lot about PIS during that long week that explained a great deal about his previous life and why he had been in Aspen for so long. It was also information that he shared with no one. Buck wasn't sure if PIS was aware of everything Buck had learned, but he had too much respect for PIS to reveal his secrets. Secrets that could prove to be deadly.

Buck knew if anyone could find the missing hiker, it would be PIS. He had mad skills, and he wasn't afraid to get in the middle of whatever was going on.

He gave Bax a quick update on what now seemed to be their three prime suspects and about the disappearance of VJ's parents.

"You figure the parents are dead?" asked Bax.

"Dead or running. I think they crossed paths with the Russian. Which means they are all in danger. So, what's the plan?" Buck asked.

"We're grabbing some food that the resort just sent up, and then we'll let PIS do his thing. I'll call you later with an update."

"Okay. Be careful. VJ and her friends are still out there."

Bax hung up, and Buck took another gulp of Coke. He would have liked to grab some more sleep, but things were moving fast, and they had to get ahead of Victor Poroshenko.

His phone buzzed with a text notification from Dr. Parkinson. The autopsy for Mark Kearney was scheduled for noon today. He texted back that he would be there. He finished the Coke, grabbed a quick shower, found his cleanest jeans and T-shirt and headed for the sheriff's office to see if they'd had any luck finding VJ's friends—but first, he needed to eat.

He left Paul a text message to meet him at the cafe for breakfast and left his room. He had a feeling today was going to be another long day.

CHAPTER FORTY

B uck had just sat down at the cafe and ordered the scrambled egg and bacon plate and a glass of Coke when Paul walked in. He looked like he hadn't gotten much sleep either since he had gotten to the motel about the same time Buck had. He ordered the same thing, except he asked for black coffee instead of Coke.

Buck filled him in on the conversation he'd had with Bax. "How did PIS find out what was going on? There's been a lot of news coverage, but how would he find out where she was?"

Buck was about to say something when a crazy thought crossed his mind. He hadn't revealed the information he had found out about PIS's background to anyone. Bax and Paul had been privy to small pieces of the information, but no one had the whole picture.

"I find it intriguing," said Buck, "that PIS shows up right after we found out that Victor Poroshenko was supposedly on his way here."

"You think this has something to do with PIS's past? I have often wondered if he is more tapped into the world than most homeless people."

"He could be tapped in more than we think," said Buck. "The only ones who had that information were Jess and her team and my contact at the U.S. Marshals Service."

"Sounds like someone might be spying on some of our government's departments and passing along information. I wonder what his real reason for being here is?" asked Paul.

Buck laughed. "We might never know. You know how mysterious he is."

But Buck thought that Paul's speculation might be right on. He was the only one who knew that PIS might still be connected to the British government. He wondered if PIS was working under orders from someone outside the United States. Someday he would have to ask him.

Buck's phone rang, and he looked at the number. "Hey, Max."

"Hi, Buck. How's my favorite cop?"

"Good, Max. Things have gotten kind of crazy here. What's up?"

"We got back the DNA from the samples Franklin sent over. There are no matches in the criminal databases and no matches in the private, for-profit DNA databases. None of these people ever checked their ancestry. Once you get a suspect and get us some DNA, we can match that to our samples.

"Second. I have some fingerprint information for you. Fingerprints recovered from the home of Mitchell Groves are a match for Victoria Jean Florence. Her prints are on file because she has a health card. The other two sets of prints are unidentified. The same prints for all three individuals are all over the Carrollton house. It's like they didn't even try to hide their identities.

"Besides Victoria Jean's prints and those of her parents, who both have prints on file, the two unidentified prints are all over her bedroom and the kitchen. This would make sense if they were friends of hers. These same two prints were found on the shell casings and the drugs at the scene of the sheriff's shoot-out. Whoever these two people are, they sure get around."

"Did you get the prints from the Florences' family room that Franklin took last night?" asked Buck.

"Yes, we just received them, and they are in process."

"Max, if you find an unknown set of prints, you might want to check whatever international databases you have access to."

"Okay, Buck. Any reason?"

Buck filled her in on the possible involvement of Victor Poroshenko and the speculation about his background.

"Shit, Buck. Do you ever get involved in a simple case? So besides ritualistic Viking murders and drug manufacturing, you may have a Russian hit man chasing the same people you are? Good god."

"You know me, Max. Never a dull moment."

Paul nodded his head, and Buck laughed.

"Okay, Buck, watch your back." She ended the conversation the way she always did. "You're a good man, Buck Taylor. God will watch over you."

Buck disconnected the call and finished his breakfast. "So, no joy on the prints or the DNA except for VJ Florence. We have suspects but no evidence."

The waitress brought the bill, and they both left twenty dollars on the table and headed for the door. Paul held the door open for a man who was just entering. Something looked familiar about the man, but he couldn't put his finger on where he had seen him before. He did note that the man had impeccable taste in his clothes. Paul also thought the guy was a little overdressed for the locale.

The man thanked him, and Paul and Buck walked down the street to the sheriff's office.

They were half a block away when they heard the yelling coming from the office. As they approached the door, Buck spotted a black Cadillac Escalade parked in front of the office. He wondered who would be yelling at the sheriff this early in the morning. He pushed open the door, and the bell announced his presence. Everyone stopped and turned.

"Am I interrupting something, Sheriff?" asked Buck.

Sheriff Willets and his two deputies were trying to calm down the man standing in the middle of the room. His red face indicated that he was the person doing most of the yelling.

"Agent Taylor. This is Mr. Talbot. His daughter and son-in-law, McKenzie and Mark Kearney, might be missing on the Continental Divide Trail."

"Not might be missing, Sheriff. Are missing, and I'd like to know what the hell you people are doing to find them. For Christ's sake, I gave you their coordinates. How hard could it fucking be to locate them?"

He looked at Paul and Buck.

"Since the sheriff is incompetent, are you the person I need to talk to, or do I have to call the governor to get someone to pay attention? Richard and I go way back."

Buck smiled. He loved people who threw names around. Next, thought Buck, he'd be yelling, "Do you know who I am?"

Buck stepped up to the man. He looked like an ad for L.L.Bean or some other expensive men's clothing store. Buck wouldn't have been surprised if some of the tags were still on the jeans or light flannel shirt. He also noticed that his boots must have cost a fortune.

"Mr. Talbot," said Buck, lowering his voice below normal. Buck had learned over the years that one of the best ways to deal with someone yelling was to talk softer, so the person had to focus on listening. It could result in one of two things happening. Either the person slowed down and stopped yelling, or he would get frustrated and leave. Buck didn't care what happened. It was always up to the other person.

"Buck Taylor, Colorado Bureau of Investigation. I'm in charge of the ongoing investigations in this town, and I would be happy to talk with you."

Buck pointed towards a chair by the empty desk. "Please have a seat, sir."

Talbot looked around and sat down. Buck sat in the chair on the opposite side of the desk.

"Your daughter is McKenzie Kearney, and her husband is Mark?"

"That's right, and two days ago, I asked the Conway Resort if they had shown up. I also gave them the last GPS coordinates, which hadn't moved since Friday night. I assumed the resort would call the sheriff, who would put together a search party. I arrived here this morning. I flew into Durango on my private jet and drove out here only to find that nothing's been done to locate my daughter."

"Or your son-in-law," said Buck.

"Yes, or him."

Talbot lost his temper again and sprang from the chair. He raised his voice. "I demand to know what is being done to locate my daughter. It is obvious"—he looked at the sheriff—"that things get done a little slower out here in the West. Well, I'm here to tell you that's going to change. If I don't get some immediate satisfaction in the next ten minutes, I will get on the phone, and within three hours, I will have a team of a dozen retired Navy SEALs scouring that trail to locate her. You mark my words."

Buck sat quietly during the tirade, and before Talbot could say another word, he stood up.

"Your son-in-law was found dead this morning."

Buck didn't say another word and watched Talbot as all the color drained from his face.

"What are you talking about? He can't be dead; we just talked a week ago. You must be mistaken." Talbot sat in the chair and stared at Buck.

"Sir, have you spoken with Mark's family? They were notified early this morning. I will be attending his autopsy in a couple of hours."

Talbot was quiet for a minute. He shook his head. "My wife and I don't socialize with Mark's relatives." He hesitated. "What about my daughter?"

"Right now, there is a search team looking for her. She was not at the site where the GPS was found. We only found Mark."

"How did he die? Was it an accident or a wild animal? I told my daughter when she proposed this stupid trip that Mark wasn't the outdoors type, and she should rethink their honeymoon."

"Mark was murdered, Mr. Talbot. Along with five other people, including the sheriff. Mr. Willets is the acting sheriff."

Talbot sat in disbelief. He looked at Buck. "Is my daughter dead too, Agent Taylor?" All the fight left him, and he slumped in the chair and put his hands over his eyes.

"We don't know that yet, sir. The searchers are following her trail, and we hope to have more information sometime later today. They have a huge area to cover, and it's not all easy terrain."

Talbot mumbled, "He was murdered. Oh my god. I need to call my wife." He pulled out a cell phone and dialed a number.

Buck and the team stepped aside to give him some privacy. Buck looked at Sheriff Willets. "See if you can get him a room at the resort and make sure he gets there. And keep an eye on him. The last thing we need is him traipsing around the trail getting in the way."

Buck took Sheriff Willets by the arm and led him into the coffee area. "Any luck locating Nelson or Kolchenko?"

"Neither one was home. We checked with Nelson's mom, and she hasn't seen him in a couple of days. I guess that's not unusual for him. No one has seen Kolchenko around town since Saturday morning. What do you want us to do?"

"Keep an eye out for either of them. We need to talk to them before the Russian finds them."

Buck took Paul aside. "See if you can find Jess and see how they are doing with their investigations, then meet me at the resort. I'm gonna head to Gunnison for the autopsy. I'll be back as soon as I can."

Buck walked over to Talbot, who had hung up his phone. "Mr. Talbot, the sheriff will get you a nice place to stay. Please stay there, so I can find you if I get any information." He introduced Paul. "Mr. Talbot, if you need anything or need to get hold of me, please call Paul, and he will take care of whatever you need. I will be back in a couple of hours."

Talbot nodded, and Buck headed for the door. This was the last thing he needed on an already full plate.

CHAPTER FORTY-ONE

"It's just like we figured," said Dr. Parkinson. "This poor fella was attacked with the same ax as the other four, but the brutality was much more intense. They almost chopped him up into pieces."

Buck took a closer look at the body now that the autopsy was finished. He noted that in this case, the head was severely damaged, almost unrecognizable.

"Are you sure about the identity?" asked Buck.

"As sure as we can be until the DNA comes back. Most of his teeth are gone, so we can't use dental comparison. I was able to match an old break in his leg that had healed. I spoke with his mother, and she confirmed the break. She and her husband are going to the local hospital to have swabs taken. His fingerprints are a match, but I want the DNA to be sure."

"I wonder if the poor guy knew what hit him?" asked Buck.

Dr. Parkinson looked up from the paperwork

he was working on. "I hope the first or second blow killed him. It's impossible to say with this much damage."

Buck took a few more photos with his phone and then clipped it on his belt. He pulled off the blue nitrile gloves and put them in the trash.

"Buck, do you think his wife is still alive?"

"I don't think so, but until we have something to go on, we treat her as a missing person and do whatever we can to find her."

Buck pulled out his phone and turned it back on. He had four texts from Bax. He knew this couldn't be good. He dialed her sat phone and waited for the connection. It rang once, and she answered.

"Hey, Buck."

"Sorry, Bax. I was at the Mark Kearney autopsy. What's going on?"

"We found her," said Bax.

"I'm going to assume the worst. Where was she?"

"She covered about five miles on foot, but with the injuries and disorientation, she ended up about two miles from where we found her husband and about two hundred yards off the trail. They hunted her for hours."

"How bad?" asked Buck.

"She's been hacked to pieces, literally, and the birds and ground critters had a field day with all the open wounds. There's not much left, and we will need DNA to positively identify her. We're gonna need Dr. Parkinson and forensics. I left a message for April Yang, but she's probably sleeping. They were up most of the night with the rest of us, but they spent their time looking for evidence while we fended off crazies."

Buck told her that McKenzie's father was in town, blowing his top. "I asked the sheriff to get him a room at the resort so that we could keep him close. He did a lot of yelling and threatening. This is going to hurt him badly. I'm heading back to Silver City now. I'll stop at the resort and make the notification. Are you heading back?"

"Once we wrap up this crime scene, we should be able to head back."

"Is PIS still with you?" asked Buck.

"He wandered off. Said he wanted to check something out. I suspect he'll be back in a little bit."

"Okay, Bax. Keep me posted, and I'll get Dr. Parkinson headed your way. Send me the GPS coordinates."

Buck hung up and looked over at Dr. Parkinson, who was staring at him. "That didn't sound good. I guess we're not done yet?" said the doctor.

Buck gave him the bad news.

"Okay. Let me get a shower and some food, and I'll head to the resort. You sure know how to keep people busy, Buck."

He signed the death certificate and gave it to one of the orderlies to file it with the state. He hadn't written as many death certificates in the last couple of months as he had written in the past four days. Like everyone else, he was tired, but also, like everyone else, he had a job to do. And his job was as important to the families as it was important to the investigation.

Buck swung by the cafeteria in the basement of the hospital, grabbed a roast beef and cheddar sandwich to go and a bottle of Coke and headed for his car. He would have liked to run home to shower and grab a quick nap, but things were moving, and he didn't want to screw with the momentum.

He dialed Director Jackson after he slid into his Jeep and filled him in on the missing woman hiker. The director listened and then asked Buck if he needed more help.

"Not right now, sir. If we run into a problem, I still have a large team from DEA that I can latch on to if needed. They should be wrapping up. I asked Paul to find Jess and get an update from her."

"Can you get someone from the U.S. Marshals

Service to help?"

Director Jackson had been at the Marshals Service office the day, several months back, when the U.S. Marshal for Denver presented Buck with a badge and credentials, making him a full-fledged deputy marshal with all the powers that came with the title. It was the service's way of honoring Buck for saving the lives of several deputies during a wild shoot-out in the federal courthouse parking garage.

The honor was rare and only happened with the cooperation of Colorado Governor Richard J. Kennedy, the United States Attorney General, and the director of the Marshals Service.

"They have a team standing by," said Buck. "So, I think we're covered."

"Okay, Buck. You let me know if you need any help, and I'll have a team there in a heartbeat."

Buck thanked the director and hung up. He pulled out of the parking lot and headed back to Pine County. Now he had to let Mr. Talbot know that his daughter was dead. That was a conversation he was not looking forward to.

Buck had been planning to head straight to the resort until he got the call from Sheriff Willets.

"Buck. You're not going to believe this. Gerald Nelson just walked into the station and turned himself in. I've got him in our interview room and wanted to wait until you got here. What's your schedule?"

"I'm almost to the resort turnoff, so maybe ten minutes. Has he asked for a lawyer?"

"Not yet," said Sheriff Willets.

"Good. Don't let anyone talk to him until I get there."

Buck disconnected the call and headed towards town instead of the resort. Mr. Talbot would have to wait. This might be their first break in the investigation.

CHAPTER FORTY-TWO

Bax and the rangers approached the rock outcropping with caution so as not to disturb any evidence that might be on the ground. They stepped around the rocks, causing the ravens to scatter, some carrying off various bits of entrails. They were not happy about leaving their meal.

The lump that was McKenzie Kearney lay about fifteen feet past the rocks. The body was unrecognizable, the birds and animals having a field day with all the open wounds. She was lying on her back. It appeared to Bax that she had been hit in the thigh with a crossbow bolt. The bolt was gone, but Bax recognized the hole it had left.

She walked around the body, using her cell phone as a video recorder. When she found something of interest, she videoed it first and then took still photos from several angles.

The body was almost split in half, one leg was lying next to it, and her lower right arm and hand were missing, most likely dragged away by some animal. From what Bax could tell, she was wearing a T-shirt and blue panties, and, unlike the footprints they had followed, she was now wearing hiking boots.

Bax walked back to the rock outcropping. She could see spots of blood scattered all over the rocks. PIS walked up next to her.

"I'm sorry, Agent Baxter. No one should be allowed to do something like this to another human. If I may speculate. I believe she took refuge behind the rocks, probably thought it gave her some protection from her pursuers. From where the body is located, she stood up to continue her walk and was shot in the thigh. She had no idea they were sitting close by, waiting for her to make her next move. Once shot, she went down, and they were on her in an instant."

Bax looked at him. "I read it the same way— damn shame. I've seen her picture. She was a beautiful woman."

Bax called the rangers together and laid out a plan to search the immediate area for evidence. She also wondered if it would be worth having the pathologist come to the site, with the body in this condition. While the rangers fanned out, she pulled a silver survival blanket out of her backpack and covered the body. She wanted to at least keep the birds from doing any more damage.

Bax noticed that PIS was quiet and seemed to

be preoccupied. She walked over to him.

"You okay?" she asked.

"I am quite well, Agent Baxter, but I wonder if you would excuse me for a little while? There is something I want to check out back up the trail."

Bax nodded and watched PIS head back the way they had come. She wondered what that was all about, but with PIS, you never knew what was going to happen next.

She pulled her sat phone out of her backpack and called Buck.

"Hey, Buck."

"Sorry, Bax. I was at the Mark Kearney autopsy. What's going on?"

"We found her," said Bax.

Bax filled him in on the details of the search and the condition of the body. She tried to keep her emotions in check, but she was angry that they couldn't save this woman.

"Is PIS still with you?"

"He wandered off. Said he wanted to check something out. I suspect he'll be back in a little bit."

Buck told her that he would get Dr. Parkinson headed her way as soon as he was finished.

Bax clicked off and looked back the way PIS was headed. She wondered what he had seen on the trail that caused him to backtrack. She turned and headed back to help the rangers, but their evidence search was fruitless. She considered herself lucky that they had as much of the body as they had. She was surprised a bear hadn't come along and claimed it for himself.

With nothing to show for their searching, Bax called a halt and told everyone to grab a shady spot and rest up. They were going to be out there for another night, and she wasn't looking forward to that unless it gave her another shot at last night's attacker. She made herself a promise that she would shoot much straighter tonight if the chance presented itself.

The day was getting long, and the team had finished off the last of the sandwiches they had brought with them. Two of the rangers had hiked back up to the trail and retrieved the remaining ATVs and what was left of their food and drinks. Bax was starting to nod off when she heard a rustling in the scrub oak. She placed her hand on her gun and was on high alert until PIS called out and identified himself. He didn't look happy as he walked to the rock outcropping.

"What's up?" asked Bax.

"I think we may have a problem, but I wanted to confirm my suspicions before I mentioned it, in case I was mistaken. I fear I was not."

Bax called all the rangers to gather around, so

PIS would only need to explain once. She looked at him and nodded.

"Earlier today, I noticed that the tracks of the attackers that we had been following had doubled back on the trail. I thought at first it might have been a trick of the light, but it was not. I was able to confirm that they did indeed backtrack. About a quarter mile from here, there is a small trail that leads east. The tracks from your attackers turned down that trail. About a mile east, those tracks intercepted two additional sets of tracks. A small print, either a woman or a child, and a print from a larger, well-worn pair of boots, most definitely a man."

"You think they met up with some more crazies?" asked one of the rangers.

Bax looked at the ranger and then back to PIS. "No," she said. "He thinks we may have two more victims." PIS nodded.

"May I see your map?" asked PIS.

Ranger Martin unfolded his map and placed it on a large rock. PIS didn't stop to orient himself the way Ranger Martin had the first time he opened the map. PIS glanced at it and pointed to the trail. Ranger Martin looked closer at the trail.

"That's the trail to Miner's Falls. There's a flat rock ledge that overlooks a beautiful canyon and the mountains beyond. A lot of hikers stop there to spend the night and look at the stars. We had reports Saturday and Sunday night of the northern lights being seen. Rare for Colorado. Miner's Falls would have been a great spot to see them."

"Okay," said Bax. She looked at the four remaining rangers and focused on two of them. "You two stay here with the body and preserve the scene. The rest of us will head for Miner's Falls. Stay alert, guys."

They grabbed their backpacks and followed as PIS led them back up the trail, the way they had come. Bax was not happy with the prospect of additional bodies. Their attackers were racking up quite a death toll. Bax hoped PIS was mistaken, but she knew that that rarely happened.

CHAPTER FORTY-THREE

B uck pulled open the door to the sheriff's office and heard the bell clang. He walked in and found Paul and Jess Gonzales sitting at the desk by the window. Sheriff Willets and Deputy Jefferson were standing in the small break room. Buck placed his backpack on the nearest desk.

"Sheriff, do you guys have video and audio recording capability in the interview room?"

The sheriff looked at Deputy Jefferson, who nodded. "Yes, sir," said Jefferson. "Sheriff Wechsler got a sweet deal on some government-issued interrogation equipment through some Pentagon program he knew about. Better stuff than we could have afforded on our own."

He walked off, and Paul followed him to a small closet next to the interrogation room. After a few minutes, Paul stuck his head out of the door and told Buck he was good to go.

Buck asked Sheriff Willets to join him, and they walked over and opened the door to the room. Gerald Nelson was startled and almost fell out of the seat. The handcuffs, locked around a big eyebolt screwed into the table, stopped him from falling. He looked up.

The first thing Buck noticed was that the guy looked like he hadn't slept in days. The bags under his eyes had bags of their own. Buck and Sheriff Willets took a seat opposite Gerald Nelson and asked him to sit back down, which he did.

Gerald Nelson was five foot nine or ten and was rail thin. He had a scruffy, half-hearted attempt at a beard on his face, and he looked like he could have passed for fifteen. He was not what Buck had expected. He wore dirty jeans and a ripped flannel shirt and smelled like he hadn't washed in days.

Buck sat and looked at him without saying a word for the next five minutes. He could see him grow more fidgety with each passing minute. He could also see Sheriff Willets looking uncomfortable.

Buck pulled a card from his pocket and read the Miranda warning. Then, he looked at Gerald Nelson.

"Do you understand the rights I have just read to you?"

Gerald nodded.

"Please answer yes or no," said Buck.

"Yes."

"Do you wish to talk with us without an attorney present?"

Another nod. "Sorry, yes."

Buck pulled a piece of paper from a manila folder he had brought in with him and slid it over to Gerald along with a pen. It was the consent form to waive his right to counsel. Gerald read it, signed it and slid it back to Buck. He left it sitting on the table.

"Anytime you want to change your mind about having an attorney present, you let us know, and the interview will end. Okay?"

"Yes, sir."

Buck leaned back in his chair. "Gerald—may I call you Gerald? Gerald, we think you've been involved in some pretty bad stuff over the last couple of days. So why did you turn yourself in today?"

Tears rolled down Gerald's face, and he wiped his nose with his sleeve. "I didn't want to do anything, but once the drugs kicked in, I couldn't help myself. She made us do it."

"What did the drugs make you do, Gerald?"

Gerald hesitated for a moment. "Kill all those people. I would never have done that if it hadn't been for that new drug she told us to try. She said it would make us feel good. She never said it would make us act like animals." He put his face in his hands and cried.

Buck gave him a few minutes and signaled for Paul to bring in a bottle of water, which he placed on the table in front of Gerald and then left the room.

"Gerald, you look like you haven't eaten in a while. Would you like us to get you something, maybe something to drink besides water?"

"No, sir." He wiped his eyes, spun the cap off the bottle and gulped down half the contents.

Buck waited patiently. Sheriff Willets shifted around in his chair. Gerald settled down, and Buck continued.

"Gerald, who gave you the drugs?"

"VJ did. She said they would make us feel great, but it didn't, and each time we took them, the effects were stronger and lasted longer."

"How many people did you kill?"

Gerald looked deep in thought. "It wasn't only me. VJ and Stefan killed some of them too."

"Who is Stefan, Gerald?"

"He is . . . was Rachel's boyfriend."

"What do you mean, was?"

"He was shot last night by that lady cop. All we wanted to do was scare them, but VJ took a couple of shots at her. Stefan was hit in the stomach when she returned fire. I think he's dead."

"Where is Stefan now, Gerald?"

"Near the old cabin. We couldn't get inside because of all the cops. The cabin was where Stefan stayed."

"Gerald, can you tell us about the murders?"

"It wasn't supposed to happen. We went to Saguache to get in a gaming tournament, but the drugs kicked in, and they told us to leave. So, we went back to Rachel's house. Her parents were away for the weekend. I figured we'd have some fun, maybe get laid and play some games, but something weird happened.

"We were playing the Viking game, and VJ brought in two cool axes and her crossbow. We had the game turned up loud and the lights off. Rachel and Stefan were having sex on the floor when her sister Jenny walked in. She screamed and started calling us names, and VJ stabbed her with a knife. She screamed, and something happened, and we started hitting them both with the axes, and VJ was yelling, and we were hollering, and the girls were screaming, and it got crazy."

"What happened next, Gerald?"

"The sheriff walked in and yelled something and just stood there. VJ picked up her crossbow and fired a bolt that went right through his vest. She yelled for us to get him, and we just lost control. It was horrible, but we couldn't stop."

Tears rolled down his face, and he emptied the water bottle and wiped his eyes with his sleeve.

"Gerald, why did you guys attack Mitchell Groves?"

"Mitch was a drug dealer, and he had a small drug lab in his house. VJ told us that the new drug came from him. She also wanted to hurt her father. He distributed the drugs for Mitch, and she wanted to take over his operation. So, we took the sheriff's car, killed Mitch and took the drugs to the root cellar at the old cabin."

"Why carve him open like you did?"

"VJ played the Viking game on her laptop while we were there, and she told us it would be cool to make him a blood eagle. She gave us another pill, and we got excited and crazy, and it just happened. I didn't realize we had done it until VJ showed us the video she posted online."

"Gerald, did VJ ever take any of the drugs?"

"No, sir."

"When did you kill the hikers?"

"That was later that night. We charged into the woods to find someone to attack. In our minds, we were Viking warriors. Nothing seemed real. It was like we were playing the game. We found that couple by Miner's Falls, and we attacked them and threw them off the cliff. The second couple were asleep in their tent when we attacked. We attacked the guy first and then had fun with the woman until she escaped. Tracking her was a blast, and when we caught her, we made her pay."

Buck looked at the sheriff, who had a surprised look on his face. He looked back at Gerald.

"You sure you killed two couples?"

"Yes, sir. The first couple was a woman older than us and a tall, skinny old man. VJ shot him with the crossbow, and he fell over the edge. The other couple were about our age. We killed the guy in his sleeping bag."

"Gerald, why rape the women?"

"That's what the Vikings in the game did."

"Gerald, are you aware that VJ's parents are missing and probably dead?"

Gerald raised his hands and covered his face. Tears fell on the table.

"We didn't know it would happen. VJ said that the people that Mitch and her father worked for would see what she was capable of and give her an area of her own. She told us we'd be rich. She didn't tell us the drugs we stole belonged to someone else until after we took them."

"Gerald, why are you here, in this room?"

"Someone was tracking us. We spotted him after Stefan got shot. When VJ said we should leave Stefan to die, I got scared. I don't want to die. I didn't know the drugs would make me crazy and not be able to control what I did. I wish I could just forget the whole weekend, but I can't. Once the drugs wore off, I couldn't believe what we had done."

Buck picked up the manila folder and placed the waiver in it. Then, he walked out the door, followed by Sheriff Willets. He looked back at Gerald, who was crying like a baby.

Jess and Paul had been watching on the closed-circuit television.

"Shit, Buck," said Jess. "This was all about ripping off her father and making a name for herself. She had no idea who she was messing with or how the Russians would react, and she let this idiot and his friend take a drug she knew nothing about and act out."

"Yeah," said Buck. "We need to call Bax and tell her about the other couple."

"Already done," said Paul. "Called her as soon as he mentioned the second couple. Bax was already on it. PIS found tracks from our friend here and his warriors, heading away from where they found McKenzie Kearney."

"Do you think the guy he mentioned in the woods is the Russian?" asked Sheriff Willets.

"That would be my guess," said Buck. "We need to find VJ Florence before he does, and we need to get back to the cabin and locate the wounded kid."

"My guys are still at the cabin," said Jess. "I'll get them started looking for the guy Bax shot."

Buck thanked her and suggested that he and Paul head to the resort and give Mr. Talbot the sad news about his daughter, and they could get an early start in the morning to look for VJ. He asked Sheriff Willets to get Gerald Nelson something to eat and put him in their only holding cell for the night.

Paul downloaded the interrogation into the investigation file and shut down the equipment. Gerald was still sitting there crying. He almost felt bad for him. The guy's life was ruined, and he would spend the rest of his life in prison if he didn't get the death penalty.

Buck hated death notifications, and he prepared himself for the wrath of McKenzie's father.

CHAPTER FORTY-FOUR

PIS passed through the trees and stepped into the clearing. The large rock shelf that lay in front of him was just like Ranger Martin had described it, including the view of the canyon below, which was spectacular.

The smell of death was strong, and as PIS stepped onto the rock ledge, he could see dried puddles of blood. He stopped. After spending years working on investigations with Buck, he knew better than to walk into a crime scene. He waited for Bax and the others.

Bax walked up onto the ledge and stopped. "I'll never get used to that smell," she said.

PIS looked at her. "The day you do is the day you should quit." He smiled, and she nodded.

Ranger Martin skirted around the ledge and looked over the edge into the canyon below. "Long way down," he said.

The noise level from the waterfall wasn't terrible, but Bax assumed that it was a lot louder later in the season when the snow melted off the mountain peaks in the distance.

Bax pulled out her phone, opened the camera and took photos of the blood puddles and blood spatter. There were small pieces of viscera dried to the rock, and it surprised her that the animals and birds hadn't stripped the rock clean.

PIS stood near the edge by Ranger Martin and looked over at the broken tree limbs. "Agent Baxter, it would appear that one of these unfortunate souls went over the edge here." He pointed to the broken tree limbs. There was no sign of a second body, unless they both went over the edge.

The sun was casting a pink glow on the snow-covered mountain peaks in the distance. It made the whole canyon glow. Bax told the team that they would need to spend the night. She wouldn't be able to get the forensic team there until first light. They all agreed, and Ranger Martin and the other ranger headed out to find some firewood.

Bax had a couple of sandwiches left in her backpack, which she shared around, and PIS took a canteen from his backpack and came back with cold water from the stream that fed the waterfall. He used the cup from the canteen to brew some hot water and made coffee for everyone but himself. PIS preferred tea.

While the others drank their coffee, PIS

reached into his backpack and pulled out a small cookie tin. Inside the cookie tin, wrapped in fine silk, was a beautiful porcelain cup and saucer, a silver spoon, a small tea ball for brewing tea and a tiny silver teapot. PIS also removed a smaller tin containing loose-leaf Earl Grey tea, which he proceeded to brew up for himself. The whole image seemed out of place there in the woods.

Bax had heard about the cookie tin from Buck, who had seen this same activity while he and PIS were looking for a missing heiress. It was Buck's only unsolved case, and he carried the file with him, as a reminder.

She had also heard that in the bottom of the tin was a worn black-and-white photo of a beautiful young woman. Buck had never explained who the woman was if he even knew, and she didn't have the nerve to ask PIS about it. She and the rangers just sat there and watched PIS bring a little civility to the wilderness.

As darkness settled all around them, they each selected a spot to rest, knowing that no one was going to get any sleep. Bax leaned back against her backpack and looked at the sky. Ranger Martin was right. This was an excellent spot for viewing the stars and would have been spectacular with the northern lights overhead.

At some point during the night, Bax must have nodded off, because she woke with a start.

Her first reaction was to rest her hand on the backstrap of her pistol. She looked around and saw Ranger Martin standing next to the fire, which, she thought, was big enough to be seen from space. They weren't taking any chances. She stood and stretched out the kinks from lying on the ground.

She walked over to Ranger Martin. "Have you seen PIS?"

Ranger Martin looked around. "He was just over from you the last time I saw him. Where the hell is he?"

Bax had to think twice about heading off into the woods to try to find him. She knew PIS could take care of himself, and she knew that he often took off on his own, especially if something attracted his attention.

CHAPTER FORTY-FIVE

PIS had waited for full dark before he slipped out of camp. Agent Baxter had nodded off, and the two rangers were sitting on the ground, focused on the fire. It was easy to slip away without being seen. He had seen another set of tracks while he was following the tracks to the overlook, and now, he was going to follow those and see where they led.

The new track PIS followed was headed back to the original crime scene, where Bax and her team had been attacked. He was hoping that this new track might lead him to where the attackers might be hiding, but mostly he was interested in who had made the new track. He made good time heading back, the tracks taking a more direct route. He was working on a hunch that he hoped would work out for everyone.

He found blood on the ground several yards from where Bax had dug the bolts out of the tree. Bax had said that she thought she had hit one of the attackers. The blood on the ground indicated that she had indeed. He began his search and soon found the trail they had used to escape the area.

He stopped short and looked at the ground near a damp spot. The fourth print was embedded in the soil, only this print was different from the other three. This was made by a boot from a manufacturer that PIS knew well. It was an expensive boot, and the tread was barely worn. Someone had purchased a new pair of boots, which would eliminate any serious hikers since no one goes on a long hike wearing new boots. That's just looking for trouble. This boot print overlapped the attackers' prints, meaning this new person had been following the attackers.

PIS followed the trail to an old cabin that sat in a clearing east of the trail. The cabin was the center of a lot of activity by a swarm of DEA agents. He backtracked and found another trail that led away from the cabin and deeper into the forest. He thought he had gone too far and was about to turn around when he spotted a dark mass propped up against a tree.

Moving cautiously, he approached the mass, which turned out to be a body. He kneeled and touched the body. It was still warm. He looked at the bloodstain around the abdomen and knew that this fella was the one Agent Baxter had shot, but she was not the cause of the red, round hole in his forehead. That was courtesy of someone else.

From the amount of blood on his shirt, he wouldn't have had long to live, anyway, so it looked like his associates had left him here to die. He guessed they thought he was a burden, bleeding all over the place. The blood on the forehead was just starting to crust over, meaning this person had been killed within the past hour.

PIS checked the victim's boots and confirmed that this was one of the attackers. There was no doubt that the person who killed this guy was tracking someone else. PIS knew who that someone else was. He also had a good idea who was doing the tracking. He spotted the fourth print in some loose dirt and followed it.

Several miles later and just off the Continental Divide Trail, he heard someone crying. He worked his way through the undergrowth until he came to the edge of a clearing. Someone had built a small, rustic lean-to between two trees. It was covered with branches, and for anyone else, it would have been impossible to see. PIS lay on the ground and watched.

A young woman was lying on the ground in front of the lean-to. She was dressed in black and had a large Celtic cross hanging around her neck. A compound crossbow lay on the ground next to her. She was in pain, and she kept putting pressure on her leg. Each time she did, she cried out.

Standing over her was a man PIS knew well, although he had never met the man, let alone seen him. It was his reputation PIS knew well. Victor Poroshenko was about the same age as PIS, his gray hair cut short. He was talking to the woman on the ground. PIS listened.

"Where is your friend?" he asked the woman.

"I don't know what you're talking about, you fuck. You shot me."

He kneeled next to her and grabbed her thigh, the one with the bullet hole in it, and squeezed.

The woman screamed and cursed him several times over.

"All you need to do is tell me where the last member of your team is. I already found the friend you abandoned. Not a very nice thing to do. That's the problem with youth. No loyalty. Now, once again, where is the third member of your team?"

He reached for her thigh. "No, don't. I don't know where he is. That's the truth. He was upset that I left Stefan to die, and he took off. I was going to shoot him myself, but he ducked deeper into the forest. I have no idea where he is. Once the drugs wore off, he got squirrely. I think he realized what we had done, and it made him upset."

Victor Poroshenko tapped her on the leg. "See, now that wasn't very hard, was it?"

PIS noticed that Victor Poroshenko spoke with almost no accent. He would be the perfect spy and assassin for both the Russian government and the Bratva, the infamous Russian crime syndicate. He looked like an everyday businessman. No bald head, no chest and arms covered in prison tattoos. From his reputation, you would have thought he wore a red cape and had superpowers—no wonder no one, including PIS, had ever gotten close to punching his ticket.

Victor stood up and walked around the woman. "Now that we are friends, tell me why you stole my employer's drugs and killed their distributor?"

The woman cried in pain and cursed him again. "You killed my parents, you bastard. I hope you rot in hell."

The silenced pistol in Victor's hand spat once, and a bullet slammed into the ground next to her other leg.

"And here I thought we were getting along so well; then you had to ruin it with your foul mouth." He turned around and walked a couple of paces away from her. Then he turned. "You are right, of course. I will rot in hell. That is my fate. What will be your fate?"

"I didn't know the drugs belonged to some

Russians. I thought Mitch and my dad were doing their own thing. Dad was making a ton of money, but he wouldn't let me into the business. I just wanted to show him and whoever he supplied the drugs to that I could be a big help. I can do the same for the people you work for. I'll give back the drugs."

Victor Poroshenko laughed. "Do I look stupid to you? The drugs you stole are now in the possession of the United States DEA. They have cleaned out your stash, and my boss's newest creation is on the way to some government lab to be replicated and used for some nefarious purpose. You stole something you knew nothing about, unaware of the dangers it posed in the wrong hands, and you let it get away from you because you liked to watch your friends savagely murder people. You, young lady, are a sick individual."

The woman cried. "I didn't know they weren't Mitch's drugs. He told me they would make the user happy. I didn't know that a game could trigger the violence. I didn't kill anyone. I never touched the drugs. I will do anything to make up for this. I'm so sorry. Ask your boss to give me a chance. You'll see."

Victor smiled. "You are the worst kind of person. You fed an unknown drug to your friends without taking it for yourself and then manipulated them into doing unspeakable things."

"Please, God. I didn't know. I have my whole life ahead of me."

Victor Poroshenko had heard enough. He stepped next to her, pointed the pistol and shot her in the head. VJ Florence died lying on the ground in the middle of the forest in the dark.

PIS was as still as he could be, but Victor turned around and stared into the wood in his direction. For almost five minutes he didn't move, and PIS couldn't be sure if Victor had heard or sensed him or if it was someone or something else that caught his attention.

Victor unscrewed the silencer and threw it as far as he could into the forest. He placed the gun into his belt holster and disappeared into the darkness.

PIS remained still for two more hours before he believed that Victor Poroshenko was gone. He headed back to the waterfall and slipped into camp just before dawn. He now knew what Victor Poroshenko looked like, and he knew what he had to do.

CHAPTER FORTY-SIX

Bax woke with a start as the sun hit her face. She looked around, unsure of where she was, until she smelled coffee brewing. It didn't matter where she was. If there was coffee to drink, then the place was perfect. She stood and wiped the sleep out of her eyes.

She glanced over and spotted PIS, sound asleep under a large pine tree. She wondered where he had gone and when he had gotten back. She walked over to the rangers and asked, and they both looked surprised that he was back, since neither of them had strayed from their spot next to the fire.

Bax pulled out her sat phone and was about to call Buck when PIS walked up and held his finger up to his lips for silence. He walked to the edge of the ledge and stopped. Bax could see he was listening for something, but she didn't want to break his concentration.

He turned. "There's someone down there," he said.

They all walked to the edge and listened, and they all heard what PIS had heard. A low, almost whisper calling for help.

PIS looked at Ranger Martin. "Is there a way to get to the bottom?" His voice had taken on a sense of urgency.

Ranger Martin looked to the opposite side of the falls and pointed. "There's a narrow path that hugs the side of the canyon wall. Used to be an old Native American trail. Wide enough for one person."

PIS grabbed his backpack off the ground and took off running towards the stream with Bax following close behind him. He splashed through the stream and stopped to get his bearings. Bax stopped beside him. Without saying a word, he pointed to a barely visible flat spot and raced off. Bax had no idea where the trail was, but she stayed on his heels.

PIS disappeared between two boulders, and for the first time, Bax saw the trail. Bax was amazed as she watched PIS run down a trail that was a foot wide at its widest. She was an expert rock climber, but this trail was unnerving. She followed PIS, who moved like a mountain goat.

After about half an hour, Bax reached the bottom. PIS had dropped his backpack next to a small, crystal-clear pool and was standing on the other side looking at something in the trees.

She walked around the icy water and walked up next to him. She looked up but at first didn't see anything. PIS pointed. "See that large branch with the double tip," he said. "There's a man up there."

Bax dropped her backpack and leaped for the lowest branch. She pulled herself up and then started to climb. PIS was right behind her.

An older man, lying trapped in the crook of a branch, reached out a hand. His mouth moved, but no words came out. Bax could see a smile cross his face. She reached the branch next to him.

"You're safe now. I'm a police officer. We here to get you out."

The man looked at the oddly dressed PIS and looked back at Bax with a question in his eyes.

Bax smiled. "He's the one who heard you call out."

The man nodded, and tears filled his eyes. PIS gave him a quick once-over and then moved next to Bax.

"He can move both his arms and legs, so I don't think his back is broken, but we need to be careful. He's got a lot of scratches, and he has a crossbow bolt sticking out of his chest. He is also severely dehydrated. We're going to need some help."

Bax climbed down to the pool and, using a cup from her backpack, scooped up some water, which she carried up to him. He tried to speak, but the look in his eyes was all the thanks she needed. She told him they would be right back, and they climbed back down.

She looked around and spotted PIS standing next to the pool at the edge of the waterfall. She walked over and stopped. Lying on the edge of the pool, partially covered by the water, was a woman's body. She had been hacked to death before she had gone over the edge. She was missing her clothes. PIS looked away and walked closer to the cliff. He came back moments later with two backpacks.

"Found these against the rock face. They're covered in blood. What do you want to do about him? He won't last much longer up there, but if we try to move him, we could kill him."

"We need some professional help," said Bax.

She pulled out the phone and dialed Buck. This was going to be another long day.

CHAPTER FORTY-SEVEN

B uck and Paul were sitting with James Talbot in the bar at the resort. They had just told him that his daughter was dead, and he was not taking it well. First, there was the stomping around, cursing and threatening anyone who had anything to do with it; then came the tears and the sorrow. He had just finished his third vodka on the rocks when he stood up, staggered a little and told Buck he needed to call his wife and let her know. He left the bar and headed for the front doors and some privacy.

Buck's phone rang as they were getting ready to leave.

"Hey, Bax."

Bax cut him off. "Buck, we found a live victim, but he's wedged in a tree. Fifty feet off the ground at the bottom of a two-hundred-foot cliff. We can't risk moving him because we can't tell how bad he's hurt, but he's very dehydrated. PIS is taking water up to him. We're gonna need some serious rescue help and air evac."

Bax took a breath. Buck said, "Stay where you are. I'm on it."

He hung up, and his phone chimed with the coordinates. He speed-dialed the director.

"Sir," said Buck. "We have a problem. Bax found a live victim, but he's severely injured and trapped in a tree. I'll explain it all later. Can you get the governor to authorize a Colorado Air National Guard rescue team and an air evac?"

"I'll call you right back." The director hung up.

"A live victim," said Paul. "And it sounds like it's going to be tough to get him out. Bax gets all the fun." Though he wasn't laughing.

They were walking out of the bar when they heard the ATVs coming back.

"Shit," said Buck. "Talbot's outside, and that will be April and the doc bringing in his daughter."

They ran out the door just as April and the doc stopped their ATVs, and Talbot made a beeline towards the body bag. Buck intercepted him.

"Let me go, goddammit. That's my daughter."

He tried to push Buck away, but Paul grabbed him in a bear hug and held on to him.

"Mr. Talbot. You don't want to see her this way."

"But that's my daughter. I have a right to see

her."

"Mr. Talbot," Buck said, lowering his voice. He pointed to the doctor. "This is Dr. Parkinson. He's going to take your daughter to Gunnison for an autopsy. He will take good care of McKenzie. He will also help you make arrangements with a local funeral home to cremate your daughter if you want so that you can take her ashes home with you. You don't want to remember the woman in the body bag, the way she is now. You want to remember the fun-loving, adventurous McKenzie."

Talbot looked at Buck as Paul let him go. "It's that bad?"

"Remember your daughter as she was," said Buck.

Dr. Parkinson stepped over and took Mr. Talbot's arm. "You can ride with me, sir. I promise we will treat your daughter with respect and dignity." The doctor nodded to Buck, and they headed for the car.

April Wang walked up and gave Buck a hug. "That poor man. I can't think of anything worse than not being able to say goodbye to a loved one. Bax called to say that she had another crime scene. So, we're gonna grab some food and water for the team and head back out there. It's been a hell of a couple of days."

"Well," said Buck. "If it's any consolation, this

should be the last one. We have one of the doers in jail. He didn't mention any more bodies. Franklin's team left this morning to get some rest. If I need a team, I'll call him first. Give you guys some time to rest."

Buck's phone rang and he looked at the number. He pushed the green button.

"Yes, sir," he said.

"Choppers warming up on the field right now, and the rescue team has been mustered. They should be off the ground in five minutes. ETA to you, fifteen minutes later."

"Thanks, sir. I'll let Bax know."

Buck was about to call Bax when his phone rang with a number he hadn't seen in quite a while.

"Cobra?" he asked with surprise.

"The one and only, on our way to save you from the mountains once again. How have you been, Buck?"

"Grateful to hear your voice. My associate, Agent Baxter, is on the scene." Buck gave her the phone number to Bax's sat phone and the coordinates.

Colorado Air National Guard Captain Elena "Cobra" Milhouse and her copilot, Lieutenant Tommy "Tomcat" Parkinson, had worked with Buck on a crazy case outside of Creede, Colorado.

Buck was investigating a group of missing scientists and students that had been found dead along another section of the Continental Divide Trail. It was determined that their deaths were attributable to a freak situation, and they were killed by naturally occurring infrasound waves.

During the investigation and with the help of Cobra and Tomcat, they had recovered all the bodies, found a Cold War bunker that was being secretly converted into a fail-safe bunker by the government and dealt with a bunch of conspiracy theorists. It had been a strange case.

Buck heard the engines rev in the background. "We're leaving the field. ETA seventeen minutes."

Buck thanked her and called Paul, who was helping the EMTs load the body bag into the ambulance.

"Let's head up there," he said.

They grabbed their backpacks and climbed into the ATV that the doctor had used to bring out the body. Paul hit the gas as Buck pulled out his GPS and plugged in the coordinates.

They spotted the chopper coming over the trees and heading east. Paul kept to the trail, and they made good time, arriving a half hour after the chopper got there. Once again, Cobra had shown her skills as the pilot of a Sikorsky UH-60 Black Hawk. She had set down right on the ledge over the waterfall with about a foot of clearance between the rotor and the trees. Buck counted six CANG rescuers, who were already setting up a lift, while two of their team worked their way down the cliff face to the tree. Above them, on its own cable, was a fiberglass bodyboard.

Bax was standing next to the chopper talking to Cobra when Buck walked up, and Cobra gave him a hug.

"Here we are once again, Buck. The first time we ever pulled a body out of a tree in a canyon. You guys lead an interesting life," she said.

Buck laughed, and then he spotted PIS standing at the edge of the forest. He walked over and hugged him. PIS hugged him back.

"Agent Taylor, how wonderful to see you again. We have been having a most interesting adventure."

Buck had tried for years to get PIS to call him Buck, but every greeting between the two was the same.

"PIS, what are you doing here? I'm glad you are, but how . . . what?"

"All in good time, my dear friend. All in good time. Right now, we need to focus on Mr. Dirt Crusher."

Buck looked at him cross-eyed. PIS smiled. "That's his trail name. I don't know what his real name is. He passed out before I could ask him.

He did tell me that the woman he was with was called Snowflake. She's also at the bottom of the cliff. In much worse shape than he is."

"Well, I appreciate your help, but how did you know we were out here?"

Buck stopped talking and got a serious look on his face. "You're not out here for us. You're after the Russian."

"Agent Taylor, some things are better left unsaid."

He waved over Bax and Paul.

"Agent Baxter, would it be all right if I borrow Agent Taylor and Agent Webber for a little while? We might want to bring the forensic team along."

April and her team had just arrived with the food and drinks and heard PIS ask Bax the question. "Where are we going?" she asked.

"Only a few miles. We should only need part of your team," said PIS.

April pulled the cooler from the ATV she was driving and grabbed one of her techs. They climbed onto the ATV, and she followed behind Buck, Paul and PIS as they headed back up the trail.

They had traveled about four miles when PIS pointed to a side trail. Buck followed his directions and headed that way. Buck recognized the dirt road they came to. He knew that the old cabin was just up ahead. PIS asked him to stop.

PIS jumped out of the ATV and headed up the trail. Everyone followed, wondering where they were going. Paul was the first one to spot the body.

"Oh, shit. We've got another body."

They gathered around the body, and Buck kneeled next to it. "Gut-shot and head-shot. This must be the one Bax shot, but he didn't get all the way here with that hole in his head. Who finished him off?" He looked at PIS.

"He was still warm when I found him. He had been left here to die, but someone found him before he completed his journey to the other side and helped him along."

"The Russian?" asked Paul.

Buck nodded.

PIS stepped next to Buck. "There's one more body up ahead."

PIS led the team another couple of miles, and they entered the small clearing with the lean-to and the body of VJ Florence.

"Fuck," said Buck. "He got to them first." He looked at PIS. "How did you find them?"

"I was hoping their tracks would lead me to a hiding spot. I figured if I could find them, it would save you some time and avoid any additional bloodshed. I'm afraid I was too late."

"Did you see anyone?" asked Buck.

PIS shook his head. Buck pulled out his phone and called Sheriff Willets. He asked him to meet the forensic team near the old shed. Buck, Paul and PIS left April to her job and headed back to the waterfall. It was time to wrap this investigation up.

CHAPTER FORTY-EIGHT

The ledge area was a buzz of activity as Paul pulled the ATV to a stop. Tomcat was using the winch on the chopper to help lift the paramedic and the backboard with Dirt Crusher securely fastened to it.

Paul and PIS went to watch the rescuers, and Buck took Bax aside.

"PIS found VJ Florence and Stefan Kolchenko. They're both dead."

Bax didn't look surprised. "I wondered where he disappeared to last night. I never got to ask him before we found the body in the tree. Suicide?"

"No, someone killed them both. The one you shot, Kolchenko, was left to die in the woods. I think he encountered the Russian. VJ had been shot once in the thigh and once in the head. We weren't close enough to save them."

Bax smiled. "I wish we knew who this Russian is, but I'll bet he's long gone by now. By the way. The rescue team brought up Snowflake first. Her body is in the chopper. The team leader says they should have Dirt Crusher up in the next few minutes. They're going to fly him to the level one trauma hospital in Colorado Springs. I called the director, and he'll have someone there to meet them and get his statement as soon as he's able. He's in rough shape."

"You guys did great work over the last couple of days. I'm proud of you and the rest of the team."

Bax nodded, and they walked closer as the backboard arrived at the top of the ledge. The rescue team made fast work of getting him into the chopper, and then they all climbed aboard, and Cobra gave the thumbs-up sign. She fired up the engines, and everyone stepped back as the chopper lifted off. Cobra gave Buck a salute as she swung around and headed out the way she had come in. She made it look so easy.

"She's nice," said Bax. "Pretty too. Sounds like you guys worked well together in Creede."

Buck laughed. Bax hated the fact that Buck was alone, but she also knew he was still mourning the loss of his wife, even after all these years.

The rest of the team gathered their gear and climbed into the ATVs. Buck looked around.

"Where's PIS?"

Bax and Paul looked around and then at each

other.

"He was here a minute ago," said Bax.

Buck shook his head. It was just like PIS to disappear when his job was done.

Buck thought back to the question he had asked PIS earlier. He wondered again if PIS had come to help them or if he came to stop the Russian. Buck knew a lot more about PIS's past than Bax or Paul did, and he wondered if he was there, in the woods, at the request of the British government.

He figured he would never know the answer, but he was glad PIS had been there to help them.

Buck climbed into the ATV, and Paul headed for the resort. He was looking forward to a hot shower, some food and some sleep.

Once they arrived back at the resort, Buck pulled out his phone and called Dr. Parkinson, who was not happy that he had three more bodies to pick up. He told Buck he would send one of the ER residents because he needed to get some sleep or he was going to run off the road. Buck told him he knew how he felt.

Bax went up to her room to grab some sleep, and she was out before her head hit the pillow. Buck and Paul drove back to the cabin to check on April and her team.

Sheriff Willets was standing next to his old

Bronco when Buck drove around the cabin and stopped next to him. He and Paul slid out of the Jeep.

"I can't believe they're both dead. My gosh, the body count is huge. Is it over?"

"I think so," said Buck.

"But what about this Russian guy?"

"I think by now, he's long gone. I think he did his job and punished everyone responsible. I doubt we'll be seeing him again."

Buck thanked Sheriff Willets for standing by until the doctor arrived. Then, they slid back into Buck's Jeep and headed back to the resort. They checked into the rooms that they had barely used in three days and agreed to meet in the morning for breakfast.

Buck had every intention of updating the investigation file, but he looked at the clock and decided it could wait. He grabbed a quick shower, lay down on the bed and was asleep in minutes. He slept until almost noon, when his phone woke him up. His first thought was, "What now?"

He saw the number and answered.

"Hey, Jess."

Jess Gonzales told him that her team was wrapped up, and they were heading back to Grand Junction. She told him to call if he needed anything to wrap up the case. Buck filled her in on what had been going on while they were dealing with the drugs.

"So, they're all dead," she said, "and there's no sign of the Russian? The guy really is a ghost. I can't believe all this death was because one woman wanted a piece of her daddy's business, and he wouldn't allow it. Fuck, Buck. We really live in a screwed-up world."

Buck thanked her for their help and asked her to upload her reports to the investigation file. He hung up, grabbed a long, hot shower, dressed in his cleanest clothes and headed downstairs to the restaurant for some much-needed food.

He found Bax and Paul sitting in the dining room.

"We thought you were going to sleep all day," said Bax.

"Wish I could have," he said and sat down at the table.

"Don't forget we have a funeral to attend at two," she said. "Sheriff Wechsler and the two Carrollton women."

Bax could tell from the look on his face that he'd forgotten about the funeral. "I was going to head to Gunnison for the autopsies of VJ Florence, Stefan Kolchenko and Snowflake." He looked at his watch, pulled out his phone and called Dr. Parkinson.

"Hey, Garrett. Can you hold off on those autopsies until a little later? I have the sheriff's funeral service at two."

"No problem, Buck. That will give me a chance to finish filling out the death certificates on all the others."

Buck hung up and ordered a large glass of Coke and the mountain man breakfast platter from the waitress who appeared at the table.

Mr. Conway stopped by the table to talk about the past couple of days. "I hope this doesn't stop people from hiking this section," he said. "There are a lot of posts on the CDT social media pages telling hikers to avoid this section."

"You can go ahead and post that everything is good if you want," said Bax.

He thanked them for all they had done and told them to come back and enjoy the hospitality anytime. He headed for the kitchen. Looking around at the staff, Buck could tell everyone was in a somber mood. He hoped their little town could recover.

The waitress brought his breakfast and his Coke and placed them in front of him. Bax was always amazed that he could eat as much as he did and not gain a pound. She figured his metabolism was working overtime.

Bax and Paul left him so they could check out of their rooms. He took time between bites to look around the room. He noticed the older gray-haired man he had seen at the cafe in town. He was very distinguished-looking, and Buck wondered what had brought him to the resort. He liked to play that game in places he visited. Try to figure out people's stories. It was a fun way to kill some time.

He finished his meal, added the charge to his room and headed to the front doors. Once outside, he called the director.

"You get any sleep, Buck?" asked the director.

"Yes, sir," said Buck. "We're wrapping up here. Jess and her team left this morning. I'm going to head home after the sheriff's funeral and witness the last three autopsies. Paul and Bax are heading home later today as well. We'll package up the investigation file and send it over to the district attorney by the end of the week. I'm hoping they can work a deal with Gerald Nelson. That drug really messed with his head. He's gonna have to live with what he did for the rest of his life."

"Hopefully, this whole incident will delay any more of the drugs from landing in Colorado, or anywhere else in the country," said Director Jackson.

"You know drug dealers, sir, especially the big guys. They're already working on filling the shoes of Mitchell Groves and the Florences. I have a feeling we are going to see this drug again, soon."

"You guys did great work, Buck. I'll call Bax and Paul and thank them later today. Once you wrap up the files, have the team take some time off. Catch a few trout for me."

Buck hung up and headed for his room to check out. It had been a long couple of days, and it wasn't over just yet. The paperwork would take the rest of the week. He stopped at the front desk and turned in his room key.

Once outside, he stood by his Jeep and looked around. He wondered where PIS had gone.

CHAPTER FORTY-NINE

Buck had called the special U.S. Marshals phone number and told Harriet that he would like a couple of deputies to come up to Silver City and pick up Gerald Nelson. He was concerned that if the Russians found out that he was in custody, they might try to kill him. She told him they would be there in a couple of hours, and they would take him to the federal lockup in Florence, Colorado, to await his arraignment. Buck thanked her and pushed open the door to the sheriff's office.

Sheriff Willets and Deputies Tortelli and Jefferson sat at their desks talking to Bax and Paul. The deputies had on their class A uniforms. Sheriff Willets wore a tailored three-piece suit. Next to them, Buck, Bax and Paul looked underdressed, but they didn't think anyone would care. They were there to show their respect for a fallen officer. That's what was important.

Sheriff Willets walked over and reached out his hand. Buck shook it. "I'm not sure I can ever thank you enough for all you did here. I would have been lost without you and your team. What a crazy week. I'm not sure the town will recover."

Buck smiled. "You guys were a big part of what went on here. You should be proud of your contribution. This was a lot more than any of us expected."

"I can't believe in the end, it was all about the money. VJ Florence just wanted what her dad had," said Deputy Tortelli.

"It wasn't just in the end. It was always about the money. You guys are all relatively new. Take it as a good lesson. If there's money involved, it's usually always about the money," said Buck.

Paul and Bax nodded.

"What happens next?" asked Sheriff Willets.

Buck sat on the edge of the desk. "Bax, Paul and I will finish putting together the investigation file; we'll gather all the physical evidence together and send a summary to the district attorney. They'll review it, ask to see some or all the evidence and then decide what charges to post. Since the only person still alive is Gerald Nelson, his fate is in their hands."

"I feel bad for him," said Deputy Jefferson. "He got more than he bargained for, all because of VJ."

Deputy Tortelli laughed. "You think he should get off? He killed a bunch of people. With luck, he'll get the electric chair."

"That's not a decision we get to make. That's for the district attorney and eventually a jury to decide," said Bax.

Sheriff Willets looked at his watch. "We should get going. We don't want to be late."

They all stood and walked out of the sheriff's office. Buck stopped Sheriff Willets at the door. "Marvin, what about you? You never asked for or wanted this job. What are you going to tell the county commissioners?"

"My wife asked me the same question last night. I think right now, this county needs me. I'm going to ask them to give me six months. If I'm still feeling the same way, I'll go to the academy and learn to be a real sheriff."

"I think you made the right decision. You're a good man, Marvin. I think you'll do fine. If you ever need anything, even just to talk or ask for advice, you call me."

Buck headed for his Jeep and followed the others to the funeral home in Saguache. The procession from Saguache to the cemetery just outside Silver City was over a mile long. One news channel estimated there were over four hundred law enforcement vehicles from all over the state. It was a tremendous outpouring of respect for a young law enforcement officer.

It was always impressive when all those officers snapped to attention and saluted as the flag-draped casket was carried past the crowd. It always brought a tear to Buck's eyes.

Buck, Paul and Bax stood at the back of the crowd gathered around the gravesite and listened while Marvin Willets gave a touching eulogy and then presented the American flag to Sheriff Wechsler's wife. She held on to her two children through the entire ceremony, never once letting go. Buck hoped she would be okay, but he knew from personal experience that time does not actually heal all wounds.

Buck spotted Director Jackson and the lieutenant governor, Constance Mondragon, standing next to the family. He nodded, and the lieutenant governor smiled at him and mouthed a silent thank-you before turning her attention back to the ceremony. Buck knew it was time to go, and they headed for their Jeeps before the crowd broke up.

He huddled up with Bax and Paul. "You guys take tomorrow off. Get some sleep and clear your minds. I've got three autopsies to witness, and then I am going to do the same. My youngest granddaughter wants to learn to fly-fish, so that's where I will be tomorrow. Let's meet at the office on Thursday morning and close this investigation. You guys did a great job, as always."

"I wish we had figured out who the Russian was," said Paul. "It would have been nice to close that part out as well, but I guess we will never know."

They laughed and said their goodbyes. As Buck walked to his Jeep, he thought about what Paul had said. He thought about the gray-haired man he had seen in the resort's restaurant. The man who looked out of place. He thought about PIS showing up out of the blue to help them find the bodies. And he wondered about the real reason PIS might have been there, and if maybe the Russian part of the case had already been solved. He hoped he would see his friend again.

He slid into his Jeep and pulled out of the lot, heading for the hospital in Gunnison. It had been a long week, and he couldn't wait for it to be over.

EPILOGUE

Victor Poroshenko sat in the restaurant at the resort, looking out the huge windows at the snowcapped mountains in the distance. The view reminded him of home. Not the home in Moscow that he never lived in, but the villa in the mountains of Italy, where he lived in secret with his wife.

He knew he should have left the day before, but it was his usual MO to stay a day or two to let things calm down. He had only been to the United States once before, and he'd spent that time in New York City. He had no idea Colorado was so beautiful, and he wanted to enjoy it.

He knew he would never get back here again. The chemo wasn't working, and the doctors had told him that his time on this earth was drawing to a close. He had never expected to live as long as he had, always figuring the next up-and-comer would take him out. He'd never expected to get taken out by colon cancer. He had hoped to retire and spend the rest of his life with his wife, watching his nine grandchildren grow up. Fate is a funny animal.

He let go of the melancholy and was about to take a bite out of the T-bone steak that sat in front of him when a shadow passed by him, and a man sat down in the chair opposite him.

Victor looked at the man. He appeared to be around the same age as Victor, and he looked like he belonged at the resort. He had on jeans and a blue polo shirt and he had long gray hair tied back in a ponytail. When he spoke, he had a silky-smooth British accent. He kept one hand under the table.

"Please keep your hands where I can see them, and don't make any sudden moves."

"Do we know each other?" asked Victor.

"Only by reputation," said the man. He pointed to Victor's plate. "Please, finish your dinner."

Victor smiled. "Can I offer you a glass of wine? It is a wonderful vintage."

He called over the waiter, who poured a glass of wine for the stranger and asked if he would like to see a menu. The stranger declined, picked up the glass, swirled it, sniffed it and tasted it. The wine was excellent.

Victor drank some of his wine, put the glass down and looked at the stranger. "I assume you are here to kill me?"

The stranger smiled. "In due time, but please

enjoy your meal. It would be undignified to take away the pleasure of such an excellent meal."

Victor's hand moved towards the steak knife. "Please be very careful of your next move," said the stranger. "I will not hesitate to kill you right here, but I would prefer not to."

Victor slowly picked up the knife and cut up his steak. He never took his eyes off the stranger. "I feel like our paths have crossed," said Victor.

"I've been searching for you for a long time," said the stranger. He reached up and pulled the collar of his shirt to the left side, revealing a jagged X-shaped scar over his heart.

Victor looked at the mark and at the stranger. "You were a guest of General Nguyen an Dung. I *have* heard of you. For some reason, you did not die like the others."

"An oddity of birth," said the stranger.

"Would it help my cause if I told you that I killed the general a year later? He was a monster. So, this is personal?"

The stranger shook his head. "Not at all. Vietnam was a long time ago. No, this is purely business. There are extermination orders for you in nine different countries. I just happened to be the closest person. Besides, I've seen firsthand your brutality."

Victor smiled. "It was you who was in the

woods last night?"

The stranger nodded.

"I could sense you. You must be very good to get that close without me seeing or hearing you. Why did you let me live?" asked Victor.

"The time wasn't right."

"The time is almost past. If you wait any longer, the cancer will beat you," said Victor.

The stranger gave him a questioning look. Victor put down his fork and rolled up his sleeve, revealing a port embedded in his skin. "Colon cancer. This was my last job. The payoff that would allow me to retire from the Bratva. I was hoping to see my grandchildren again, but I guess that is not to be."

The stranger smiled. "Trying to tug at my heartstrings, Victor. How long do you have?"

"The doctor says a couple of months." He put on a thick Russian accent. "What do doctors know. I am Russian, strong like bull." He laughed.

The stranger laughed as well. They sounded like two old friends reminiscing.

"I can see in your eyes that no amount of pleading would matter. Men like you and I have seen and done too much to beg for mercy in the end. We always knew our end would come from a gun or a knife."

The stranger took a drink. "Our paths have crossed many times. I almost killed you several times, but you always managed to escape. The closest I came was in Rwanda when you killed that British diplomat. You might be interested in knowing that the British agent who helped you escape died the next day."

Victor laughed. "He was a Soviet mole, trained from birth to be a British spy. He was expendable."

"We knew that all along," said the stranger. "I do have one question that has been bothering me for years. How did you get into the holding cells at Scotland Yard to kill that Russian defector? We had that whole building locked down tight."

Victor smiled. "That, my friend, is a secret that will go with me to the grave."

Victor finished his meal and the last sip of wine and looked at the stranger. "I guess it is time for us to go?"

They both stood up, the stranger never taking his eyes off Victor. Victor reached for his wallet, but the stranger beat him to it and left a hundred-dollar bill on the table. They walked to the front door and out into the fading light. The stranger pointed to a trail, and Victor headed that way, followed by the stranger, who kept his distance.

Ten minutes later, they came to an overlook,

and Victor stepped up to the low rock wall and stared at the view of the mountains. While they were walking, he had heard the stranger screwing the silencer onto the small pistol. Victor silently asked God to watch over his wife and family.

"Thank you," said Victor as he faced the mountains. "For allowing me to die with dignity in this beautiful place."

The stranger raised the pistol and pointed it at the back of Victor's head. He pulled the hammer back to the half-cocked position . . . *click* . . . and then to the fully cocked position . . . *click.* Tears fell from Victor's eyes as he watched the sun set over the mountains.

Acknowledgments

A special thank-you to my daughter Christina J. Morgan, my unofficial editor-in-chief. She devoted a significant amount of time making sure the book was presented as perfectly as possible.

Thanks to my editor, Laura Dragonette, whose efforts helped turn my manuscript into a polished novel. Her help is greatly appreciated. Any mistakes the reader may find are solely the responsibility of the author.

Also, I would like to thank my family for all of their encouragement. I have been telling them stories since they were little, and I always told them that someone should be writing this stuff down. I decided to write it down myself.

I want to thank my closest friend, Trish Moakler-Herud. She has been encouraging me for years to write my stories down. I hope this will make her proud.

A special thanks to my late wife, Jane. She pushed me for years to become a writer, and my biggest regret is that she didn't live long enough to see it happen. I love her with all my heart and miss her every day. I think she would be pleased.

Finally, thanks to the readers. Without you, none of this would be important.

About the Author

2019 Pacific Book Awards Best Mystery Finalist . . . *Crime Delayed*

2020 Pacific Book Awards Best Mystery Winner . . . *Crime Denied*

2020 Chanticleer International Book Awards: 1st Place Blue Ribbon, CLUE Book Awards for Suspense, Thriller Fiction . . . *Crime Denied*

2021 Chanticleer International Book Awards Finalist, CLUE Book Awards for Suspense, Thriller Fiction . . . *Crime Conspiracy*

2021 Chanticleer International Book Awards Finalist, Book Series, CLUE Book Awards for Suspense, Thriller Fiction . . . Crime Series, The Buck Taylor Novels

Chuck Morgan attended Seton Hall University and Regis College and spent thirty-five years as a construction project manager. He is an avid outdoorsman, an Eagle Scout and a licensed private pilot. He enjoys camping, hiking, mountain biking and fly-fishing.

He is the author of the Crime series, featuring Colorado Bureau of Investigation agent Buck Taylor. The series includes *Crime Interrupted, Crime Delayed, Crime Unsolved, Crime Exposed, Crime Denied, Crime Conspiracy, Crime Unknown & Crime Exploded.*

He is also the author of *Her Name Was Jane,*

a memoir about his late wife's nine-year battle with breast cancer. He has three children, three grandchildren and a Siberian Husky. He resides in Lone Tree, Colorado.

Other Books by the Author

"Crime Interrupted: A Buck Taylor Novel by Chuck Morgan is a gripping, edge-of-the-seat novel. Right from page one, the action kicks off and never stops, gaining pace as each chapter passes." Reviewed by Anne-Marie Reynolds for Readers' Favorite.

Finalist . . . 2019 Pacific Book Awards Best Mystery

"This crime novel reads like a great thriller. The writing is atmospheric, laced with vivid descriptions that capture the setting in great detail while allowing readers to follow the intensity of the action and the emotional and psychological depth of the story." Reviewed by Divine Zape for Readers' Favorite.

"Professionally written in the style of a best-selling crime novelist, such as Tom Clancy, Crime Unsolved: A Buck Taylor Novel by Chuck Morgan is a spellbinding suspense novel with an environmental flair. Intriguing subplots of fraud, survivalist paranoia, and murder weave their way through the fabric of the plot, creating a dynamic story. This is an action-filled, stimulating tale which contains fascinating details that are relevant in our present climate." Reviewed by Susan Sewell for Readers' Favorite.

"Chuck Morgan has a unique gift for plot, one that makes Crime Exposed: A Buck Taylor Novel a hard-to-put-down book. From the start, readers know what happens to Barb, but they become curious as they follow the investigation, wondering if the characters will find out what happened to her. The descriptions are filled with clarity, and they offer readers great images. The

prose is elegant, and it captures both the emotional and psychological elements of the novel clearly while offering vivid descriptions of scenes and characters. This is a fast-paced thriller with memorable characters and a criminal investigation that is so real readers will believe it could happen." Reviewed by Romuald Dzemo for Readers' Favorite.

Winner . . . 2020 Pacific Book Awards Best Mystery

2020 Chanticleer International Book Awards: 1st Place Blue Ribbon, CLUE Book Awards for Suspense, Thriller Fiction

"It's really progressive to see a female serial killer portrayed with such intelligent writing and depth of character, and the cat and mouse chase dynamic is thrown off nicely by the switching of genders. What results is a really enjoyable thriller and crime mystery novel, and overall Crime Denied is certain to please fans of both hard-boiled detective tales and action/adventure crime novels." Reviewed by K.C. Finn for Readers' Favorite.

2021 Chanticleer International Book Awards, Finalist, CLUE Book Awards for Suspense, Thriller Fiction . . . *Crime Conspiracy*

"This makes for a truly dynamic story where anything is possible, and a hero you can root for even when it looks like all is lost." Reviewed by K.C. Finn for Readers' Favorite.

"This is a book you can't put down, which will entertain you on many levels, and at times make your skin crawl; the kind of book that remains in your thoughts long after you finish reading." Reviewed by Steven Robson for Readers' Favorite.

"I read Crime Unknown in one sitting. The plot is intense and the main character agent Buck Taylor is a hero like no other. This book has everything a thriller

needs to be and more. I thought I knew the story at the beginning. Buck will solve a tricky murder case, I thought. But Chuck Morgan adds a twist to this story that expands it and makes it one of the most enjoyable books I've read in this genre. I loved that the lead was such an awesome well-rounded fellow but that he also had a support team who were just as important to the story." Reviewed by Maureen Dangarembizi for Readers' Favorite.

"Crime Unknown is a thoroughly enjoyable read and I would not hesitate to recommend this book to fans of the crime genre and those looking for a gateway in." Reviewed by K.C. Finn for Readers' Favorite.

"Action-packed and fast-paced, I was sucked into the story the moment I opened the novel. The author built the story to perfection. Chuck Morgan gave just the right amount of suspense, mystery, and action to keep readers' attention on Buck and his team. There was never a dull moment in the story. The narrative ran smoothly until the end; it followed the development of the story and the pace set by the characters. I enjoyed the twists and turns. What I loved more than anything else in the plot was how calculating Buck was. He was smart; he didn't let the FBI discourage him and kept his

head in the game. The action gave me an adrenaline rush. Absolutely brilliant!" Rabia Tanveer for Readers' Favorite.

www.ingramcontent.com/pod-product-compliance
Lightning Source LLC
Chambersburg PA
CBHW072111250626
47159CB00007B/2399